DEADLY BOND

A Selection of Recent Titles by Christine Green

Kate Kinsella Mysteries

DEADLY ADMIRERS
DEADLY BOND*
DEADLY ERRAND
DEADLY PARTNERS
DEADLY PRACTICE

FATAL CUT*
FIRE ANGELS*

** available from Severn House*

DEADLY BOND

Christine Green

This first world edition published in Great Britain 2001 by
SEVERN HOUSE PUBLISHERS LTD of
9–15 High Street, Sutton, Surrey SM1 1DF.
This first world edition published in the USA 2002 by
SEVERN HOUSE PUBLISHERS INC of
595 Madison Avenue, New York, N.Y. 10022.

British Library Cataloguing in Publication Data

Green, Christine, 1944–
Deadly bond
1. Kinsella, Kate (Fictitious character) – Fiction
2. Women private investigators – Great Britain – Fiction
3. Detective and mystery stories
I. Title
823.9′14 [F]

ISBN 0-7278-5783-5

Typeset by Palimpsest Book Production Ltd.,
Polmont, Stirlingshire, Scotland.
Printed and bound in Great Britain by
MPG Books Ltd., Bodmin, Cornwall.

For my dearest husband, Tony,
with much love and appreciation
for everything you do

One

Most people need a sabbatical at some time in their lives. I've just come back from mine, thinking it would be a long rest. My Medical and Nursing Investigation Agency had reached a nadir – the only client for a month being an elderly man who wanted a nurse 'with bounce' to find his long-lost sweetheart. He was an odd little man and I didn't give him the satisfaction of asking him exactly what he meant.

My 'long rest' was anything but. I went to New Zealand. My mother was still living in Australia and I suppose I thought meeting up with her would be like island-hopping in the Med. In the event she came to New Zealand to see me. I was working in a geriatric facility for the mentally frail where some of the staff could have easily qualified for a bed.

Anyway, she turned up, fifty-something and looking the complete tart. Short skirt, high heels, tight top, bleached hair and dark glasses plus red lips with a cupid's bow well past its line of origin. She insisted we went clubbing together and she got all the attention. I like to think it was because the lights were so low they couldn't see her wrinkles.

When my mother acquired a job at the same hospital, as a care assistant, I knew I should be thinking about my return to the UK. My mother's idea of caring is handing over a fag and a pint of lager. She wasn't always the same, at least until she was forty-five; then she went into her prolonged adolescence, slimming down to a size ten in the process. I can squash myself into a size fourteen but if shops sold a fifteen I could probably keep my skirt buttons done up after a meal. I'm a redhead with blue eyes, five foot four, and a man once called me 'well-proportioned with good child-bearing hips' – I think it was meant as a compliment but I still felt like slapping his face.

Meanwhile my mother tells everyone she was a child bride and that I'm twenty-five but look older. She's ashamed of me, of course. I'm a thirty-something with no man and hardly any money. Only on rare occasions do I look glamorous.

New Zealand's Wellington had everything: great restaurants serving huge portions, easy parking – a traffic jam is four cars moving slowly – and good weather except for the strong winds and a tendency for the earth to shake. I got used to the tremors and could almost guess the strength. After the last quake, when I'd finished shaking, I murmured dementedly to myself, 'Four point two on the Richter scale.' And I was right.

The men are toned and mostly good-looking, Maori men being my mother's current favourite. It was when she tried to persuade me *I* needed to be more fit and toned and that joining a gym and taking up scuba diving would be the answer that I finally decided to return home.

I rent my office from Hubert Humberstone, Funeral Director of Longborough, and although I hadn't paid any rent for a year he'd written and phoned and assured me I had a place in his premises until 'the grave'. His age is a dark secret but he's definitely twenty years older than I am so I presume he meant his end and not mine. Hubert is a friend as well as a landlord. When I left for New Zealand he was happily 'courting' an attractive transsexual whose only giveaway on the physical front was a man-sized Adam's apple. His last letter concluded: 'The silly trollop has abandoned me for a butch gay biker leaving me with ten pairs of size eight shoes and eight pairs of worn fishnet tights.' For Hubert platforms with skyscraper heels or shoes with rapier heels, preferably with steel tips that click suggestively, are a major part of feminine allure. Being more worldly-wise now, I realise he is not alone.

At Heathrow I left the plane feeling ten years older. I'd spent the flight next to a man who overflowed into my limited space. His round head, as smoothly polished as a marble paperweight, emerged above a thick neck and several chins. He reminded me of a too well-risen Yorkshire pudding in a bun tin. He *was* from Yorkshire, and he had a fear of food he wasn't used to. He managed to overcome the fear but one meal, consisting of savoury pancakes, really flummoxed him. 'What is it?' he asked me, giving the pancake a flip with his plastic fork.

'A pancake with vegetables in.'

'I've never seen one before,' he said, suspiciously. 'I like mine with sugar and oranges or lemons.' Then he added, in his slow way, 'I do hope this isn't the last thing I eat.'

'Eat it quickly,' I said. 'Then that chocolate muffin will be the last thing you eat.'

He peered at the wrapped muffin and ate his pancake in three mouthfuls.

I spent nearly twenty-four hours in this man's company. For twenty of those hours he had his shoes off. The smell of his feet would have stopped a charging rhino in its tracks.

I'd followed the advice 'wear something comfortable', so I'd bought a pair of trousers with an elasticated waist my mother wouldn't have been seen dead in. And they were comfortable, at least for the first four hours. After that my stomach, instead of being like a slightly inflated balloon, became fully inflated, the waistband struggling to contain me. I squashed myself past Pudding at regular intervals for nasal and bodily respite and skulked in the claustrophobic loo for as long as possible. I did at least remember not to make the mistake of flushing whilst sitting. I'd read about a disaster some years before where a woman had done just that and her bowels had been sucked out of her. Was it an airline myth or the wishful thinking of someone whose bowels were in such torment they longed for a good clear-out?

As we neared Heathrow I thought it the longest twenty-four hours of my life. I wanted to go back to New Zealand one day but in my present discomfort colonic irrigation seemed like more fun and needed a lot less stamina. My preoccupation with bowel function is perhaps due to my recent nursing experience – or it could be that trapped wind, like a pregnancy, focuses all thoughts below the waist.

The UK came as a noisy shock. There seemed to be more people in Heathrow than the whole of New Zealand. I struggled out with two suitcases into the rain and waited for my coach. No one spoke in the queue and the coach was an hour late. Hubert had offered to meet me but I'd declined, knowing that it was winter, it could have been snowing and the death rate was always highest after Christmas. He was needed. At the moment no one needed me.

I dozed on the coach for some time with the comfort of an empty seat beside me and struggled not to give in to proper sleep. As we neared Longborough, I squinted and saw the rain galloping across the coach windows like thousands of speeding spermatozoa. I closed my eyes, my eyelids no longer under my control, weighed down as though gravity itself was forcing them shut. I thought of the sunshine I'd left and the friends I'd made and the wonderful food and the 'barbies' and the sound of the sea and I felt a real pang – a longing for a country that in some ways had become in retrospect more like home than home.

Staggering from the coach in Longborough, my spirits lifted as I saw Hubert walking towards me under a black umbrella. I was so glad to see him I didn't even mind the fact that he was also dressed in black, wearing the white wing collar he often wore for the more traditional funerals. I can't imagine the grim reaper being dressed in any other way.

He gave me a big smile, slapped me on the back and said, 'You look rough, Kate.'

'So would you if you'd been sat next to a Yorkshire pudding for twenty-four hours.'

He didn't know what I was talking about so he picked up my cases and we advanced towards the Daimler. 'I've got a job on in twenty minutes,' he said as he offloaded my cases into the back seat. 'Office or home?' he asked, then, as an afterthought, added, 'Are you glad to be back?'

'Mildly ecstatic, thank you.'

'Kiwiland hasn't changed your sarcastic bent,' he said. 'Strange I could miss trouble so much.'

I said nothing. I'd missed Hubert too. As a friend he could be critical at times, was obsessive about shoes, had the misfortune to look like an undertaker and tried to organise me all the time, but I knew he was as reliable as Big Ben and had the kindest of natures.

I own a small terraced house in Farley Wood, a few miles from Longborough, that I'd rented out via Hubert, who'd acted as my agent. In the year I'd been away, the first tenants hadn't paid any rent for three months, the second lot were busted by the police for drug use and the last tenant had been on a short lease. I presumed she'd left. 'I can go to my own place, then?' I queried.

Hubert, negotiating a bend, nodded in the mirror. I noticed now that his long face looked thinner and his prune-coloured eyes were set deeper. All over he looked thinner, which didn't seem possible. Sod's law. The thin get thinner and the fat just carry on eating. Emotional trauma for me is just another excuse for a jam doughnut.

'Your tenant was all packed up yesterday,' said Hubert.

'So you could go there. But I've got something to show you at the office.'

'Should I be worried?'

'I didn't say it was bad news.'

'So it's good news?'

Hubert raised his eyebrows. 'Let's call it a surprise.'

And it was. At the side entrance of Humberstones is my door. My door with my mock gold plaque. Except that it had now become a silver plaque with black lettering, and 'Medical and Nursing Investigation Agency' had become 'Kinsella Investigations, Prop. Miss K. Kinsella, Private Investigator, DR (NZ)'.

I was still staring gormlessly at my new sign when Hubert began explaining, 'You won't get work if you restrict yourself. Let's face it, you're the only PI in Longborough.'

'What the hell does DR stand for?'

'Didn't you tell me you'd done a course in reflexology in New Zealand? It stands for Diploma in Reflexology.'

'Hardly a course, Hubert – one session with a friend does not qualify for a diploma in any language or country.'

'Maybe not, but who's going to ask?'

'That's not the point.'

He didn't let me finish. 'I know you can do reflexology.'

'I can give a good foot massage,' I admitted, 'but I don't know which toe correlates with which bit of the body.'

'Does it matter?'

I looked at him as sternly as anyone can with drooping eyelids. 'Of course it matters.'

'It wouldn't to me.'

'That's true, Hubert; your foot agenda is simply for pleasure. For some people it's medicinal.'

'The sensual delights of a foot massage,' he said earnestly, 'are very therapeutic, with or without the technicalities.'

'If you think I'm going to massage your feet you're going

to be disappointed. But as for Kinsella Investigations,' I admitted grudgingly, '*that* could be a good idea.'

Hubert opened the door then to the narrow staircase that led to my office rooms. With a flourish of his hand he signalled me inside. Gone were the gothic purple walls and the purple lampshade that had always hung at an angle. Instead the walls were pale cream, with stylish mirrors on either side. A luxurious cream carpet covered the stairs and a chandelier had replaced the lampshade. The whole effect said 'Here dwells a successful PI'. 'It's brilliant – it's a different place. Why?'

'Why not? I want you to be a success.'

'You're not that hard up for my rent money, surely.'

'I've had my best year ever,' said Hubert, miffed. 'And it's all down to my marketing techniques.'

'Kills people off, does it?'

'Don't be such a smart-arse. As a businesswoman you make a good nurse.'

He was right of course but at that moment I was too exhausted to be as grateful for his DIY as I should have been. 'Haven't you got to do the honours somewhere, Hubert?'

'Christ,' he muttered. 'I'll see you later.'

'Don't wake me.'

He didn't answer. He left the suitcases and me at the bottom of the stairs and I realised I hadn't got the strength to carry them up. I slipped off my trainers for fear of marking my posh new stair carpet and made my way slowly up to my camp bed in the boxroom. When I opened the door I thought I'd made a mistake. Gone was the camp bed, replaced by a smart divan smothered in black and gold cushions. The walls were now magnolia; the window, which looked out on to the car park, now shimmered with silvery drapes. There were even white roses in an elegant glass vase on a new bedside table. A large mirror on the wall opposite enlarged the room and my feet appreciated the soft pale green carpet. (Would I ever keep it clean, though?) The old sink had been replaced and now I had one with gold-coloured taps and a silk screen with a Japanese theme giving a little extra privacy. All in all the difference seemed as great as previously living in a cardboard box and now having a room at the Ritz – not that I'd ever seen a room at the Ritz.

I longed for a bath. I could have used one of Hubert's but I made do with a quick wash because I couldn't wait to lie down. Lying prone after so long being cramped and uncomfortable was – orgasmic. My pleasure was curtailed by instant sleep.

I woke once in the dark to find Hubert standing in the doorway, still in black. If he *had* been the Grim Reaper I wouldn't have minded. I tried to speak but my lips wouldn't move.

I woke a second time to the sound of church bells and Hubert saying, 'Thank God for that.'

I had to prise one eye open with a little finger. 'What's happening?' I asked through a tongue that had sucked sand.

'I thought you were in a coma,' he said. 'You haven't stirred for eighteen hours.'

'I *have* stirred,' I said. 'Once or twice.'

'I've brought you some tea.' He handed me a mug of tea and, managing to open both eyes, I struggled to sit up, forgetting I wasn't wearing anything. 'You could have put something on,' he said, averting his eyes.

'I didn't know you'd be trooping in and out all night.'

'One visit to make sure you were still alive doesn't qualify as trooping.'

I sipped the tea gratefully. 'This tea is nectar – thank you.'

Hubert sat on the edge of the bed now that I had covered myself with the duvet. 'I'll have a breakfast on the go when you're ready – unless you're on a diet.'

'You know full well I don't do dieting,' I said. 'So yes – thanks again. I'm famished.'

He grinned. 'Same old Kate, then.'

'Aren't you working?' I asked, which was a stupid question because he was wearing grey slacks and a navy-blue sweater.

'It's Sunday – which is why the bells were ringing.'

'I won't be long,' I said, hoping he'd take the hint. He didn't.

'I've been doing a bit of advertising on your behalf. Your first appointment is today at ten thirty a.m. – a woman.'

'Tell me about it over breakfast,' I said, shuffling about in the bed as if about to expose myself. He jumped from the bed as if I'd propositioned him.

'Did you say *today*?' I added, still not fully awake and my brain several revs below normal.

'I thought you could manage it,' he mumbled, looking slightly shamefaced.

I decided that I could manage one client visit and that I should be grateful. 'By the way,' I said, 'you've got great taste in decor, Hubert – I've never known such luxury.'

'If you work hard,' he said, poised to go, 'you could be the most successful PI in England.'

'In Christendom, even.'

He frowned. 'That's your trouble, Kate. You're too flippant. You just want to do the minimum. You'll never reach your full potential unless you put the effort in.'

'You sound just like an old headmaster of mine,' I said, 'and I know you're right.'

Hubert flashed me his 'I give up' expression and left.

Breakfast was a sumptuous affair. Buck's Fizz came as a prelude to a full fry-up – if there was a Richter scale for calories it would have been a national alert – but I enjoyed every mouthful.

Hubert was unwilling to talk about his being dumped and I knew how he felt. I'd met a New Zealand possum hunter, all big gun and muscles, and he'd dropped me after three months for a stick insect with blonde hair and a borderline IQ. Borderline for a possum, that is.

'Have you been into your office yet?' Hubert asked as he began filling the dishwasher.

'Not yet. Has it been revamped too? You're spoiling me. At this rate I might just become successful.'

'That's the idea. When I retire from undertaking I can run things for you.'

My heart sank. I felt like the unmarried daughter having her life mapped out by a bossy father. 'So you don't think some man will whisk me away from all this,' I said, with a hand flourish.

'He hasn't done so far, has he? And you're not getting any younger.'

'Thanks. You do wonders for my self-esteem.'

'Hard work will do that,' he muttered, as he set the dishwasher in motion. 'Anyway, let's go up to your office and I'll show you the future.'

I saw immediately what Hubert meant. My office had been revamped too but the primary change was the computer station that now, altarlike, occupied my desk.

'Should I kneel down and pray before it?' I asked. Hubert's disappointed expression said it all. 'It's wonderful,' I said, giving him a hug, 'or at least it will be when I've mastered it. How much do I owe you?'

'It wasn't exactly buy one get one free,' he said, as he stroked the computer's top. 'But I've got one and this was a bargain so one day when you're rich you can pay me back.'

'It's a deal . . . I'm really impressed by the décor, Hubert,' I said, as I took in the stylish filing cabinet, array of potted greenery, modern wall lights and new fitted carpet.

'Make sure you look after the plants and don't let them die,' he warned direly, as if I had a history of child neglect.

'Where did you get your ideas from?' I asked. 'This place is a whole new world.'

'*The House Doctor*,' he answered. I was none the wiser.

'Television programme.'

'Oh,' I said. 'I've never heard of it. The best New Zealand could export was *Shortland Street*.'

It was his turn to look puzzled. 'It's time you got to work, Kate. Let me show you your first file.'

He showed me how to switch on. *That* I could manage. And it looked easy enough to open the file he had named '1'. I was suitably impressed when the client's name and address graced the screen: Mrs Lorraine Farnforth, 3 Aspen Drive, Aspen Gardens, Longborough, followed by her telephone number and her 'Investigation Requirements', under which Hubert had typed in bold letters '**WITNESS PROTECTION**'.

Hubert sat at my desk and I stood behind him, staring at the screen. 'Estimated Fee: £750.00 per week plus expenses.' 'My flabber is gasted – since when have I done protection work?' Before Hubert had time to answer I added, 'And since when have my fees been that high?'

He didn't take his eyes from the screen. 'Since I decided to give you a helping hand.'

In the circumstances, what could I say? 'Who does she want protection from?'

Hubert shook his head. 'No idea, but she sounded scared. All she did say was that she'd been a witness to a crime and she couldn't go to the police.'

'Sounds a bit rough for me. You know I'm not too good on the strong-arm stuff.'

'You'll manage. And I'll be around for back-up.'

'Not if you're in the middle of a funeral.'

'Try being positive, Kate. She's expecting you in half an hour.'

I groaned inwardly. I still felt jet-lagged. 'Is my car still driveable?'

'Yes. I've checked it over.'

Another excuse had been blown away. Hubert thrust a mobile phone into my hand. 'No rental to pay on that,' he explained. 'You can buy cards for it anywhere.'

'You think of everything, Hubert.'

'I knew it would take you a while to adjust.'

'A whole night you've allowed me. I can only just *see*, never mind protect.'

'Don't forget to take notes,' he said, as he pushed me towards the door, 'and keep any receipts for the taxman.'

As I drove towards Aspen Drive I reflected on the change in my landlord. Had he lost his passion for shoes now that he was left with those eight empty pairs? Was that the reason he was so focused on my work? Or was he bored with uncomplicated dead bodies? Whatever the reason, he'd managed to get me working on my first day in the UK. And who in their right mind wants to see a PI on a Sunday?

Someone scared witless, I thought as I drove into the ultra-private estate of Aspen Gardens.

Two

Aspen Gardens is one of *the* places to live in Longborough, a hoi polloi-free environment. It has no shops within walking distance, nor anything vaguely agricultural or industrial. It does have some fine trees, gardens of identical neatness and bungalows with glass-encased porches and conservatories. It attracts older, richer inhabitants and only the occasional visiting grandchild or reluctant teenager is seen, delivered by car and hurried indoors.

As far as I could see the only protection anyone could need in Aspen Gardens was from stultifying boredom. Appearances can be deceptive, I told myself. Perhaps behind the glass porches extraordinary and exciting lives are lived. Somehow I doubted it. It also seemed strange that my prospective client needed protection. This was the sort of area that already had it.

Aspen Drive itself is in a cul-de-sac; each property burglar-alarmed with lockable windows and Neighbourhood Watch stickers in every window. High fences sealed off the back gardens and, although I hadn't seen a Rottweiler, I could hear the barking of small breeds, especially coming from number three, where a high-pitched yap answered the tuneful chimes.

A woman I presumed to be Lorraine Farnforth stared at me for a moment from behind the glass of her porch. A black miniature poodle barked excitedly at her feet. She pointed a finger at him and he sat down, ears cocked, still quivering. I hoped it was pleasure or excitement and not a desire to bite my ankles.

Lorraine was, I guessed, in her late thirties. She wore well-cut black trousers and a grey sweater that looked expensive. The gold watch, bracelet, necklace and earrings all suggested a woman who also carried a gold credit card. She had a slight tan, dark hair in a straight bob and plain chocolate-coloured eyes beneath heavy but well-shaped brows. She could have been Italian or Spanish but, judging by her slim figure, she was sparing with the olive oil. The poodle was as trim and well-groomed as his owner and even sported a gold name-tag.

In contrast, I wore cheapo jeans, a baggy sweatshirt and trainers. My image was *not* carefully crafted butch, but those were the only clothes I had that didn't need ironing and I wanted to convey the image of a woman who could at least manage a swift knee in the groin and then run like the clappers.

I took Lorraine's outstretched hand, which felt a little limp, and tried to convey an air of confidence and feminine strength. 'You look the part,' she said, in a girly voice.

Did that mean scruffy or down at heel, or that I looked like a force to be reckoned with? Either way, I smiled confidently and allowed the poodle to lick my hand.

'Jasper likes you.'

I patted Jasper on the head because, after all, I did need this job and it might just be a doddle.

'Come through to the kitchen,' she said, gliding along on high-heeled black mules. 'Jasper – bed!' Jasper obediently slunk away to his basket in the hall from where he eyed me cautiously.

In the kitchen we sat at either end of a table covered by a white lace cloth with a huge bowl of fruit between us. To one side was a gold-framed mirror which took up most of the wall space. It did make her average-sized kitchen look larger, and the light from the garden window reflected back on a vase of yellow roses on the sill above the sink. As far as kitchens went there was no sign of any tendency to cook. The oven looked pristine and no washing-up liquid marred the equally pristine sink. It smelt more of roses than food and it seemed there was to be no offer of a hot drink.

'You're experienced in protection work, I believe?' she asked.

I nodded enigmatically. 'But I don't talk about my previous clients. My services remain confidential.'

I was impressed with how that sounded. She murmured, 'Yes, of course,' then began absent-mindedly tracing her fingers over the lace cloth. I couldn't fail to notice that she'd bitten her fingernails to the quick. Cashmere and roses couldn't console *her* inner demons. I was in the jam-doughnut league but, somehow, a woman who is obliged to eat her fingernails appeared to me to be in real trouble.

I came straight to the point. 'Why do you need protection, Mrs Farnforth?'

'Lorraine.'

'Same question, then – Lorraine.'

She stopped tracing the lace and looked at me. 'I was a witness.'

'What did you witness?'

She stared at the lace and mumbled, 'Murder.'

'You saw someone murdered?'

'Yes.'

I waited for her to say more because silence can be like an empty stomach – it's a space waiting to be filled. Eventually she said, 'I saw a woman shot and now he's after me. He saw me, you see, and now it's my turn. He's got to silence me.' She raised her eyes from the lace and added, 'Hasn't he?'

'What exactly happened?' I asked, keeping my voice even. After all, shootings in Longborough were as rare as meteorites, but I wanted her to think such events didn't ruffle me one bit.

'I'd been late-night shopping – it was about eight thirty. I'd parked my car in the picnic area near the river.'

What river? 'You mean the stream on the Dunmore road?'

She nodded.

'That's some way from the shops.'

'I like walking and there's always a space.' Her voice sounded shaky. I tried to visualise where she meant, but couldn't. 'What did you see?'

'I was walking fast,' she said. 'I saw my car . . . there was another car parked a few yards away. He couldn't have seen me at first. A woman got out. There was a bit of pushing and shoving and I thought it was just an ordinary domestic argument but then . . . I saw he had something in his hand – she pushed him again and then a shot rang out. She slumped to the floor and he looked at me – stared, really stared.'

'What did you do?'

She shrugged. 'I just stood there. I suppose I was in shock. I thought if I ran he might shoot me in the back. Then . . . it all happened so fast. He picked up the woman's body and put her in the boot of the car and drove off – fast.'

'You took the number?'

She shook her head. 'I couldn't believe what I'd seen. I wasn't thinking.'

'The car?'

Now she was looking really miserable and chewing on her thumb. 'It was silver-grey, a four-door but I don't know the make.'

'So you phoned the police?'

There was a long, irritating pause. 'Well . . . no . . .'

'Why not? You say you've seen a woman shot and you haven't reported it.'

'I *did* see a woman shot. But I didn't have my mobile phone with me and I just wanted to get away.'

'Lorraine, I'm not disputing that you saw a woman shot but, shock or no shock, why the hell didn't you ring the police?'

'There's no need to get cross.'

I swallowed hard. And took a deep breath. 'If you want me to protect you, I have to know what's going on.'

She went back to fiddling with the lace and I grew more irritated. 'Fine. That's it. If you can't be honest with me perhaps you'd like to tell the police *now*.'

'I'd been shoplifting,' she said, abruptly.

This *did* take me by surprise. I couldn't imagine her having the guts or the need to be a shoplifter. 'Why?'

She shrugged. 'I like the buzz it gives me – sometimes I even take things back. That evening I was convinced the store detective was after me, so I'd been hurrying along, hoping I wasn't being followed.'

Warning bells rang at this point, enough to deafen me, but even they couldn't quell the thought that popped into my mind – *nutter*! And I didn't want to get involved.

I stood up to leave. 'Please don't go,' she begged. 'I'll try to explain.'

Reluctantly I sat down. I was here and I had nothing urgent to do other than washing and ironing and recovering from jet-lag, not to mention getting my life back in some sort of order. 'My husband Carl works in Saudi – he's an engineer. He'd lose his job if his employers found out his wife was a thief.'

'Is that why you shoplift?'

She looked puzzled. 'What do you mean?'

'I mean – if he lost his job he'd be here with you, so subconsciously you shoplift to increase your chances of him coming home.'

'I hadn't thought of it like that.'

'How much time does he spend with you?'

'It varies,' she said. 'On average he's home for a couple of weeks every two months.'

'Is he due back soon?'

She shook her head. 'Not for a month or so and, of course, I can't tell him what's happened. If he found out I'd been shoplifting he'd . . . well, he'd be . . . devastated.'

'Do you have a job?' I asked.

'I do voluntary work.'

'But you have a lot of time to fill – so you shoplift.'

'You despise me,' she said. 'I can hear it in your voice.'

I managed a half-smile. 'I'm just trying to work out what exactly is going on here.'

'There is something I haven't told you,' she said. 'The murderer has been phoning me – silent calls, number withheld.'

'It might not be him.'

She nodded. 'True, but I've never had silent phone calls before.'

'In all that pushing and shoving before the woman was shot did either of them speak?'

She shook her head. 'No. But when he raised the gun at *me*, he didn't need any words.'

'It's strange the woman didn't scream,' I said. 'And after all, he could have killed *you* there and then.'

She held her head to one side and rested a shaking hand on her cheek. 'I thought he was going to. I really thought he was going to shoot.'

'But he didn't,' I said briskly. 'So you could describe this man?'

'It was dark – the streetlight had failed, so I didn't see him that well. I just got a vague impression . . .'

'Which was?'

'He was about five foot ten, a white man, slim, in his forties. Dark eyes, or at least they looked dark.'

'What was he wearing?'

'One of those padded jackets with the hood up – dark blue, I think, but it could have been black – dark trousers – grey – I'm not sure, I was just so scared – my eyes were fixed on the gun.'

'And the woman?'

'What?'

'The woman – the victim.'

'Oh yes. I didn't get a good look at her either. She was about my height – five four. Late thirties, I should think. She wore a black coat and a red beret-type hat with a red scarf.'

'Distinctive, then?'

'Yes. But I didn't see her face properly. When he picked her up the beret slipped forwards – she had short fair hair.'

'There is just one more question,' I said. 'Where and when was the body found?'

She stared at me, her lips in a slight pout. 'As far as I know it hasn't been found yet. There's been nothing in the newspapers about it.'

This minor point took me a while to digest. But before I could comment, Lorraine leant forward. 'He's clever, you see – no body – no murder – get rid of me and where's the evidence?'

'I'd happily offer you my services,' I said grandly, 'but the police *need* to be informed.'

'This man is . . .' Her hand on my wrist interrupted me. 'Please, Kate – I'm begging you. There must be some way – I could give the information anonymously.'

'I've thought about that,' I said, 'but, without a body and a witness unwilling to come forward, I don't think the Longborough police will take any action.'

Lorraine's lower lip trembled and her eyes filled with tears. 'The silent calls were just a warning. Once the body is found he'll come after me. He'll have to silence me then – won't he?'

She was beginning to win. What could I do? 'Give me a couple of days.'

'Can't you stay now? He could come tonight.'

If it had only been *her* begging I might not have succumbed, but now Jasper had padded towards me and was licking my hand and even his eyes had a pleading quality. I stroked his head and he lay down at my feet. 'I think the murderer will feel safe,' I said, as Jasper watched me with pricked-up ears, 'until the body is found. And I need a couple of days to get myself organised.'

'I'll be so relieved when someone is here with me,' she said, managing a smile. 'I even keep a baseball bat under the bed.'

'That's reassuring,' I said. 'But there is one thing that I'll need to insist on.'

'Anything,' she murmured.

'I'll need plenty of tea and coffee.'

'I'll get some in – I don't drink either. I keep to herbal teas and fruit juices.'

Somehow, protecting Lorraine Farnforth wasn't going to be just a job. I sensed it would have all the allure of a protracted stay in a health farm.

When I returned to Humberstones I could see Hubert watching me from my office.

'I thought I'd give you your first lesson in keeping files,' he said. I mumbled about washing, ironing and unpacking. He swung round on my office chair to appraise my appearance. His eyes fixed on my feet. 'The only place you'll get in life wearing trainers,' he said, 'is an offer of half a pint of shandy from an elderly drunk.'

'Sounds okay to me in my state of social purdah. But what you really mean is, I won't find a *permanent* man unless I go all frou-frou and feminine.'

He nodded. 'Got it in one, Kate. If only you'd give high heels and short skirts a chance you'd see I was right.' He signalled for me to come closer. 'Now look – here's your first file, LF. What do you want me to add?'

I stared at the screen. 'Lorraine says she witnessed a shooting and she thinks he's after her.'

'You don't sound very convinced,' said Hubert.

'Has a woman's body been found?'

Hubert shook his head. 'Not round here.'

'Precisely. No body – no case.'

'She imagined a murder, then?'

'I didn't say that.'

'I've heard of people being convicted of murder without a body. Years ago there was a kidnapping case and the body was fed to the pigs.'

'Trust you to come up with something like that, Hubert. Want to swap jobs?'

He grinned. 'No. I like doing yours by proxy.'

'I've got two days' grace,' I said, 'but I'll have to start ferreting for the names of missing women in the area.'

'I'll see if I can find anything on the Internet.'

While Hubert did his fact-finding I switched the kettle on. I've got things wrong, I thought, as I waited for it to boil. How come I was making the coffee?

'Here's a selection,' he said a few minutes later, handing me sheets of paper listing details of local missing persons. The quality of the print was fine, but the photographs were dark, which seemed to add to their gravity. Alongside their faces and descriptions were pleas to get in touch from anxious parents or distraught partners. None fitted Lorraine's description of the victim, but then maybe she hadn't been reported missing yet.

'What do you think?' asked Hubert.

'I didn't realise there were so many missing people.'

'I meant the facility – the quality.'

'Great. I'm really impressed.' Hubert looked pleased. 'The Internet should be a real boon to me,' I added under my breath, 'if I could ever get to use it.'

'What was that?'

'Nothing – I just muttered that you were a dot-com whizz.'

He didn't believe me because he has ears that are primed for whispers. I wasn't sure if that was years of listening to the sad incoherent murmuring of the bereaved or just naturally healthy aural tackle. 'The Internet *is* the future, Kate. You could even find a man online – there are lonely-hearts chat rooms.'

'*You* use them, then,' I said, a bit narked. 'I want a meeting of bodies – the meeting of minds can come later.'

Hubert gave me a searching look.

'How would I describe myself, anyway?' I said. 'Struggling PI, almost past her sell-by date, wears flat shoes, likes jam doughnuts and a quiet life, seeks rampant handsome rich intelligent – ?'

'You're being daft, Kate – you don't need rampant.'

I burst out laughing and Hubert joined in, until I said, 'Hang on – it's not that funny. I *would* like someone who wanted to ravish me often.'

'You just be careful,' warned Hubert. 'Some men would take advantage of a young woman like you.'

'You mean they'd guess I was up for it.'

He shook his head disapprovingly. 'New Zealand did you no good at all.'

'You only know half of it.'

'And that's just as well,' he muttered.

Hubert continued on the Internet, although doing what, I didn't know, and I left and drove over to Farley Wood to check my little terraced house was still standing and that the tenant had gone.

It was raining again, but even in the rain Farley Wood

looked like a proper village with a church and a bit of village green. My house is one of four in a row and even before NZ I didn't spend much time there, but it was a comfort to know I had a bolt hole and that, if Hubert's info was correct, it was a steadily appreciating asset.

I knocked on the door loudly and stood waiting for a response for some time. Then, feeling a complete lemon, I realised I had my own key.

There were suitcases inside my living room waiting by the front door and a smell of cleanliness. 'Anyone there?' I called out. I wandered about, not that there was far to wander, just two small rooms plus kitchen downstairs and two bedrooms and bathroom upstairs. Everywhere had a just-cleaned appearance, even the cooker. I checked each room but there was no tenant, just the appearance of her having left everything in readiness for me. Whoever she was, the house didn't smell like mine and I felt oddly out of place. I didn't want to wait for her, so I left her a note on a scrap of paper asking her to phone me.

As I drove away, I hoped I'd see a familiar face in the village, but there wasn't a soul to be seen. The rain drizzled on relentlessly and it only served to remind me of the blue sky and sunshine I'd left behind.

Later that day, Hubert handed me a week-old Longborough News. I scanned the front page. 'What am I supposed to be looking at?'

'There.' He pointed. At the bottom of the front page were a few lines captioned 'Missing Mother'.

> Paula Jenkins (40) was last seen in Longborough three weeks ago. She has left home before, but her husband Ian (43) says he has become worried because she usually contacts her children. On the day she disappeared she was wearing a distinctive red scarf

> and beret. If anyone has seen her, would they please contact the local police.

'Well?' said Hubert.

'Well what?'

'Don't be difficult – could this be your victim?'

'Sounds like it,' I said. 'Only complicated by the fact that she's been missing three weeks and yet she was supposedly shot a mere week ago.'

'Seems simple enough to me,' said Hubert. 'You could contact this Ian Jenkins and offer your services. If she's not the victim, you have two cases instead of one. If she *is* the victim, then at least her husband will know *why* she hasn't phoned the children.'

I stared at Hubert. 'That idea *cannot* be ethical. I'm surprised at you.'

Hubert looked a little shamefaced. 'You're going to the police, then?'

I hesitated. My new case in embryo was suddenly turning into a moral dilemma. That bothered me. But what bothered me most was the red beret and scarf. Were they a fashion statement? Purely practical? Or maybe a gift that, like a hand-knitted sweater, she felt obliged to wear? Whatever the reason, she was a victim, bright as a candle in the snow, and I needed to think. 'I'm not going to the police just yet,' I told Hubert. 'I'll think about it over the ironing.'

Ironing is not my strong point, but Hubert's ironing board had a well-fitting cover, so I borrowed that and struggled with it to my back room, marvelling at the fact that bits of foam didn't creep out from under the cover. I ironed enthusiastically for at least ten minutes. Then I called out to Hubert, offering to make sandwiches.

'Sarnies for Sunday lunch? Let's go to the pub instead.'

'You're a smooth talker,' I said, grabbing my coat and

realising that moral dilemmas can just as easily be solved with a full stomach and a dash of alcohol.

Disappointingly, it wasn't that easy. The chef at the Frog and Fiddler had thrown a wobbly and walked out, so it was corned beef sandwiches and a packet of crisps. I had both food and drink and still felt none the wiser, so by late afternoon I was back ironing, but my enthusiasm had dwindled and I was in philosophical mode – 'Is ironing God's punishment for so-called civilisation? Discuss' – when the phone rang.

'Kate – it's Lorraine. Please . . . please come at once. I think he's in the garden.'

She sounded distraught, but even so, I said, 'Call the police. You can report an intruder – no explanations necessary.'

There was a short pause. 'You don't understand. I *have* called them. They won't come.'

'Why not?'

'I'll explain when you get here – please, you must help me.'

I glanced at the ironing board. Turgid ironing or witness protection? No contest – the iron was already unplugged. 'I'll be there as quick as I can.'

'Thank God.'

'Lock yourself in the bathroom.'

I yelled to Hubert that I was on my way to Aspen Drive. I was moving too fast to hear his reply, if any.

Three

The drive to Aspen Gardens in continuing drizzle took six minutes. When I arrived at number three the house was in darkness. Even the porch light had been switched off. I took a torch from my car and ran round to investigate the back fence. It was nearly six feet high and, as far as I could see, the only footprints in the wet earth were mine. I rushed round again to the front door and rang the doorbell. The chimes rang out, but there was no sign of Lorraine or Jasper. I shouted again and again through the letterbox.

'What's wrong?'

I turned to the sound of the male voice. The next-door neighbour had his head stuck out of a window.

'Lorraine phoned me a few minutes ago, so I know she's inside.'

'I'll be right down,' he said. 'I think we've got a key.'

Seeing his face for a few seconds, I wasn't able to form an opinion about his looks. But when he appeared and stood with me in the porch – thirtyish, all six foot something, dark, close-cut hair, big brown eyes and wearing a black padded jacket and black cords, my eyes clicked like a camera. Somewhere in my brain circuitry I'd had a blurred negative of my ideal man, but he was the developed image.

'Are you okay?' he asked, as he turned the key in the lock.

'Fine,' I muttered, wondering if I'd gone pale at the sight of him. 'I'm just worried about Lorraine. She thought she had a prowler.' He flicked on the hall light. 'I did tell her to lock herself in the bathroom,' I explained.

'Calling the police might have been a better idea,' he said. 'You stay here. I'll go and check.'

I waited in the hall. The bathroom was the second door on the left. He knocked on the bathroom door before turning the handle. 'There's no one here,' he called out. We checked the other rooms. There was no sign of Jasper's lead in the porch or the hall.

'Perhaps she's taken the car or she's in the garage,' I suggested. He sorted through the small bunch of keys. 'I think this is the garage key,' he said. I followed him out to the garage and he unlocked the up-and-over door. It was empty. 'My aunt told me Lorraine was having her car serviced. She knows what everyone is doing in the Drive,' he said, with a smile. 'She even knows when a resident changes the colour of their toilet paper.'

'Sounds like a handy woman to know,' I said. But what now? I thought. 'Do *you* know Lorraine?' I asked.

'Only to pass the time of day with,' he said in a deep voice, as handsome as his face. 'I'm not here that often. My aunt is a relative newcomer to Aspen Drive – she's only been here two years. She had to move – couldn't manage stairs,' he explained. For a moment I thought he wasn't going to say any more, but then he added, as he shook my hand, 'I'm Jem, by the way – Jem Harrison – Major, British Army.'

'I'm Kate – Kate Kinsella – Private Investigator – Longborough.'

I wasn't sure if he was surprised or impressed, but he was still holding my hand and smiling, so it could have been both. Being so smitten, I'd temporarily forgotten my mission. 'I must find Lorraine. She's convinced she—' I paused – 'needs protection.'

'She's not famous,' he said. 'So why?' I shrugged, unwilling to say. He waited a few seconds to see if I was going to elaborate. 'Well, then,' he said, 'I suggest I explore the garden and the shed and you check she hasn't taken all her clothes and gone AWOL.'

'Good idea,' I said, as if I hadn't thought of that.

He took my torch and went out into the garden. I went to the main bedroom and began searching her knicker drawer. She had, at a guess, sixty pairs, some with the labels still on. If an abundance of knickers were an indicator of wealth, I would be well below the poverty line, or knicker line in this case.

There were three built-in wardrobes, all crammed with clothes. I reasoned if there was anything missing from them, it would be the width of a pair of silk pyjamas. The last third of the end wardrobe held her nightwear – and what sort of person hangs up their nightclothes? I knew I wasn't alone in having just one nightie, in case of a sudden hospital admission. For normal life, wearing old T-shirts in bed works for most women I knew. Lorraine, shoplifting included, remained a complete mystery to me.

I heard what sounded like Jem stamping his feet and the kitchen door opening, then the sound of feet padding towards the bedroom door. Silence. 'Jem,' I called out. Then, a bit louder, 'Jem?'

A black gloved hand thrust through the open door and switched off the light. I ran across to the door just as it closed. Then – *wallop* – it opened again, so that it hit me full in the face. It didn't fell me immediately, but I staggered backwards trying to regain my balance and eventually, after a few seconds of tottering, sagged to the floor.

I held my head, trying to rub away the brain-numbing throbbing that banged away in my forehead. Then I felt sick. Self-preservation versus vomiting began a short-lived battle. I hadn't heard him *leave.* He could still be outside the door. Self-preservation stuck in there and won. I struggled to my feet, managed to find the light switch and looked around for a weapon. I had two choices – a heavy lamp or a hairbrush. No contest. I unplugged the lamp.

The door only faintly creaked as I opened it. The hall was in darkness. Holding the base of the lamp in a threatening manner and with the light from the bedroom behind me, I managed to find the hall light switch. Warily, I made my way to the kitchen. 'Jem!' I yelled through the open kitchen door.

I felt a bit of a fool holding the lamp, so I left it on the table and went to investigate the garden shed. The door was half open. The throbbing in my head was only a minor twitch now compared to a thumping heart and legs that had no knees. I swung the shed door open. In the gloom I could see Jem laid out on the floor.

I knelt beside him and, for the first time ever, felt no hesitation about doing mouth-to-mouth resuscitation. Except that I didn't need to – he was breathing and beginning to stir.

'What the hell happened?' he mumbled, trying to sit upright. As he lifted his head, I saw that blood had pooled where his head lay.

'I'll call an ambulance,' I said.

'No – just get me up. I feel okay.' The pool of clotting blood and the wetness of his jacket denied that fact, but since I wasn't sure where my mobile phone was, it seemed sensible to get him into the house and use the land line.

We supported each other the short distance to the kitchen. Jem put his arm round me and I struggled to keep him upright and my legs from buckling. I sat him down at the kitchen table and turned to shut the back door when I heard a noise from the hall. And there they stood – Lorraine Farnforth and Jasper.

Lorraine looked as perky as the dog. 'Oh, you poor thing,' she said, slipping off her camel coat and advancing on Jem like the angel of mercy I should have been. Worse was to follow. She took Jem's chin in one hand, whilst handing me Jasper on his lead with the other. 'Would you take his lead off and hang it in the hall and give him a rub-down with the little red towel that's in the bathroom?' Not wanting to seem churlish in front of the gorgeous Jem, I took Jasper to the bathroom and, as I rubbed him down, added a few F's to Farnforth and suggested to the dog where I'd like to hang his beloved mistress.

When I returned she was examining his head and bathing the wound. 'It's not too bad, Jem,' she was saying. 'I don't think it will need stitching.'

'I don't agree,' I said, peering at the back of his head. 'I think it needs at least two sutures.'

'Oh –' She paused. 'Well, I could be wrong. I'll call a taxi.'

'No – I'll take him in my car.'

Jem raised his head and flashed me a smile. '*You've* had a nasty bang on the head. Wouldn't you be better going home?'

Before I could answer, Lorraine turned to me. 'You *do* look pale, Kate. I'm sorry I had to leave the house, but you can understand why now. Please go home. Jem says I can stay overnight in his house.'

I stood as still as Lot's wife, post backward glance, but eventually mumbled, 'I'm surprised Jem doesn't want to call the police.'

'Lorraine tells me she has very good reasons for not calling the police,' said Jem. 'And he's gone now – the chances of the local plod being able to find him are remote.'

'The local police are as efficient as any other police force,' I replied, archly.

Lorraine took my arm. 'Please, Kate. Come back tomorrow when you're feeling better. I've explained to Jem about the trouble I've been having with my ex-boyfriend and he agrees I should take out an injunction, but these things take time and, now that Jem's staying next door, I'm sure we'll be safe.'

What a good liar she made. She'd managed to achieve more with a man in the time it takes to rub down a small dog than I could manage as a gyrating table-top dancer. Some women just have sex appeal – I obviously didn't. Perhaps Hubert was right about trainers and old jeans. I needed a new image. That was on the positive side. My negative side was muttering about a new body, a new personality and a whole new bloody life.

As I left I couldn't help wondering how I'd managed to be the one to go. I was the private investigator, after all, except that I felt as if I'd just been ejected from a quiz programme. 'You are the weakest link – good-bye!'

As I drove back to Humberstones, I did seriously wonder if I was in the wrong profession. I hadn't made it up the nursing ladder and my investigations thus far had proved fairly disastrous. There was a major shortage of nurses, except that there seemed no particular branch I was suited for. I wasn't technically minded and I had known nurses so entranced by machines that the *patient* seemed a mere attachment. Anyway, patients didn't exist any more. They were customers or clients or, even worse, healthcare recipients. If patients are in fact customers, would they, I wonder, be willing to wait two days on a trolley at Argos for a bit of service?

Hubert was in his kitchen cooking and singing 'He Who Would Valiant Be' when I arrived back.

'You've been watching *Songs of Praise* again,' I said.

He wiped his hands on his floral apron and gave me a searching look. 'You've got a ruddy great lump on your forehead – did your client bop you one?'

'I'm not in the mood, Hubert.'

'Food will make it better. Food always cheers you up.'

'I'm on a diet.'

He had the cheek to laugh. 'You don't do diets – you told me that yesterday.'

'That was before I remembered that skinny women do seem to have more fun.'

'Depends on your idea of fun,' said Hubert. 'I've cooked roast pork and the crackling is superb. You can start your diet tomorrow.'

I had to admit that, when he opened the oven door, the smell and the sight of it, surrounded by crisp roast potatoes and parsnips, won over my salivary glands. 'Is there any apple sauce?'

'You're never satisfied,' he grumbled.

'Not true.'

'Sit down,' he said, 'before you fall. Do you fancy a bottle of wine?'

'Is the Pope Catholic?'

Roast pork plus crackling and most of a bottle of white wine made the world seem a better place and I told Hubert all about the gorgeous Jem and how an older woman outshone me and was a consummate liar to boot.

'You don't have to take the case,' said Hubert, irritatingly scraping his plate with his knife, as if afraid to miss a tiny scrap. At least I'd managed to leave a sliver of carrot and five peas on *my* plate. 'She could be lying about the shooting,' he suggested.

'So you think this story about the demented ex-boyfriend is more likely?'

He nodded. 'From what I read in the papers, some men have a hard time letting go.'

'I suppose you sympathise with them?'

Hubert shrugged. 'Male pride has a strange effect.'

'But women are supposed to swallow their pride and take it on the chin.'

'Or in your case,' he said, 'on the bonce.'

'You can mock,' I said, 'but male pride is no excuse for violence, stalking and burglary.'

'What are you going to do, then?'

I thought about that for a moment. 'She's paying well,' I said, 'but I don't see why she should not only lie to me but snaffle the man of my dreams from under my nose.'

'So you have a plan?' interrupted Hubert, finishing off his wine in one gulp and pouring cheap brandy into cut-glass balloons.

'Plan?' I queried, thinking he meant had I thought of some means of Jem-retrieval.

'Yes,' said Hubert. 'You know what a plan is – it's organisation – method. Are you going to offer her live-in protection? If so, you've cocked it up once and he might well come back to see you both off.'

He was right, of course, but I wasn't going to admit it. 'You're a cheerful soul,' I said. 'I reckon *he* was more scared than us.'

'Kate – you were clobbered. An army major gets clobbered. I bet the intruder's knees were really knocking.'

There's no convincing Hubert at times. I sipped at the brandy, thinking that it tasted no better than in a tumbler, but it did have the same effect. 'If I had a *plan,* Hubert, it would involve the police and proper channels.'

Hubert nodded sagely, but didn't comment. 'Mrs Farnforth is a devious bitch,' I said, 'but she's obviously in danger and I've said I'd stay, so I'll stay – once the body is found.'

'It might never be found.'

'True, in which case I shall have to persuade her to go to the police.'

Hubert gave me a searching look. 'You don't usually call your clients bitches. This Jem bloke must have made an impact.'

I shrugged. 'Merely lust at first sight.'

'Don't let him distract you, Kate,' said Hubert, wagging

his finger at me. 'You've got to build up a reputation for being a brilliant, incisive PI.'

I laughed. The brandy, cheap and nasty though it was, had made me somewhat more resolute, although brilliant and incisive was pushing it a bit.

'You're suffering from delusions of grandeur,' I said. 'At the moment, survival is at the top of my agenda. The gorgeous Jem is a mere second to that.'

'Are you sure he's not married?'

'That's it, Hubert, try and burst my bubble. Of course he isn't married. Why else would he be staying with his aunt?'

'His wife could be on holiday.'

'She could, but I think that's unlikely.'

I watched Hubert's face carefully. His eyebrows could be expressive. His face remained deadpan and I was convinced he was winding me up. His next question proved it. 'If he's that wonderful, ask yourself why he isn't married.'

'I'm sure he's not gay, if that's what you're suggesting.'

'No need to get rattled. I'm trying to point out you don't know anything about either of them.'

'I haven't had a bloody chance to get to know anything yet. There's only so much chit-chat you can do in certain situations.'

Hubert's expression conveyed more than words.

I went, or rather flounced, to my boxroom-cum-bedroom and lay on the bed, staring at the ceiling and wondering why I wasn't sitting on the decking outside my little wooden cabin in New Zealand. There it would be sunny and warm and I could hear the sea and watch white clouds in a blue sky and breathe unpolluted air. My nostalgia, like an orgasm, didn't last long, and I was soon asleep.

I woke at three a.m. to the sound of a phone ringing. I ignored it, partly because it sounded like Hubert's phone, and partly because he was still in my bad books. What did he expect – perfection?

At eight a.m. there was a knock on my door. 'I've brought you a mug of tea,' announced Hubert, as solemnly as if he were handing me an urn containing the ashes of a loved one.

'You're an angel,' I said, absolving him from my black books. After all, he *was* usually right.

'I had a phone call in the early hours,' he said.

'And?'

'It was a contact of mine at Longborough nick. He's recommended that Ian Jenkins phone you today. It seems the police have several missing persons in the area, but they're overstretched and can't help with cases of missing adults, unless there is some evidence of foul play.'

'Foul play,' I echoed, thoughtfully. 'That's a strange expression, isn't it? I mean, play is play.'

Hubert muttered, 'Yes, yes. Don't forget to take your mobile. You can easily do the cases in tandem.'

'No trouble at all,' I said. 'And move back into my house and probably study for a degree in forensics at the same time.'

He smiled grimly. 'Is your job better than working in a maggot factory?'

'Is there such a thing?'

'Oh yes, and the smell is 'orrible.'

'In that case, Hubert, I'll stop whinging and prove I can crack the case of the missing corpse.'

'Being flippant won't help. It could be that poor man's wife.'

He was right, of course. I murmured, 'Sorry,' and drank his tea with gusto.

I was leaving at nine when my mobile rang. It was Ian Jenkins. He sounded distraught. 'I haven't slept for nights. I'm worried sick – you will find her, won't you? It's the not knowing I can't stand. I've looked everywhere . . .' His voice trailed off.

'I can only promise to do my best. When can I visit you?'

'Any time. I'm not working. I'm looking after the children.'

'I'll be there some time this morning.' I wrote down his address and telephone number.

'Thank you. Thank you so much.'

I found the call distressing. I felt like a cross between Judas and Lord Haw-Haw. What the hell was I going to do?

Four

Lorraine seemed pleased to see me. So too did Jasper, whose little body quivered with excitement, waiting for the fussing he knew was to come.

Now that Jem wasn't around, Lorraine was more anxious and keen to make amends. 'I've got in tea and coffee,' she said. 'And biscuits.' I hadn't mentioned biscuits, so she'd made assumptions based purely on my hip size. She was looking particularly svelte this morning in a navy ensemble – navy skirt and navy sweater with a blue silk scarf at her neck. She looked officer-wife material to me.

We sat in the kitchen. I drank coffee, she drank mint tea. 'Jem thinks I should inform the police about last night,' she said, watching for my reaction.

'Will you?'

She shook her head. 'I'm too scared. They won't offer me round-the-clock protection, will they?'

'They might, if you admitted being a witness to murder.'

'You know I can't do that.'

'There is an alternative,' I said. 'You could feign illness and ask your husband to come home.'

'You mean lie?' she asked, wide-eyed and innocent.

'Lying came easily enough with Jem next door.'

She sipped her mint tea and then smiled. 'Carl is my third husband,' she said, as casually as if they were holidays. How do some women do it? I couldn't manage to find one man to share my bed, never mind marry me. 'You see, Kate,' she continued, 'both divorces gave me grief, but my first husband was the worst loser and he knows where I live. Frankly, he's – unstable.'

'So you're saying it could have been him who attacked us last night?'

'I don't know. I didn't see him. Did you?'

'All I saw was a gloved hand.'

'Jem was hit from behind,' she said, 'so he didn't see his face.'

I drank my tea. Irate ex-husbands seemed preferable to a killer with a gun. 'In that case,' I said, 'the police might at least be able to eliminate one or both ex-husbands as last night's attacker.'

'You could be right, Kate,' she said, eventually.

At long last I was getting somewhere. 'I could let the police know that we suspect one of them of being responsible.'

She nibbled on her lower lip. 'Do what you think best, but please don't mention the murder. Promise.' I promised.

Later that morning I told her I was going to the police, but I'd be back before dark.

'I've got some food shopping to do,' she said. 'Is there anything you especially like or dislike?'

'You will pay for it, won't you?'

She managed a half-smile. 'I don't steal food. Even I have limits.'

'Well, in that case,' I said, 'I'll eat anything but jellied eels, whelks and caviar.'

She looked at me with ill-concealed disdain. 'They didn't feature in my list.'

The police could wait for an hour or so, I decided. In the car I checked Ian Jenkins's address and sat for a while, thinking that if Lorraine was going to cook for me, perhaps it wouldn't be such a bad assignment after all. Hubert was right. This *was* better than a maggot factory. Was he winding me up, though? Are maggots actually bred?

I was about to drive off when I decided to call on Jem. It seemed churlish not to, especially as I was next door and he was easily the most attractive man I'd seen in ages.

'Kate.' He smiled with a flash of perfect enamel. 'How are you? Are you recovered?'

'I'm fine. How's your head?'

'Great. No problem. Come on in and have a coffee.'

The bungalow was neat, but every surface was covered with white crocheted doilies. The coffee table sported three, the dining table one large one. Even the plants rested on them. 'Aunt Emily likes to keep busy,' he said, noticing my eyes straying to the doilies. 'Don't admire them or she'll make you a few hundred.'

Aunt Emily must have smelled the aroma of coffee brewing, because I could hear the click-click of her Zimmer frame approaching. She barely reached my armpit and, although she looked fragile with her thin body and waxen skin, her eyes were bright and her tongue could have won marathons. Her chat ranged from yesteryear and the war to yesterday and the price of cod. I sat bemused, while every so often Jem winked at me.

'Next door is after my Jem, you know,' she continued. 'Mind you, a woman like her' – she managed to make the word *woman* sound like an insult – 'chases anything in a pair of trousers.'

At this point Jem interrupted her flow. 'Auntie, Kate has to go now.'

'Well, you come back soon, dear,' she said, patting my arm. 'It's been so nice talking to you.'

As Jem opened the front door he said, 'We must get together for a drink sometime.' My hopes rose, only to be dashed immediately when he added, 'I'll keep an eye on Lorraine and I'll ring you.'

I knew, of course, that he wouldn't.

The Jenkins house was in Pinecroft Road, just off Longborough High Street – an Edwardian villa with bay windows and the occasional splash of stained glass. Ian Jenkins looked older than I expected, but perhaps that was due to the bags under his eyes. He was in his forties, medium height with fair hair, going grey. Without the eye bags he would have been quite attractive.

He'd opened the door, a child in one arm and one hanging on to his jeans. Both were in mid-scream. 'It's a bloody madhouse,' he said, as he ushered me into a land of strewn toys, packets of nappies, potties and plastic beakers. The child he held was about two, with chubby, bare legs and a red face. The one attached to his leg was four or five, a girl with fair hair. I couldn't see her face, since she was crying and wiping her face on his jeans.

Minutes later I was the one holding the baby and, while the children's attention was taken up with a video, Ian talked and talked. He told me how he had first met Paula – in the Accident and Emergency department of the local hospital. He'd been in a road traffic accident and Paula had been the first nurse he saw when he came round. It had been love at first sight. He was in hospital for a few weeks and, when he came out, she moved in with him. Three months later they were married.

'Daddy,' called out Alice, the little girl, plaintively, 'I want a biscuit.'

'You know where they are.'

Alice left the room and Steven clambered from the sofa and toddled behind her.

'Does Paula still work at the General?' I asked.

Ian shook his head. 'No, I –' He paused. 'We agreed that she should give up work. I run my own business making surgical precision instruments. She didn't *need* to work, but she missed it.'

'Do you think she was depressed?'

He shook his head. 'Sometimes she was nervy and anxious, but I wouldn't say she was *depressed*.'

'She's left home before, hasn't she?'

'Daddy! Daddy!' came a high-pitched scream from the kitchen.

'Oh God! Here we go.' Ian left the room and returned with Steven under his arm and Alice declaring loudly, 'It wasn't *my* fault, Daddy – he grabbed *all* the biscuits. *He* made the mess all over the floor. It wasn't *me*!'

'It never is,' he said wearily. 'Just sit down and watch the video.'

'I don't like this video,' she said, stamping her feet. 'Mummy knows I don't like it.'

'Mummy – Mummy,' called out Steven.

I shifted uneasily in my chair. I wanted out too. 'Have you thought about getting some help with the children?' I asked.

Ian patted Steven on the head and set him down on the floor, where he began a tantrum. Above the noise he nodded. 'I'm interviewing nannies at the moment.'

'If you get a chance,' I said, 'we can meet up in my office for a proper chat. Just ring me on my mobile.'

'I *hate* this video,' yelled Alice. 'It's only for *babies*. Mummy—'

'Mummy isn't here,' snapped Ian.

'Why *not*?'

Ian shrugged miserably and I left, shaking his hand and wishing him the best of luck.

Outside in the cold fresh air I thought about the joys of parenthood. Is it merely a rumour cast by harassed parents to convince the childless they're missing out? Or is it simply that other people's children are never that appealing unless asleep? Either way, a proper conversation between two adults isn't possible with young children present, but at least I'd learnt that Paula wasn't a happy stay-at-home mum. Was she dead, though? How many women wear a red beret and scarf? Ian Jenkins seemed a nice enough bloke, so why would an ex-nurse be shot in a car park? Could it be a love triangle, or had she got involved with drugs? The drug angle was a possibility, but I wasn't convinced. And does a woman with two small children *have* extra-marital opportunities? Where would she meet a man anyway? On the school or playgroup run? At aqua aerobics? Was there something wrong with me, I wondered – pre-New Zealand I'd been round and about and hadn't managed much in the way of any sort of sex.

I drove directly to the police station. Sleet accompanied by general winter drear made even the local nick seem quite warm and welcoming. And at least it was open. Due to only intermittent crime, the station now closed at weekends and then an officer living in the police house at Dunmore could be called out.

Since Saturday night and subsequently drunken Sunday mornings are sometimes quite riotous (in Longborough a riot is four or five youths tanked up on three strong lagers) it seemed a bit short-sighted for the station to be closed then. On a Monday *nothing* happens in the town. Tuesdays are more lively – it's pension and market day. Otherwise muggings and bank robberies are relatively unknown. But now a woman had been shot dead and, as yet, only three people knew. I, being one of them, was worried. Dead bodies *do* keep their secrets. People *do* disappear never to be seen again.

'Can I help you, madam?' asked the PC at the desk.

'Yes,' I said, wondering how old you have to look before being called *madam.* 'I wish to report a crime.'

'What sort of crime, madam?' He was young, about

twenty, fresh-faced and earnest-looking. The type who might join the Salvation Army and bang a tambourine. He had a supercilious edge to his tone, as if somehow *my* idea of a crime might be double parking.

'Burglary and GBH,' I answered, crisply.

'That would be CID you want then, madam,' he said. 'Sit down in the waiting room and I'll call you when someone is available.'

I sat down and waited. And waited. My normal lunchtime came and went. My blood sugar took such a serious dive that I began to shiver. I can barely function without food every three hours or so and I began to feel cold, sick and irritable. I went back to the PC at the desk. 'Is there any chance I might see someone this century?'

I knew it was a mistake as soon as I opened my big mouth. Police constables, especially young ones, don't like a smart arse. His eyes narrowed as if I'd banged his tambourine. 'You'll have to be patient, madam. We are very busy.'

I couldn't help it – I was hungry and I had a headache starting. 'Has there been a crime wave?' I asked.

This time his eyes narrowed and his lips tightened. I wasn't doing myself any favours. Now his indignation was akin to his tambourine being stolen. 'Not that I know of,' he said, between clenched teeth. 'You'll just have to sit down and wait your turn.'

My turn? There was no one else waiting. Hubert's funeral parlour was more active. The thought of Hubert gave me an idea. I wandered outside to use my mobile phone.

'Yes, Kate,' he said. 'What can I do for you?'

'Just give me a name,' I said. 'I've been stuck in Longborough nick for hours.'

'DCI David Todman.'

'Cheers.'

'I hope it helps.'

I went back to the desk. 'Officer,' I said, with a friendly

smile, 'would you know if DCI David Todman is in his office?'

He nodded, still peeved.

'Would you tell him Kate Kinsella from Humberstones is here, and that I'd be grateful if I could have a quick word.'

He was about to answer when I said, 'I'll sit down and wait, shall I?'

'You do that, madam.'

I waited another fifteen minutes before a man in a grey suit appeared and introduced himself as DCI Todman. Lean with hazel eyes and dark wavy hair, he was younger than I expected and better looking. I was also quite impressed by his aquamarine shirt and grey and black striped tie. 'Kate,' he said, shaking my hand. 'I've heard so much about you.'

'You have?' I was astounded.

'Come on up to my office.'

I couldn't help giving the constable on the desk a wink as we passed.

DCI David Todman listened to details of the assault and keyed them into the computer in front of him. 'So, in fact, you only saw a gloved hand,' he said, when I'd finished.

That sounded feeble, I knew, but it was the truth.

'What puzzles me,' he said, staring at me, 'is why the next-door neighbour didn't report his injuries. After all, *he* could claim compensation.' I muttered about him being home on leave and that Lorraine had asked the police to visit but they had refused. There was a pause while the DCI looked at his computer. 'In the past three weeks Mrs Farnforth has allegedly seen prowlers at least twice a week.' He looked across at me and smiled. 'No evidence of a prowler was ever found.'

'So that's why the police didn't come.'

'I see you have a razor-sharp mind, Kate.'

'Very funny.'

'I can be,' he said, 'given half a chance.'

'There *has* been a prowler this time, and Jem Harrison next door has injuries to prove it.'

'And *this time*,' he said, 'we'll investigate.'

'What about her ex-husbands?'

He checked the screen. 'On the first two occasions they had alibis. The first husband is happily remarried and the second husband denies either wanting her back or even wanting to see her again.'

'So you think she's a liar?'

He shrugged. 'Neurotic and lonely would be my opinion. Husband away weeks at a time. Her imagination works overtime.'

'Except for this time.'

'Okay – I agree. She cried wolf once too often, but we don't have the numbers to personally visit every worried, home-alone woman. My advice to them would be to buy a Rottweiler.'

'Very practical. Anyway, she does have a dog.'

'What sort?'

'A poodle.'

He laughed. 'Could give a nasty nip on the ankles.'

'This isn't funny.'

He sat looking mock solemn. 'We'll pay her a visit.'

By now I was feeling twitchy and I sat poised on the edge of my seat, longing to tell him about the shooting. It was on my conscience. Someone had been killed – maybe Paula Jenkins – and I was doing nothing. Just as I was about to ask about police policy on missing adults, he leant back in his chair and said, 'How is the old boy?'

For a moment I was mystified, then the penny dropped. 'Hubert? He's fine.'

'I've known him for years,' he said. 'He buried my dad

ten years ago and just recently my mum. He always does a good job.'

This really was a conversation stopper. I shifted in my seat. 'Thanks for your help.'

As he showed me to the door he said, 'I suppose Hubert told you I was divorced.'

I shook my head.

'Well, I am and I was . . . wondering if you'd like to have a drink with me sometime.'

Strange, I thought, that when a man does ask me out, I always hesitate. My social diary remained as virginal as a nun's wimple and yet I mumbled something about being busy. Who was I kidding? 'You could phone me on my mobile,' I mumbled.

'Will do. Number?'

My memory bank foreclosed on that one. 'I'll ring *you*,' I said, 'if that's okay.'

'Fine by me.'

As I walked out of the station I thought – choice is power. If he *really* wants to see me, he'll find out my phone number. I still had the option to ring him, and I might – and then again I might not.

Hubert was just returning from a funeral when I arrived at Humberstones. His face had a set expression, but he didn't go into details. Some funerals really got to him and I guessed this was one of them. Sometimes he told me about them and sometimes he didn't.

I updated my two files and waited for him to appear. When he did, he'd changed from his black work suit to a dark grey, which meant an alternative funeral was in the offing. 'I've been to the police,' I said, 'about the assault.'

'That's a start.' He sounded glum and his expression remained set.

'Anything wrong?'

He shrugged and cast me a pleading expression. 'I've got

a booking for the catering suite after the next funeral and the caterers have let me down.'

'Don't look at me like that, Hubert. I've got to get back to my client.'

'I can't let people down,' he said, 'and no other caterers can manage it.'

'What about the bakers?' I suggested. 'There's two in the High Street – I was a good customer once. They do sandwiches and baguettes and some lovely cakes.'

Hubert's face brightened. 'I'll give them a ring.'

'Now that's settled,' I said, 'what exactly did you say to DCI Todman?'

'What do you mean?'

'Don't play the innocent – you know what I mean. He gave me the old *I've heard so much about you* routine, so I know you've said something.'

'Did he ask you out?'

I nodded. 'I said I'd phone him.'

'You're a hussy,' said Hubert, with a smile. 'And he could be useful.'

'I think a course in martial arts might be of more use.'

Hubert was about to leave the room when thoughts of the baker's made me think of food. 'Could you order me a ham salad roll and a jam doughnut?'

'I don't know how long it will be.'

'I'll wait.'

Whilst I waited I stared at my computer screen. I was typing in David Todman's name when my mobile rang. I scrabbled around dementedly in my shoulder bag, like a ferret up a trouser leg, and eventually found it.

It was Ian Jenkins.

Five

'I've thought of something,' shouted Ian excitedly, above the sound of his screaming kids.

'What's that?' I yelled back.

'The afternoon Paula went missing, she left the house wearing that red beret and scarf—' A wailing sound from Steven interrupted him.

I waited until the noise lessened. 'You were saying?'

'I've just found them in a plastic bag at the bottom of the children's cupboard.'

'What do you think it means?' I asked, as I moved the phone further from my ear. 'That she wasn't wearing them? Or could she have returned to the house?'

'No, no.' His voice lowered now as the children became ominously quiet. 'I don't think so, but it explains why nobody saw Paula in the town. After all, they would have noticed her in that gear, but – Alice, put Steven *down*!'

I wasn't quite sure what to say now. I waited for him to say more, but general mayhem in the background gave me time to think. Had the gunman managed to return the beret and scarf and if so, why? It would be useful to have them forensically examined, but what could I say that didn't give my knowledge away?

'I've made contact with a police inspector, Ian, so I'll get in touch with him and try to chivvy them into action.' It was only after I'd promised to visit him ASAP and put the phone down that I wondered why *he* hadn't immediately contacted the police. Was he merely disenchanted with their reaction or was there a good reason she'd left in the first place?

My more immediate concern that day was Lorraine and, after all, I was being paid to protect her.

I returned just before dark in slow-falling sleet. Aspen Gardens seemed already tucked up for the night with drawn curtains and soft lights from lamplit rooms. Lorraine, wearing a black velvet ensemble, smiled at me in a relieved fashion and Jasper nuzzled a wet nose just above my ankle. It seemed he too had accepted me because he didn't yap once.

'We'll eat about seven,' she said. 'Some pasta with a home-made sauce – will that be okay?'

'Sounds fine by me.'

We sat in the lounge – she and Jasper on one sofa and I on the other. There was a hiatus of silence which went unrelieved for a few minutes until she said, 'Do you fancy a drink?'

I smiled and nodded, hoping she meant alcohol. I had a feeling that I would relate better to Lorraine if I were a tad mellowed.

Pre-pasta she managed to down two large vodkas and half a bottle of wine. If she'd shown any real signs of getting plastered I wouldn't have been concerned but she merely became more talkative. In comparison to her I was virtually teetotal and yet she avoided caffeine as though her enemy lurked in a cup of coffee.

'Carl chose to live here,' she confided, 'because he thought it was a safe area, especially as I'm on my own so much.'

'Where did you live before?'

'London. Harrow. We had a lovely town house there. Big bay windows, a huge garden and a great social life – theatres, art galleries – so much to do and see. I loved it.'

I'd been to Harrow once. It was leafy and pleasant

and it certainly wasn't the crime centre of the Western world. 'Harrow isn't exactly Manchester's Moss Side or London's Tower Hamlets,' I said, 'so what was your husband afraid of?'

'We were burgled twice,' she said. 'It seemed to worry him more than me.' She sipped at her wine thoughtfully and I wondered if she'd drunk as much then as she did now. Perhaps she'd been too pickled to worry overmuch about mere burglaries. 'Carl was in the UK both times,' she said. 'We'd been out for the evening and when we came back we'd been turned over. Literally. Every drawer, every cupboard, even the beds had been upended.'

'What did they take?'

'That's the strange thing – absolutely nothing. Not even my jewellery, and I have some nice pieces.'

'You mean you were burgled twice and both times they took nothing?'

Lorraine chewed on the remains of a fingernail. 'I suppose I wasn't that worried, because I thought it likely it was someone we knew being vindictive.'

'Like an ex-husband?'

'Possibly.'

'Do you still think that?'

She examined her gnawed fingernail with interest. 'I'm not sure,' she said, eventually. 'Either of them might have trashed the place, but there was no real damage done.' She paused. 'It was as if whoever it was – was looking for something.'

'And you have no idea what?'

She shook her head. 'Carl has no idea either.'

It was when she progressed to another fingernail that I began to view *my* nails with interest. I had to say something. 'For God's sake,' I snapped, 'can't you *sit* on your hands?'

'I can't help it,' she said. 'My nerves are in tatters. It isn't every day I see someone murdered and know the murderer is after me.'

I murmured a lukewarm apology and she retreated to the kitchen to make the pasta she'd promised me.

When it did arrive half an hour later it was an overcooked carbonara (she announced it as that) with the spaghetti clumped together in a gelatinous sauce that could compete with some of my worst culinary disasters. Whatever it was it tasted truly awful. 'I only eat once a day,' she said moving the food around the plate. If her daily meal was generally on a par with this one, I wasn't surprised that one was more than enough. I felt relieved my portion was so small but I managed to eat it and began to feel like someone trapped in a pretentious wine bar longing to escape to the local chippy.

No dessert other than either more wine or vodka was offered so I drank wine and began scribbling notes that I hoped I'd be able to read later. 'Could you tell me a little more about Carl?' I began, pen poised. It seemed innocuous enough.

'Why?' she snapped. 'He's got nothing to do with this.' Her hand slipped to her right side and she grimaced.

'Are you okay?' I asked.

She shrugged and continued to hold her side. 'It's just a pain I've been getting now and again – it passes.'

'It could be your appendix,' I suggested.

'I'll be fine,' she said briskly. She drank more vodka in silence and afterwards I could tell by her relieved expression that the pain had finally gone.

I wondered if the vodka was masking the problem but I knew she wasn't going to stop drinking just because I didn't think it was a good idea. As her expression relaxed I continued with, 'If you don't want to talk about Carl, let's talk about your ex-husbands.'

'What for? It wasn't anyone I knew who killed that woman.'

'You're sure?'

'Of course I am. I think I would have recognised someone I was married to.'

'They could have changed. How long is it since you saw your first husband?'

She paused momentarily. 'About ten years.'

'And your second?'

'Just before I married Carl.'

'Which was?'

'Seven years ago.'

She finished her vodka and placed her glass on a silver coaster on the coffee table. Then she sat back on the sofa, closed her eyes and murmured, 'I'm sure it couldn't have been either of them. Anyway, they might kill me but why would they kill her?'

It was the way she said '*her*' that puzzled me. Not '*that poor woman*' or '*that girl*'.

'You knew her, didn't you?'

'I didn't recognise her, if that's what you mean. But if she's the missing woman Paula Jenkins, I *did* know her.'

I gulped the rest of my wine, resolved not to have any more because I needed a clear head. Lorraine Farnforth was full of surprises and I didn't need any help in dulling my senses. With or without alcohol I could cock up.

'How did you get to meet her?' I asked casually. A mother of two young children and a shoplifter with none. It seemed strange that their paths should have crossed.

'I know her,' she said cagily. 'Ian Jenkins and Carl once worked together on a project.'

'What sort of project?'

Lorraine shrugged. 'Some sort of precision engineering. I really don't know. I'm not that interested in Carl's work.'

'What *are* you interested in?' I asked.

She chewed on her index finger and stared at me. 'You think I'm a selfish, bored, spoiled woman, don't you?'

'I didn't say that.'

'You didn't have to.'

'If you want me to help catch the killer,' I said, 'then you'll have to cooperate.'

'You mean go to the police?'

'You could give me more details of that evening. I could then relay it to the police anonymously. Of course, they might well investigate all Paula and Ian Jenkins's known associates, and they may well get round to you – and then, of course, you'll have to make a choice.'

'If Carl lost his job because of me he'd divorce me, you know.'

'Are things that rocky?'

She smiled at me grimly. 'He's my third husband, so I'm obviously not good wife material.'

'Or a poor judge of men,' I suggested.

'No, it's me,' she said miserably. 'My marriage to Alan was very happy for the first two years, until I mentioned having a family. Then over the next year it broke down. I rushed into a second with Sean because he wanted children as much as I did.' She paused, staring at the remnants of her fingernails. 'He refused to have any tests, convinced it was my fault because he'd fathered a child before. So that was marriage number two out of the window. Then a couple of years later I met Carl.' Her eyes filled with tears. 'I'm such a bloody failure – I still couldn't get pregnant.'

'Isn't there anything that could be done?'

She shook her head. 'Over the years we've considered surrogacy and adoption – but had no luck with either. Carl wanted his own child anyway, and since he's been working in Saudi he seems to have lost interest altogether.'

'I'm sorry.'

'Don't be. I've money in the bank, my health, and

Carl is very loving and kind, so I do have a lot to be grateful for.'

She refilled her glass; a third vodka topped up with orange juice, and invited me to have one. I declined and she sat next to Jasper who lay asleep on a miniature duvet, stretched out in sublime contentment.

'Do you have any family?' I asked.

She shook her head. 'My parents are both dead. My mother died in a road accident. My father was driving. He hung himself from the rafters. I was the one to find him.'

'Have you ever recovered from that?' I murmured.

'Yes . . . I—' She broke off. 'No one's ever asked me that before. I hadn't thought.' She gulped down some of the vodka. 'I'm still angry, I know that. The selfish old sod.' She began to laugh, the sort of hysteria that is a prelude to tears. 'He knew I'd be the one to find him. I know he cared about my mother and I thought he cared about *me*!'

'Perhaps it was a spur of the moment thing.'

Lorraine's eyes flashed at me, bright with tears. 'The bastard bought the rope a week before. He planned it.'

The phone rang, startling us both. 'Oh my God,' she said, as if it couldn't be a normal phone call.

'Do you want me to take it?'

She took her last gulp of vodka and shook her head. 'Hello.' There was a moment's pause during which I stood up, as if it would make a difference. 'Carl,' she breathed in relief. 'How unexpected. Is everything all right?'

I made my way to the kitchen and began washing up. I noticed there were more vodka bottles in her kitchen cupboards than on a supermarket shelf and that her fridge was empty apart from a hunk of Parmesan cheese, a carton of milk and a bottle of champagne. I wondered idly if I'd lose a few pounds in weight if I kept my fridge virtually empty. Perhaps that was the answer to all weight problems. Or at least mine.

I was closing the fridge door when I realised Lorraine was right behind me. I spun round. She was smiling broadly. 'He's got a bonus so he's taking an extra week's leave instead.'

'That's great. When will he be arriving?'

'In a few days, depending on flights and things.'

Although I didn't want to burst her bubble at that moment, I knew I would have to sooner or later. And only a little later she decided to have a nightcap, so I sat opposite her with a glass of fizzy water and said, 'Let's talk about the shoplifting, Lorraine.'

'What is there to say?'

'Have you ever been caught?'

She shook her head.

'Not even cautioned?'

Again she shook her head but now she looked nervous. Even though she was holding her glass of vodka she was staring at her fingernails.

'I'm finding it odd,' I said, 'that you would be worried about Carl losing his job when you've never been either convicted or cautioned, and although you thought a store detective was following you that night you were obviously wrong.'

'I *do* shoplift but, as I said, I take most things back.'

'But you don't fear being caught enough to give it up?'

'I suppose not.'

'The night you saw the shooting, which shop had you just left?'

'Boots.'

'What had you stolen?'

'A lipstick.'

'Describe the store detective to me.'

She took a swig of vodka. 'He was—'

'Don't bother lying, Lorraine. I don't believe a shop that size even has a store detective.'

She didn't answer, just stared into her glass.

'A store that size,' I said, 'would rely on CCTV or mirrors. There are no shops big enough in Longborough to fund a store detective.'

'How do you know?' she snapped. 'You've been away.'

I didn't know, I was just guessing, but her reaction proved I was right.

'I think you're genuinely scared, Lorraine,' I said quietly. 'But if you lie to me about the shoplifting, how do I know you're telling the truth about the shooting?'

Lorraine reacted with a big sigh. 'I'll tell you, but you must swear to me that you won't tell a soul.' I was just about to swear when she added, 'Someone might die if you did.' I nodded solemnly and promised.

The vodka was at last beginning to take its toll and Lorraine's face had a rosy glow – or was it the lamplight?

'I wasn't shoplifting that afternoon,' she said. 'I was with a man and I'd had quite a bit to drink.'

I wasn't that surprised. Lorraine having an affair and drinking seemed far more in character than shoplifting. 'I'm not in love with him,' she said. 'But he thinks I am.'

I kept quiet while she stared at me, waiting for a reaction. 'He's a good man and I'm using him.'

'He's married?'

'Oh yes. He's got three children. If anyone found out it would ruin his marriage and his career.'

She was watching me like a hawk. 'It's not an *affair* as such. The only reason I'm doing it is to get pregnant.'

'And then you'll pass it off as Carl's.'

'Yes. Does that shock you?'

I shrugged. 'No, I'm not shocked. Just surprised you're willing to take such a risk in a small town. Sooner or later you'll be caught.'

'I do know that – but I'm desperate. I don't see him when Carl comes home, of course.'

'Are you going to tell me who he is?'

There was a short pause before she said, 'He's my doctor.'

I didn't ask his name. The chances of there being more than one male doctor with three children in Longborough was pretty remote. When I re-registered with a doctor I'd make sure *he* wasn't the one.

'There's something else.' Lorraine stood up, swayed a fraction as if she were on board a ship in a choppy sea and left the room.

She returned in a few minutes and stood in the doorway. This time I *was* surprised. My mouth dropped open. She was smiling a grim 'I told you so' sort of smile.

Six

Lorraine stood in the doorway for a few seconds. Even in the dimness of the hall she shone like a beacon. She wore a red beret forward over her left eye, and a red scarf she'd wrapped around her neck. 'What the hell is going on?' I demanded, as my left knee trembled and my stomach jigged up and down like the needle on a sewing machine.

'I thought you might be able to tell me,' said Lorraine, removing the beret and the scarf. 'How do you think I felt seeing a woman shot wearing an identical scarf and beret?'

'Why didn't you tell me before?'

'There was plenty of time,' she said, handing me the beret and the scarf. 'They were sent to me in the post. I hadn't ordered them. They were wrapped in a plastic bag, no order form with them. The name and address on the parcel was correct so I put them in the back of a drawer and forgot about them. After all, I wouldn't be seen dead . . . oh my God.' She paled and sank down on the sofa. 'Do you think I was meant to wear them as some sort of signal?'

'You mean a contract killer?'

She nodded and I thought about it for a moment. 'It seems a bit unlikely,' I said, 'in Longborough, and anyway why would anyone want you dead?'

She shrugged mutely.

'The scarf and beret could just be a horrible coincidence.' Who was I kidding? I was just grateful I hadn't mentioned the mysterious return of the same items to the Jenkins house.

'I need another drink,' she said. 'Will you have one?'

This time I needed one.

I sipped my vodka and fresh orange in a ladylike fashion and thought about the alternatives and any plan A or B. Of course there was really no option – she, or we, had to go to the police.

'In the morning,' I said firmly, 'we go to the police. You say you were shopping on that Thursday evening. The fact that you were screwing your GP has nothing to do with them. After all, it isn't a criminal act. The BMA might not approve but you've been discreet and neither of you are going to admit it – are you?'

She nodded. 'I was very careful but the police think I'm a nuisance – I've rung them so many times about prowlers.'

'Paula Jenkins is missing – they'll have to take notice.'

It was now past midnight and I wanted nothing more than sleep. Lorraine still looked pale and occasionally in pain and was once more anxiously scanning her fingernails for a chewable morsel. It did cross my mind that if her GP lover couldn't cure one simple habit then he wasn't up to much, except of course in the bedroom.

I checked the doors and the window and the burglar alarm and by the time I'd done that Lorraine was asleep, curled up on her side on the sofa. The alcohol had finally closed down her brain. I tried to wake her but although she stirred slightly it was just to mutter, 'Piss off and let me sleep.' I didn't need telling twice so I took the duvet from the bed, draped it over her and slipped off her mules. Only Jasper stirred and, seeing an opportunity, snuggled under the duvet beside her.

My single divan with pale blue duvet and embroidered pillowcases looked inviting and within minutes I was asleep. And within a few more minutes, or so it seemed, Jasper had jumped on my bed and was licking, sniffing and whimpering at me.

'Want a change of venue, do you?' I murmured through dry lips before falling asleep again. When I woke again Jasper was at the doorway huffing and puffing. 'Do you want to wee?' I asked, as though he could understand my every word. I switched on the bedside light, staggered out of bed and lurched somewhat unsteadily towards the kitchen.

I knew immediately something was wrong. Cold air wafted through my T-shirt and I walked towards the draught. The back door was wide open and swinging free. Shards of glass glinted on the kitchen floor. 'Lorraine!' I yelled, dashing into the lounge. She was still lying on the sofa, the mauve duvet just falling short of her feet. 'Lorraine!' I shrieked again as I yanked back the duvet. She lay on her back, her eyes wide open. Vomit had trickled from her mouth and pooled in the groove between her collarbone and her neck. I felt her hand – it was so cold it hurt.

In real life a scream can be hard to find and, although I was screaming inside, on the outside I stood unmoving. Then, in what seemed like slow motion, I walked over to the phone and began dialling. Why I dialled Hubert's number I don't know. Was it because I knew he was always calm in the face of death? Or was it because I thought he'd get to me sooner? Either way it didn't matter. I wanted to hear the sound of a friendly, calm voice.

'I'm on my way,' he said. 'I'll ring the police. Just don't touch anything.'

'I'm supposed to be the detective,' I said, then found myself on the verge of tears and saying, 'It's all my fault – I didn't hear a thing. I was supposed to be protecting her and now she's—'

'Stop it, Kate. Just pull yourself together. You've seen dead bodies before.'

'I'm not a bloody undertaker, though, am I?' I snapped back.

'That's more like the Kate I know,' he said briskly. 'Now make yourself a cup of tea and before you've drunk it I'll be there.'

And he was. 'You could have got dressed,' he said as I opened the front door. I hadn't realised that I wasn't properly clothed. It seemed a minor consideration in the face of sudden death or murder but at least my T-shirt was mid-thigh length, and my legs are easily my most presentable part. I dressed quickly, leaving Hubert to fuss over Jasper, who did now seem to realise something was drastically wrong because he'd leapt into Hubert's lap and was whining piteously.

It was another ten minutes before an assortment of police personnel arrived, DCI David Todman amongst them. 'What's been going on?' he asked me mildly enough, but suspicion shone in his eyes as brightly as sunlight on morning dew.

'How long have you got?' I asked.

'As long as it takes,' he said. 'Do you want to answer questions here or at the station?'

I looked around. Already the bungalow was crowded and that was before the forensic team had even arrived. 'I didn't hear a thing,' I found myself saying loudly. So loudly a hush fell on the room and all eyes seemed to be on me. 'I didn't,' I repeated lamely.

'Not even when the door was jemmied?'

'I was tired.'

'Must have been in a bloody coma,' said a male voice.

David Todman took me by the arm and I looked across at Hubert, who had, it seemed, so bonded with the dog that he was standing but still holding Jasper in his arms. 'Were you on a social visit?' asked Todman.

'Working,' I answered.

'What sort of work?

'Protection,' I mumbled.

The bastard pretended not to hear. 'What was that?' he asked. This was a man I had considered phoning.

'You heard the first time.'

'A little louder, please, Kate, for the benefit of my colleagues.'

'Protection,' I repeated.

There was a little ripple of laughter. 'It's not funny,' I said. 'At least I took her seriously. You lot refused to make an appearance the last time she called.'

The arrival of the forensic team and the police doctor focused attention back where it belonged – on Lorraine. I tried to eavesdrop but all I could manage to gather was that she'd been dead for at least four hours and, in official jargon, the 'actual cause of death' could not be ascertained.

Quite unnecessarily DCI Todman took down my address and phone number at Humberstones, said I could go and told me he'd give me a ring when he was back at the station.

'What about the dog?' I asked.

'The police dog pound?' he suggested.

Hubert stepped forward then, clutching the dog to his bosom. 'I'll take him,' he said.

There was no murmur of dissent so we began sidling towards the door. 'If Jasper's sick in your car don't be surprised,' I said as we walked outside.

'I've always wanted a dog,' said Hubert, stroking the head that nuzzled into his chest.

'Don't you think you've been a tad impulsive?' I asked.

Hubert smiled down at the dog and I knew in that instant that Hubert had fallen in love. I felt a totally unreasonable pang of jealousy.

'I'll go back and collect his lead and his duvet, his dog bowl, his brush and . . .' I tailed off as he put a restraining hand on my arm.

'Don't go on, Kate,' he said. 'I'll go straight to the pet shop and get him everything he needs. New life, new gear. I'll see you back at my place.'

I'd been dismissed by Hubert, of all people. Didn't he realise I was feeling fragile? I hadn't known Lorraine well, hadn't even liked her at first but I'd warmed to her, we'd shared a meal, a drink, her troubles, and I'd failed her. The only thing she'd wanted from me was protection and I'd slept through the sounds of the back door being jemmied and her dying. There *had* been a prowler and he'd ended her life somehow. It was possible, I supposed, that she'd choked on her own vomit – the post-mortem would reveal that – but I was convinced she had been murdered and I resolved, come what might, to find her killer.

For some time I sat in my office staring at the word 'Protection' on my computer screen. My mind was blank and all I wanted was for Hubert to come back so that we could talk it over.

I saw his car arrive, but he didn't come straight up to me. He had Jasper on a new lead and was introducing him to the car park. It was more than an hour later by the time he finally appeared.

'I've just been introducing Jasper to his new home,' he said proudly. 'I've left him downstairs with Elvie.' Elvie was his new receptionist.

'Are you sure he'll cope without you?'

Hubert opened his mouth to reply but closed it again. 'I had you going there, Hubert. You've really got it bad. Love at first sight, was it?'

'You're jealous.'

'I am not!'

'Oh yes you are,' he said, wagging his finger at me. 'Jealous of a little dog. You should be ashamed of yourself.'

'I'm contrite,' I lied. 'If you can spare a few minutes from your canine duties I'd be grateful for your help.'

Mollified a little, Hubert sat down. 'Apart from your little barbed comments, you know I always have time for you, Kate.'

'I'm in a rotten mood – I feel such a failure.'

'You can't help that,' he said. 'You *are*.'

It seemed from dry eyes to a bucketful of tears took no time at all. Hubert faffed a bit patting my back and then brought me tissues and a large brandy. The brandy did the trick. 'There, there,' he said, giving me a final pat. 'I was only joking. Think of it this way, Kate. If you *had* woken up you could be dead too.'

That thought didn't make me feel any better but telling him about Lorraine did. 'I reckon I know who that doctor is,' said Hubert. 'There's only one in town with three kids – Reece Gardener. He's fortyish and used to play cricket with the local team.'

'Is he attractive?'

'How would I know? He wears glasses and he's medium build and he's got a full head of hair.'

'Where's his surgery?'

'On the Dunmore road – just a two-man practice in a large house.'

'Does he live there?' I asked.

'I don't know. Couldn't you have found all this out from your client?'

'That's hardly fair,' I said. 'How could I have known she wouldn't survive till morning? I thought time was on my side.'

Hubert shrugged. 'He could be a suspect, anyway – he might have got scared his wife would find out.'

'Using a jemmy on the back door seems a bit crass for a GP when he could have managed something medical.'

'Like Dr Shipman?'

'Precisely, and as she was his patient he could have got away with it.'

'Do the police know about him?'

'No, and I don't intend to tell them.'

'Is that wise?'

'What's wisdom got to do with being a PI, Hubert? Nothing. I wouldn't want to wreck his marriage when a few questions might be all that's needed.'

Hubert gave me a quizzical look. 'Don't get above yourself. Since when has a few questions sorted anything out for you?'

I had to agree he was right, but I was still adamant that Dr Reece Gardener's involvement shouldn't be mentioned – it was bad enough to have to disclose a shooting.

Hubert looked a little restless and I guessed he'd remembered Jasper. 'Do you realise,' I said, 'Jasper probably knows who the killer is.'

'Did he bark?'

'I don't know. He did come into my room – he was whimpering a bit, but I don't know much about dogs. I thought he wanted a wee.'

'If he didn't bark, maybe he knew the intruder,' suggested Hubert.

'In that case,' I said, 'in a police line-up he'd be able to pick him out on a three woofs basis.'

'Don't be so daft,' said Hubert, but I had the feeling he thought Jasper *was* bright enough to do just that.

'I did find out something else.' Hubert raised his eyebrows in anticipation. 'Carl Farnforth knew Ian Jenkins.'

The eyebrows stayed raised. 'That gives us something to go on,' he said. 'I'll see what I can find out about Ian Jenkins.' I noticed the 'us'. Usually it irritated me – this time it didn't, for I finally had to accept I needed all the help I could get.

'I know he runs a surgical instrument business locally—' I broke off, interrupted by the telephone.

It was DCI David Todman requesting my attendance.

I decided the walk would do me good. It also gave me more time to think and worry. My stomach seemed to flutter about in my chest like a trapped bird. The sort of feeling I get on planes whenever turbulence strikes. I didn't know DCI Todman and at this stage I didn't want to. He wasn't going to be best pleased with my revelations. I'd failed Lorraine but I'd also failed Paula Jenkins. It was payback time.

Seven

David Todman met me in reception with his tie askew and his brow furrowed. 'The interview rooms are full,' he explained as he elbowed me out of the door. 'It's bloody bedlam in there so I'll take you out for that drink and a chat.' I'd imagined sackcloth and ashes in some windowless room with a po-faced WPC standing by. Somehow an intimate tête-à-tête in a pub seemed just as scary.

We were already outside when I said, 'Look, I don't think this is a very good idea.'

'From where I'm standing,' he said, straightening his tie, 'getting out of a madhouse for a few minutes with an attractive woman seems like a very good idea.'

A little bit of flattery is nearly as good as finding plenty of jam in a doughnut so I didn't argue any more. 'You'll like this place,' he said as he walked with long strides into a side alley a few hundred yards away, which, pre-NZ, had been virtually derelict. Now we passed a boutique and a china shop and there, instead of the pub I was expecting, was Monica's Tea Room.

'I thought you'd be a pub man,' I said.

He shook his head. 'I'm an oddball – I don't drink.'

'Not at all?' I asked, amazed.

He shook his head and opened the door; a bell above announced our arrival.

Monica's had an atmosphere of reconstituted yesteryear. The waitresses wore frilly white aprons over black dresses and, to complete the look, black court shoes. The tablecloths were embroidered and the cups and teapots pure white china. There were six tables, only two of which were occupied, but we were directed to a corner table as if it were the holy of holies and left with a tasselled menu. I couldn't help comparing prices – in New Zealand for the cost of Monica's cream tea you could have eaten sirloin steak, chips and salad washed down with a glass of wine – which is why I was nudging diethood. I hesitated over the menu, the sight of food alone having settled my stomach. The home-made scones with clotted cream sounded good and I was genuinely hungry.

I put down the menu. 'Inspector – I have a confession to make, and I can't sit here drinking tea and not being straight with you.'

'Let me guess,' he said. 'In New Zealand you secretly married a huge tattooed Maori and now all covered parts of your body are decorated with matching tattoos.'

'I'm being serious.'

'Yeah. I can tell that by the look on your face. Get it over with.'

I explained briefly why I was supposedly protecting Lorraine. I expected him to be furious that I hadn't reported the shooting but his reaction was worse. He was disappointed in me and he said so. 'Christ Almighty, Kate. Didn't it cross your mind that a gunman would come after a witness?'

'I suppose I wasn't totally convinced.' I said. 'No body had been found and she did lie to me.'

'What about?'

'She said she'd been shoplifting just before seeing the shooting.'

He smiled. 'Maybe she was telling the truth all along. She was certainly telling the truth about her retail therapy – she's been shoplifting from Harrods to M&S. We found drawers full of small items plus a few trinkets from local shops. We've got someone checking out her activities as we speak.'

'She was a troubled woman,' I said, feeling I had to defend her now that she was dead.

'Most women I know are troubled but they don't go out nicking.'

'You know a lot of women, then?' I asked.

He managed a smile. 'I've got four sisters and a gran and if they're not troubled, trouble troubles them.'

A middle-aged waitress with swollen ankles and a fixed smile approached the table for our order. 'Don't even think about saying no to the full Monty,' he said. 'Women on diets get on my nerves. I'm paying anyway. Tea?'

I nodded.

'And we'll have Monica's special for two,' he added. The waitress's fixed smile didn't flicker.

There's something about a man, I thought, who, in the midst of a murder enquiry, is good-natured enough to buy sustenance for a woman who has failed to disclose information and probably allowed a murderer to get away. I could fall for a man like that if I allowed myself to.

'There is something else,' I said.

'What is it this time – not another missing person?'

'No. It seems that Ian Jenkins and Carl Farnforth knew each other. They had some sort of business connection.'

'Thanks so much for telling me *now*.'

He took a mobile from his jacket pocket, jabbing at it in irritation. 'Bring in Ian Jenkins for questioning,' he said into the phone, 'and search his house.'

'I'm sorry, sir, no mobiles allowed here,' said the timid voice of our smiling waitress.

'Police business,' he said, flashing his warrant card. That seemed to be enough and she slunk away as if insulted.

I already felt sorry for Ian. His wife had disappeared and

was probably dead and suddenly he was being interviewed and his privacy violated. Also troubling me was the information I was still withholding about Dr Reece Gardener. I decided David Todman would be in info overload if I said any more. Lorraine had been using the doc as a sperm bank, and a wrecked marriage and career wasn't something I wanted to be responsible for. So I kept quiet on the doctor front.

'We've contacted Carl Farnforth's company in Saudi,' David informed me. 'An American outfit called AAE. American Arabian Engineering.'

'Is he on his way?'

'No idea. Cagey sort of place by all accounts. They'll take messages but won't put anyone through direct. Nature of the business, I suppose.'

'Which is?'

'Weapons and highly secretive.'

'Do you think that has any connection?'

'With what?' he asked. 'The shooting or Mrs Farnforth?'

Our tea trolley arrived at that moment and its mouth-watering selection momentarily blotted out my cares. The sandwiches were genteel and crustless, the cakes large and creamy. 'Tuck in,' said David. 'I love to see a woman eat well.'

I was hungry and I didn't need telling twice.

'Are you sure you've told me everything?' he asked.

I nodded.

'You'll have to come back with me to the station to make a statement.'

I nodded again, my mouth still full.

'It'll mean dragging rivers and lakes to find Paula Jenkins.'

I stopped eating. The thought of watery graves and bloated bodies made my appetite give way as fast as a dodgy kneecap.

'I wonder if Paula Jenkins was having an affair,' muttered David. 'Did the description of the bloke she saw with the gun match Ian Jenkins and did Mrs Farnforth ever meet the Jenkinses?'

'I did make notes,' I said, scrabbling around in my bag.

'Don't worry about it now, Kate. We have to be getting back to the nick.' He looked at my plate and my half-eaten cream cake and tutted. 'You can tell you don't come from a big family. "Eat it quick or someone else will" was the motto in ours.'

Back at the station general chaos reigned and amongst the throng toing and froing was Ian Jenkins, who was being led to an interview room. He turned to look at me, his face full of anguish. 'Help me,' he mouthed.

I stood transfixed to the spot until David led me upstairs to an interview room. 'I'll be back as soon as I can,' he said. Luckily he left the door slightly open otherwise I would have felt claustrophobic. I sat and waited and waited some more. I'd often wondered how I'd fare under intense questioning if I *had* committed a crime. After an hour and a half's wait I knew that boredom and restlessness would lead me to admit to a crime I *hadn't* committed.

I stood up. I sat down. I even wandered outside in the corridor. Eventually DCI Todman returned. His face was stern. 'I've swung it for you, Kate. God knows how. But I have to caution you about the withholding of information in your line of work. Don't do it again.'

I smiled apologetically but he didn't smile back. 'Can I go, then?'

He nodded. 'Yeah. Don't leave the country. I'll ring you.'

Outside I breathed the air of freedom. It didn't smell fresh, though. It had a dank wintry smell and the blackish sky added a gloomy feel to match my mood. I'd blown my career in so-called protection and I assumed

I'd blown it with David Todman. It hadn't been a good day.

Don't give up on the day yet, said a little voice in my brain that occasionally got it right. It was time to have a crack at Dr Reece Gardener.

'It's a personal matter,' I said to the young receptionist with blonde hair that had more tendrils than a sweet pea and whose large frame dwarfed the stool she sat on. She seemed dumbfounded at that.

'Are you a patient here?' she asked.

I looked at my watch – it was six thirty. Only three patients sat staring into space. 'I don't mind waiting,' I said.

'Well, you'll have to – he's a busy man.'

'Yes, indeed he is.'

'Name?' she demanded, eyeing me with deep suspicion, but I didn't mind. Her bum was much bigger than mine and quite unreasonably I felt that gave me an advantage.

She paused to sort a few files and to let me know she wasn't going to dance to my tune, but after a few minutes she walked off to an inner sanctum, came back and said, 'He'll see you at the end of surgery.'

'Jolly good. Thank you.'

She pursed her lips and I joined the others in the waiting room and stared into space with them. In a strange sort of way it was quite companionable.

Dr Reece Gardener sat at his desk signing prescriptions. Half-glasses perched on the end of his thin nose. His hair, long at the back, curled on to his collar but had ceased growing on the top of his head. 'Hello,' he said with a pleasant smile. 'Do sit down.'

I sat down. Okay, the man had a deep voice and quite attractive blue eyes, but he seemed more the academic type than stud. I felt I had to tread carefully. Unless *he* had murdered Lorraine, there was no way he could know of her death.

'What can I do for you?' he said.

'I believe you have a patient – Lorraine Farnforth?'

'Who are you?'

'My name is Kate Kinsella and I'm a private investigator.'

His expression mirrored his thoughts – *Oh my God, my wife knows.*

'Recently I met Lorraine,' I continued, 'and in confidence she told me of your relationship.'

His glasses slipped further down his nose but he didn't speak.

'I have some bad news.' I paused. 'She was found dead this morning – there had been an intruder. Cause of death isn't known at the moment.'

His right hand trembled as it rested on the desk, rustling the prescription sheets. With his left hand he snatched his glasses off. His thin lips had whitened but he struggled to speak. 'I can't believe it. I knew she worried about burglars but I never expected this.'

'Where were you last night, Dr Gardener?'

'Oh, Christ, it wasn't me. I was at home. My wife is ill – I don't do any "on calls".' He rested his head on his hands. It was some time before he spoke again. 'I've never—' His voice cracked. 'I've never been involved with a patient before. We only ever met in the day.' I wasn't sure what he meant by that. Perhaps he thought adultery didn't count in the hours of daylight. Or, more likely, he was telling me that as he didn't see her at night it couldn't have been him.

'I don't intend to tell the police,' I said, having made up my mind that though Reece Gardener *might* be capable of murder, I didn't see him climbing fences or using a jemmy. Doctors use the front door. 'But,' I added, 'I don't know if Lorraine may have left a diary or any other item that may implicate you – so you may be paid a visit by the police.'

He lowered his hands. 'This will kill my wife. She's severely depressed. Has been for three years.' He looked at me with misty eyes. 'It's no excuse, I know, but I was so lonely. I was tempted and I succumbed.'

'I'm sorry.'

'I loved Lorraine in my own way,' he said. 'She made me feel alive again – a man—' He broke off. 'You'd better go.'

I repeated that I was sorry, and I was, because I had a feeling his grief was only a part of the troubles he now had to face.

I stood up to go but as I got to the door he said, 'Should I tell my wife?'

I shrugged, unsure. 'It might be for the best . . . but then, I often get things wrong.'

Walking back to Humberstones I tried to focus on something positive to do to save me from seeing life in general as a black pit of thwarted hopes and lives cut short. Even so, my first thought was a negative one. It seemed I was now without clients. Compared to being a PI, nursing seemed a good paying option, but it could be just as depressing as attempting to do a job which was obviously too much for me. So much for positive thinking.

As I arrived at the side door Hubert was just leaving – with Jasper. 'Come with us, Kate. A brisk walk to the park will do you good.'

It was the last thing I wanted, but at least I could fill Hubert in on my latest catalogue of doom and disaster. I began my update but Jasper, sniffing at trees and wagging his tail, was as much a delight for Hubert as a child's first steps or first smile is for its father. Perhaps if Jasper had been mine I would have felt the same, but now I wanted a power walk, not a pissing tree to pissing tree meander.

Hubert got the drift of my mood. 'Look here, Kate. Lorraine's number was up long before you came on the scene. It wasn't your fault. Your mere presence wasn't going to stop it happening. You could be dead too – you'll have to remember that and snap out of it.'

Although Hubert wouldn't have looked out of place as an usher at the pearly gates he could talk sense on occasions and I had to accept that this might be one of them.

When Jasper was let off the lead in the park and there was a bigger selection of trees, I took Hubert's arm in case he needed something to hang on to whilst Jasper ran free.

'Ian Jenkins has asked me to help him,' I said. I didn't mention that he was between two burly coppers at the time.

'I thought he was already a client.'

'Well, yes, but no money has changed hands.'

'Better get in touch with him quickly, then.'

'I'll do that,' I said. 'I told the police about the shooting,' I added.

'And?'

'I think David Todman got a bollocking and I suspect I'm persona non grata with him now.'

'I'd be surprised at that,' said Hubert, as he scanned the park for a sighting of Jasper.

'Why?'

'You're the absolute image of his favourite sister.'

'You set me up, didn't you?'

'I wouldn't put it as strongly as that. I just said you were free most Saturday nights.'

'You sod. I bet he thinks I'm pathetic.'

'No,' said Hubert. 'He told me himself he likes a well-covered woman with a good appetite.'

'In that case sod the both of you. Makes me sound like a breeding sow in a field. Makes sexy shoes seem normal.'

'Nothing wrong with sexy shoes,' said Hubert, unruffled. 'You should try them. You wouldn't be in any Saturday nights then.'

'I'm going home,' I said. 'And I don't mean back to the office. I'm going to Farley Wood, and if my tenant hasn't gone I'll remove her bodily.'

Of course by the time I'd stomped back to Humberstones and packed a small suitcase I'd calmed down. But pride wouldn't let me stay so I drove to my house, looked through the letter box, saw that my tenant had gone and stepped over the threshold into my living room, it being too small a house to have a hall. I checked everything was still working, turned the gas fire up full blast, switched on the TV and decided to chill out with a bottle of wine I'd bought as a present for Hubert.

By the second glass I was feeling more mellow and looking forward to supper and a good night's sleep. The overly loud ringing of my phone startled me. It could only be Hubert. 'There's no need to apologise,' I said. 'I know you mean well.'

'I wasn't going to. David Todman rang. He wants to speak to you.'

'He's got my mobile number.'

'You left that here. And I didn't give him the Farley Wood number because I live in fear of your wrath.'

'Ha, bloody ha. I'll ring him, then, but I suppose *you* know what it's about.'

'I'm not an oracle.'

'Seems like it as far as I'm concerned. When you're not seeing to the dog, that is.'

'I didn't realise, Kate, you had such a jealous nature.'

I was about to blast a retort but Jasper *had* got to me. I was no longer Hubert's main concern. Once we'd been like lame ducks together; now he had a real animal to take care of.

'I'll give him a ring – thanks, Hubert.'

I rang David straight away. 'I want you to come to the nick,' he said.

'Why?' I asked.

'Ian Jenkins is refusing to answer questions unless you are there. He doesn't want a solicitor. He wants you.'

'Does he need a solicitor?'

'Oh yes.'

'You don't think he shot his wife?' I asked in amazement.

There was a short pause. 'He could have done, and as yet the post-mortem on Lorraine Farnforth is inconclusive.'

'I've had a drink,' I muttered.

'I'll send a car for you.'

'David, what the hell can I *do* for him?'

'Encourage him to confess. It'll save us a lot of time.'

'But I don't think he did it.'

'The husband is always the most likely perpetrator.'

'Are you a betting man?' I asked, wondering if he'd like to risk a fiver on a gamble with me.

'I don't drink, smoke or gamble.'

'Should have been a bloody monk,' I muttered to myself as I put down the phone. I poured myself another half-glass of wine to while away the waiting time and sprawled on the sofa.

A knock at the door surprised me. I slipped on my coat, thinking there might have been a police car in the area. As I opened the door my question, 'What the hell are—' went unfinished as the man at the door roughly pushed past me.

Eight

'You can't stay,' I said nervously. 'I'm waiting for the police.'

'It won't take long,' said Reece Gardener. 'I was in the area and I followed you.'

I backed away from him. Ever since Dr Shipman, 'home visits' had taken on an entirely new meaning, and Dr Gardener had a wide-eyed and frantic look.

'I've fixed it with my partner at the practice, Dr Ali,' he began in a rush. 'New notes – I only saw her as a patient twice – but she has got a prescription with my name on and if the police haven't found it yet—'

'Calm down,' I said, stopping him in mid-flow. 'Let me get this straight – you've fixed the paperwork so that Lorraine was never your patient.'

'Yes. But she does have a prescription and a note I sent her.'

'What did you prescribe for her?'

'The pill. Well, I couldn't risk her getting pregnant, could I?'

'No indeed,' I said. What else could I say? 'What do you want me to do?' I asked.

'Find it and destroy it.'

'If the police have already taken it away how can I do that?'

His head dropped despairingly. 'They may not have thought it was important. They miss things, don't they –

maybe you could have a look round.'

'You mean breaking and entering?'

He nodded. 'I'm desperate – please. If I'm struck off what will happen to my family?'

'I think you're just making things worse,' I said. 'But I will tell you I'm almost sure that Lorraine would have destroyed both the prescription and the note.'

He looked up swiftly. 'What do you mean?'

'I mean she would never have collected that prescription. She *wanted* to get pregnant by you.'

His lower lip dropped in surprise. 'How do you know that?'

'She told me.'

For some time he didn't speak. 'I didn't know her very well, did I?'

'Lorraine was a complicated woman.'

'You won't tell the police, will you?'

I shook my head. 'I shall feign total ignorance of you and her medical history – but of course they may find out anyway.'

'Thanks,' he murmured.

I heard a car draw up outside then, so I opened the curtain a fraction. 'It's the police. Stay here and wait until I've gone before you leave.'

He nodded. In such a short space of time he'd aged. His eyes had a haunted look. The wages of sin and subterfuge, I thought. Let that be a warning to me.

I opened the door, smiled broadly at the uniformed PC driver and crossed my fingers that Dr Gardener wouldn't decide to hang himself from *my* rafters.

At the station I was treated to a proper mug of coffee instead of the usual plastic cup that now had a new innovation – the plastic holder. Either way I always seem to dribble using plastic. I was grateful, even though I was left to drink it in a room no bigger than a cupboard.

Eventually David Todman appeared. 'Hi there, Kate. Sorry to drag you back here, but Jenkins insists on seeing you.'

'Has he been charged yet?'

David shook his head. 'We've got forensics on a fast track but it looks like he's our man.'

'What do you mean?'

'You'll find out. He wants to see you alone and we've agreed. It's irregular, but I trust you to tell us what he says.'

Ian Jenkins sat, head in hands, in an interview room with a uniformed PC sitting in the corner. David signalled for him to leave and as I sat down he closed the door on us.

'You wanted to see me?' I asked.

He looked up. He'd been crying. 'They say Paula has been shot. I can't believe it. I just can't. Christ, I'm in a mess – what am I going to do?'

'Have the police got any evidence?'

'On a plate – the gun, a jemmy and pairs of gloves.'

'Where did they find them?'

'In the garden shed underneath a load of old newspapers.'

'Would your fingerprints be on any of them?'

'No, of course not. I've never seen them before – it's a bloody set-up.'

'Who would want to set you up?'

'How would I know? I run a small company – I'm a family man. For God's sake, I loved my wife. There was nothing I wouldn't do for her.'

'Tell me about that red beret and scarf.'

'What?' He rubbed his face in agitation as if trying to remember. 'She said they came through the post – she hadn't ordered them – they just arrived. She loved bright colours—' He was sobbing too hard to say any more.

I sat for a while then leaned across and patted his shoulder. He stiffened. 'Don't touch me,' he said, sharp-eyed and harsh-voiced. So, there was a side I hadn't seen before.

Had he experienced a surge of choking anger with a gun in his hand? But of course that meant he'd coldly and deliberately loaded the gun and to do that there had to be malice aforethought. And where were the children that evening – and what could Paula have done to incur such a terrible retribution?

'Where were the children the evening Paula went missing?' I asked him briskly.

'At my mother's,' he said. He was calm now, his voice normal. 'She often had them – when Paula wanted to go shopping or to her aerobics class.'

'How many times had she left you before, Ian?'

He didn't need to think about that. 'Four times.'

'Where did she go?'

'To her mother; she lives in Northants. She always rang the children from there.'

'How angry did you get about that?'

'I was annoyed with her but I knew she found being alone with the kids a strain. She said she wasn't *leaving* me, just having a break. And it wasn't that I really minded. It was just that she'd up and go without any warning.'

'Did she take her car that day?'

He shook his head. 'Paula walked into the town – she often did that.'

'Would she have visited Lorraine Farnforth?'

'No!' The answer was far too brisk.

'You didn't approve of their friendship?'

'As far as I'm aware Paula wasn't friendly with Lorraine.'

'Why was that?'

'That's our business. And now Lorraine and Paula are both—' He broke off, his voice croaky.

I'd run out of questions anyway. Not having met Paula, I knew only that she was an ex-nurse who didn't find motherhood totally absorbing. But what had she been doing by the river? And how much had Ian been told about her actual death? I glanced at my watch, trying to suggest my time might be better spent elsewhere.

'Don't go, Kate. I'm trying to hold myself together, but I didn't kill my wife.'

'You must cooperate with the police and tell them the truth.'

'I've told them the truth. I'm innocent!'

I stood up. He grabbed my arm. 'Please – don't abandon me. Try to find out who did it – please. I'll pay anything.' I had to prise his fingers away. I wasn't scared. I was embarrassed. My mind had blanked. He slumped forward, head in hands. 'I didn't do it,' he muttered. 'I didn't do it.'

As I came out a young PC went back in and David, waiting outside in the corridor, took my arm and said, 'Come on. I'll buy you a coffee.'

The police canteen was unmanned and the coffee came from a machine via a plastic cup. 'Once upon a time,' said David, 'Enid or Liz cooked us hot meals at night. Not any more. Now it's chilled sandwiches and microwaved chips.'

We sat by the window well away from the three occupied tables. 'Well, what did he say and what do you think?' asked David.

'He says he's innocent.'

'He would.'

'Even if he did shoot his wife, what reason could he have for killing Lorraine? A woman he says he never even met.'

'So you think he might have shot his wife?'

'No, I didn't say that.'

'What else did he say?' asked David, staring at me as if somehow I might have been told something he hadn't.

'I'm not an experienced questioner,' I said. 'For the past year my best interviews have revolved around bowels, sleep and bodily fluids. Even then I rarely got a straight answer.'

David smiled. 'Don't underestimate yourself.'

'I'm not. The only thing I did notice was that he said you'd found "*the* gun". Did you tell him it was the murder weapon?'

'No. I said we'd found a gun.'

'What sort of gun?'

'I can't give you that information, Kate, but we'll soon know if it's the murder weapon.' He sipped at his coffee. 'If I were you I'd forget all about this case. Why don't you stick to medical stuff?'

I didn't answer immediately because I'd have said, 'Bollocks,' and I only swear amongst friends. At that moment he didn't qualify. 'Why don't *you* go back into uniform?' I asked, pleased with my composure.

'I don't want to.'

'Precisely. You do what you want and I'll carry on doing as I want.'

'No need to get in a strop,' he said. 'You'll just be wasting your time on this one.'

'It's mine to waste.'

I was getting a bit childish now and trying to score points, so I thought it best to quit before our chat disintegrated completely.

'I'd better go,' I said. 'I'm sure you're very busy.'

I sipped at the last of my coffee, misjudged once again the plastic rim and dribbled down my chin. 'Here,' he said, handing me a paper tissue. I took it with a forced smile, dabbed my chin and stood up. 'What's your next move?' I asked.

'On you or Jenkins?'

I gave him a look that should have withered a smart arse. It had no effect on him. I supposed being surrounded by women had lowered his susceptibility to female ire.

'Jenkins,' he said, 'has to tell us what he's done with his wife's body. We can't drag every lake and river for miles around.'

'He won't confess to something he hasn't done.'

'No, but if he doesn't, we'll start digging up his garden and his allotment.'

'I didn't know he had an allotment,' I said. 'I wouldn't have thought he was the type or had the time.'

'Bet you didn't know that he owned a black anorak or went jogging at nights either.'

He was the one scoring points now. 'Of course I knew that,' I said swiftly. A little too swiftly to be convincing but I couldn't let him think I knew sod all about Ian Jenkins. I'll show you, I resolved – I'll show you.

Back at Humberstones I sought out Hubert. His accommodation above the business was Tardislike in its surprising space. He had two living rooms, both with huge TVs and videos, probably three bedrooms and at least two bathrooms with bidet and Jacuzzi. Mostly he used a small room that looked out on to the High Street. For some reason his main door was open and I crept along the corridor, not exactly nervous but a little apprehensive.

I found him sprawled on the sofa with Jasper lying sound asleep on his chest. He put a finger to his lips and mouthed, 'Shush.'

'Jasper is *not* a baby,' I said.

'He's the nearest I'll ever get to one,' whispered Hubert.

'I'll come back later, then.'

'No, I'll shift him,' he said, lifting Jasper as carefully as a terrorist handling Semtex in the middle of a firework display. Once the sleeping dog had been resettled in an armchair he said, 'Do you fancy a nightcap?'

I nodded. 'A big one.'

'Case not going well?'

'What case? The police think they have the evidence to convict Jenkins.'

'And you don't agree?'

I shrugged. 'It seems to me that they have too much evidence. He can't be that stupid.'

'So what's your theory?'

'I don't have one.'

'Why not?'

'I'm confused.'

'Nothing unusual about that.'

I didn't rise to the bait but simply waited for my drink, which turned out to be Baileys on ice, his left-over Christmas tipple. 'The trouble is,' I said, sipping quickly at my drink, 'I didn't have enough time to get to know either Lorraine or Ian, I never met Paula and now all three are beyond reach.'

'You're being defeatist,' said Hubert. 'What do PIs do?'

'Can I phone a friend?'

'I'm being serious,' he said. 'They snoop. If you want to solve anything you have to ask questions, lie through your teeth and rely on someone like me who can help you with local knowledge.'

'You're too busy, Hubert,' I said, 'flogging funeral bonds and looking after Jasper.'

'What if I was to tell you Jasper has already found something out about Lorraine?'

'I'd say you were winding me up.'

'Nice little dogs are a talking point.'

'Really?'

'Don't be cynical,' said Hubert, looking disapproving. 'You try it. Go out and about with Jasper and you'll hear everybody's life story.'

'I know Jasper is golden but what little nugget of info did you find out about Lorraine?'

'Someone saw her in the office at IJ Precision Instruments.'

'With Jenkins?'

'No, she was seen leaving on her own.'

I had nothing to say to that. Hubert's information had silenced me.

We both had another Baileys and, after finding out that his informant was a traffic warden who'd noticed Lorraine walking her dog, I asked, 'How big is the Jenkins factory?'

Hubert thought for a moment. 'I'd say there were fifty employees with an annual turnover of at least four million.'

My mouth dropped open. 'Surely not,' I said.

'The workforce is highly skilled, very well paid and share prices are rising.'

'You've obviously looked it up.'

Hubert smiled in smug satisfaction. 'I took to dabbling a bit while you were away. I think I have a financial flair.'

'Strange that Ian Jenkins lives in such a modest house.'

'Maybe he ploughs all the profits back into the company.'

'Is that what you do, Hubert?'

'Business is booming,' he said, proudly. 'Our reputation is second to none.'

'Better than the Co-op?'

'We've overtaken the Co-op.'

'I'm impressed. So are you investing heavily?'

'Why do you ask?'

'Lorraine's death and Paula being shot might not have such a domestic angle. Maybe someone will benefit, and not by peanuts.'

'Do you know how much Lorraine was worth?'

'More dead than alive, I should think.'

'Like most people,' muttered Hubert.

I'd had a drink or two and had no option but to spend the night at Humberstones, not that I minded. I was feeling tired now, and yet Hubert looked wide awake. He could drink and just become more talkative. Alcohol merely sank my IQ and numbed my upper lip.

I didn't lie awake worrying about my next move and when I heard a ringing noise I assumed it was my alarm clock. It wasn't, it was the telephone. It was six a.m. My throat was so dry I didn't give my name, I just picked up the receiver.

'This is Carl Farnforth. I believe you were with my wife the night she died.'

I managed to utter a gravelly, 'Yes.'

'I think we should meet. Will you come into town? Say ten o'clock? Outside Monica's Tea Room.'

'You mean today?'

'Yes. Is that a problem?'

'No. I'll be there.'

'Good. See you at ten.'

As I put down the phone I realised it wasn't worth going back to bed now. I was wide awake. Wide awake enough to recognise in the crisp cool tones of Carl Farnforth that he wasn't heartbroken at the death of his wife.

Nine

With a strong wind whipping around my ears I loitered outside Monica's Tea Room. I'd arrived ten minutes early and, with arms folded around me, I either walked on the spot or gazed into the tea room wondering if he could have slipped in without me noticing. I hadn't seen a photo of him but I imagined him as slim and tanned. Ten minutes seems a long time in cold winds and a further five seemed interminable.

'I'm sorry to keep you waiting,' said a deep voice behind me. 'It is Kate Kinsella, isn't it?'

Carl Farnforth was, for some reason, far larger than I'd expected: well over six feet, tall and broad with wide shoulders. His grey hair had been close-cut and his wide face sported a light tan. With a gold necklace and bracelet he could have passed for an East End bouncer.

'Thanks for coming,' he added. The crisp phone tone had gone. His lips were fleshy, as was his nose; he wasn't good-looking but he had presence and he looked supremely fit, perhaps an impression aided by the fact that he wore a black tracksuit and trainers and carried a squash racquet. 'I'm not posing,' he said. 'There's a squash club round the back of Monica's. Keeping busy is my way of coping.'

The same waitress with the horribly fixed smile served us with a pot of coffee. She flashed me an enquiring glance as if wondering how I'd managed to find two different men in two days.

Carl sat, hands at peace, lightly resting on the table. He had long fingers on squarish hands but it was his fingernails I noticed – they were manicured and buffed to perfection.

'I expect you're wondering why I wanted to see you?' he asked, as he poured the coffee. There was something about him that made me nervous, not just the situation but something in his voice. The low tones, soothing but mysterious. It was then I realised I fancied him – he had that dangerous edge.

'Well, I was the last person to see Lorraine alive – bar the intruder, of course,' I blurted out. 'I'm just sorry I heard nothing.'

He smiled. 'You were trying to help her,' he said. 'I wanted to see you to find out exactly what happened that night.'

I told him Lorraine had been drinking heavily and that she had probably suffered little. It didn't sound much of a comfort and I added lamely, 'Although there was an intruder, her death may have been accidental. The post-mortem reports haven't been completed yet.'

'I'm glad she didn't suffer,' he said, sounding genuine enough, although he certainly didn't appear upset. 'I'm not going to pretend I'm heartbroken,' he said, as if reading my mind. 'I'm not a hypocrite and I'm sorry she's dead – but my life will go on.' He drank more coffee and then stared at me. His eyes, I noticed for the first time, were dark blue, the colour of a fading bruise. 'She was having an affair,' he said abruptly.

'You knew?'

'I might be working in the Middle East but I did know what was going on. Not *who* this time, but Lorraine and I had an arrangement.'

'Which was?'

'We asked no questions.'

'Did you know she'd been shoplifting?'

He nodded. 'I've paid off shops to stop her being prosecuted.'

'She told me if your employers found out about her stealing you might lose your job.'

'My firm doesn't worry about what happens as long as it's not on Arab territory.'

'So why would she lie?'

He laughed. 'Lorraine was nuts. Neurotic, manipulative and she couldn't have kids.'

'Why did you stay with her?'

'I didn't, did I? I hardly saw her. I'm not a saint either – I've had other women.'

'So why didn't you divorce?'

'Why should I? I enjoyed seeing her. Made me realise how lucky I was to be working abroad. I was fond of her. I didn't wish her dead. Our arrangement suited us.'

'Will you benefit from her death?'

He nodded smugly. 'Of course I will. She had money in the bank and a good life policy taken out years ago. Nothing to do with me – her previous husband encouraged her to do that.'

I'd known him five minutes and had gone from initial lustful twinges to thinking he was quite capable of murder or at least arranging a murder.

'Why did you ask me here, Mr Farnforth?'

'I want you to work for me, of course.'

'Doing what?'

'Finding out who killed my wife.'

'The police seem to have that under control at the moment. Death could have been from natural causes—'

He didn't let me finish. His hand clenched into a fist and I thought he was going to strike the table. 'Some bastard came into *my* house and left *my* wife dead – and I want to know who.'

'Of course you do,' I murmured.

He stared at me for a moment, took a deep breath and unclenched his hands. 'I have my suspicions,' he said.

'Who?'

'Ian Jenkins.'

'Why would he kill your wife?'

'The bastard wanted everything – my wife included.'

'I thought you were friends.'

'*Once* we were, but he's greedy.'

'In what way?' I asked.

'That's for you to find out. His wife is missing and I'm sure the bastard has killed her too.'

'I need to tell you that Ian Jenkins has employed me to . . . find his wife.'

'Really! He's a devious sod.'

'You sound bitter.'

He shrugged. 'He's a liar and a cheat and he's dangerous. He has no conscience.'

I thought that was a bit rich coming from someone who worked making weapons. 'Are you going to tell me about the aggro between you?' I asked.

He ignored that question. 'I'll pay you over the odds,' he said with a sly smile.

'I can't work for both of you.'

'I don't see why not. After all, solving crime is what you do.'

I smiled. 'The police solve crimes. I can only deal with side issues.'

He patted my hand. 'This is your chance, then, to bring a criminal to justice.'

I didn't answer. I had already decided that working for Carl Farnforth would be about as worthwhile as being bath attendant to Saddam Hussein.

'I'm sorry,' I said, 'but at the moment I have a full list of clients.'

He looked slightly surprised at that. 'I'm offering a

reward – ten thousand pounds. You could take a long holiday.'

'I've just come back from one.'

I stood up to leave and he stood up at the same time, moving closer to me, so close I could smell his aftershave. 'Think about it. I reckon Jenkins was my wife's lover.'

'I got the impression,' I said, trying to keep my voice even, 'that she hardly knew Ian Jenkins.'

He laughed softly in my ear and I took a step backward. 'You're gullible, aren't you? Lorraine knew him all right. She was always a good liar.'

Part of me was intrigued. I needed time to think.

'You want to find out the truth, don't you?' he asked.

I stayed silent. It felt as if he were reading my mind.

'Don't you?' he repeated quietly.

'I want to find the truth, but on my own terms.'

He shrugged and moved even closer. 'Have it your way. The police will find out and you'll miss out on a handy bit of cash.'

'Although you said you were fond of your wife,' I began, 'I can't understand why you think I'm necessary. The police—'

'Sod the police,' he snapped. 'Someone killed my wife and I want the bastard caught. No one takes what belongs to me.'

I walked towards the door. 'You think about it,' he called after me. 'Money up front and a reward. There are other investigators, you know.'

'Quite!'

For a few seconds outside I took some deep breaths. He'd made no mention of Jasper and I was very glad about that – Hubert's adoption seemed safe. The obnoxious Carl made Ian Jenkins seem a saint in comparison. Dosh or no dosh, Lorraine and Paula deserved justice. And whatever I could do I would do for them.

Back at Humberstones there was no sign of Hubert and the funeral cars were out. Elvie sat at her desk with Jasper on her lap. Her mother had been a Presley fan and Elvie had taken up the mantle. She knew the words of all his songs, she could do the hip actions and play air guitar. The only thing she couldn't do was sing. But she did create a niche for Elvis music and Humberstone funerals had far more than most.

''Ello, Kate,' she said, with a toss of her long ponytail. 'Hubert says, 'ave you got time to walk Jasper. 'E's a lovely little dog – the customers love 'im.'

Jasper heard the word *walk*, sprang from Elvie's lap and stood wagging his tail and shaking his body. There was something about the enthusiasm in his small, eager face that was infectious. I bent to stroke his head and he rolled over on to his back so that I could rub his tummy. Dogs have that trusting capacity and it hooks you just like a drug. I hadn't wanted to get involved with Jasper but dogs, like men, grow on you. One minute they are vaguely attractive, the next you're afraid to leave the house on the off-chance they'll ring you. Which is why the mobile phone is one of women's greatest liberators. No longer do women have to make excuses not to go out with girlfriends because of a man they met only once but who could be *the one*, they can be out and about and still be on the lookout. It must at least treble the chances of meeting other men and it softens the blow when he doesn't phone.

Jasper's enthusiasm meant his legs worked liked pistons at first until we met a tree or a scent he had to define. Then, if that was satisfactory, it was leg-cocking time. I'd planned to walk to the Jenkins factory but I soon found dog walking is not the same as power walking – he wanted to stop every few yards. Eventually his little legs gave out before mine and he refused to go any further. I wasn't sorry about that. There was a chill wind blowing and so I tucked him under the crook of my arm where he was happy and I had a bit of extra warmth.

On Longborough's small industrial estate I found IJ Precision Instruments. The main building was single storey, more like offices than a factory. Opposite was a similar block and between the two, at the entrance, was a glass-fronted security office.

The hefty security man inside slid open his window. 'What can I do for you, miss?' he asked. I adjusted Jasper so his cheeky face could be seen more clearly. 'She's a lovely little dog,' he said. He came out of his side door carrying a half-eaten digestive biscuit.

'It's a he,' I said. 'Jasper.'

'Hello there, Jasper – like a bit of biscuit?' Jasper obliged and nearly nibbled his fingers in the process. 'Now then,' he said, stroking away and allowing Jasper to lick his fingers, 'who did you want to see?'

'I wondered if there were any jobs going at the precision factory.'

'For you?' he asked.

'No. My boyfriend.'

He shook his head. 'Nah – not at the moment, love. It's very skilled work.'

'Well paid?'

'Certainly is – best paid in the town.'

Jasper was by now gazing adoringly at the man – or was he merely pleading for another biscuit? 'He's had experience.'

'He could try. They might put him on the waiting list – you never know.'

'Who's the best person to get in touch with?'

'That would be the personnel officer. Hang on a minute.' He returned to his booth and studied a clipboard. Then he wrote something down on a scrap of paper. 'Here you are,' he said, handing it to me through the window. He'd written her name and office telephone number down. 'I hope your boyfriend gets lucky.'

'Thanks.'

'Cheerio, Jasper.' Jasper obligingly gave a departing woof. Hubert was right. Dogs, especially small pretty ones, did seem to encourage friendliness.

I wasn't sure exactly what I hoped to find out now that I'd got a name and telephone number, but it was a start.

I'd expected Hubert to be around when I got back, but he wasn't. I was glad to put Jasper in his basket near Elvie, who was busy taking details from someone enquiring about a funeral bond. I glanced at the brochure – *A funeral for the future at today's prices.*

In the late afternoon, I began to worry about Hubert. I knew there were no funerals in progress because I'd seen the drivers leaving for the day. When my phone did ring I was expecting it to be him, but it wasn't – it was David Todman.

'Do you fancy a meal later tonight?'

'What do you call *later?*'

'I should be finished by nine.'

'I'll be on my knees by then.'

'Praying?'

'You know what I mean. I eat about seven.'

'Have a snack. There's a new curry place just opened – great food. And I've got some forensic news on Jenkins.'

'This is blackmail.'

'No, just the way to a girl's heart.'

'We'll see,' I said, grudgingly.

Strange that although I sometimes thought I'd like a man in my life – other than Hubert, who doesn't really count – when push came to shove I was scared of getting involved. As far as I could see all David Todman had in his favour was the fact he was teetotal and liked to see me eat. The last police inspector I'd known in a biblical sense was drunk most evenings and was killed by falling masonry on his way home. My only comfort in the darkest of times afterwards was that he was too drunk to have felt a thing. David, I reasoned, must have a weakness: maybe he was gay. But if he was, at least I could relax and enjoy having him as a friend.

By six thirty I was worrying more about Hubert. I checked with Elvie at her home and she promised to phone a peripatetic embalmer called Charles Dearborn who it seemed was quite likely to know.

''Ave you met Charlie?' she asked.

'Haven't had the pleasure,' I said.

'You will, Kate. He keeps snakes and bloody great tarantulas and he'll offer to show you 'em.'

'Thanks for the warning.'

'If I 'ear anything I'll let you know.'

By eight thirty I was ready to go out. I'd fished out a pair of 'proper' shoes with heels, given them a polish and put on a decent black skirt and lowish-cut mauve jumper. I even put on full make-up. I blew myself a kiss into the mirror and told myself this was the best I could look and if he didn't make a pass it wasn't my fault.

At nine thirty I was still waiting. My emotions veered between worry about Hubert and real irritation at David Todman for keeping me on date alert. By nine forty-five I was more cross with myself for having bothered to tart myself up. I was convinced something awful had happened to Hubert and in comparison being stood up wasn't a big deal.

When the phone did ring it was Hubert. 'Hello, Kate. How's Jasper?'

I paused. I wasn't going to give Hubert the opportunity of thinking me jealous again.

'At my last check he was asleep in his basket,' I said. 'He hasn't run off with a German Shepherd – or should that be Shepherdess? – and all his vital signs seem normal.'

'You're in a mood,' he said.

'I think I've been stood up.'

'Who by?'

'DCI Todman.'

'He's a busy man, but he's reliable.'

'A matchmaker you are not,' I said. 'He's not my type. He's too squeaky clean.'

There was a pause.

'Let me tell you, Hubert,' I continued, 'if I find out he's a member of a happy-clappy church I won't speak to you ever again.'

'He doesn't go to any church.'

'Just as well,' I muttered.

'I didn't ring you for idle chat,' said Hubert, sounding peeved. 'I've been to Harrow on your behalf.'

'The Farnforths' old home?'

'They were burgled a couple of times.'

'I know that. Lorraine told me.'

'Did she tell you the Jenkinses used to live nearby? And that according to the neighbours they were quite friendly?'

'No, she didn't tell me,' I said, wearily wondering what the hell I was doing on this case. 'I'd be better off serving writs,' I said, 'and following errant husbands.'

'Just as likely to be wives these days.'

'Thank you for that, Hubert. This case is a pain in the neck.'

'Don't start getting emotional, Kate. You can do it.'

'Carl Farnforth wants me to work for him. He's offering a reward.'

'Go for it.'

'I don't like or trust the man.'

Hubert laughed. 'Since when do PIs have to like their clients?'

Perhaps I *was* being choosy and, after all, without Hubert I'd have had to take almost any kind of work to keep going. 'I'll think about it,' I said, reluctantly.

I'd almost forgotten about DCI Todman when the doorbell rang. 'I think he's here – must go – see you.'

As I got to the door I felt guilty for ending Hubert's call so abruptly and merely for a man who'd kept me waiting.

Ten

DCI Todman, I'd thought, would apologise profusely. He didn't. 'Couldn't be helped,' he said cheerfully. 'The super wanted to see me.'

I picked up my handbag and didn't say a word.

In the car he switched on the radio and said, 'If you sulk it'll spoil your appetite.'

'I'm not sulking.'

'Good!'

Jamal's Palace paid homage to elephants. Stone-cast pachyderms guarded an ex-fireplace, murals decorated the walls and gold creatures embossed the menus and the napkins. A waiter in a white turban with a broad Birmingham accent greeted David like an old friend and led us to a corner table.

'Would you like some wine?' asked David.

I nodded. I don't get out much and I intended to make the most of it.

He asked me about New Zealand and I rabbited lyrically for a while, especially when the wine hit my empty stomach and made a quick exit from there to my brain. When I'd exhausted my anecdotes of life down under and he'd finished a glass of mineral water and a nargis kebab I asked him about the case. 'It's not going too well,' he said. 'We've had to let Ian Jenkins go for the time being.'

'I'm not that surprised,' I said. 'I didn't think he'd killed Lorraine or Paula – what possible motive could he have?'

David smiled wryly. 'There's quite a few men who don't need a motive to murder their wives.'

I ignored that and stifled a response about wives who kill husbands getting longer sentences than vice versa.

'Anyway, motive apart,' he said, 'forensic found nothing on those items taken from Jenkins's shed. No fingerprints, no DNA – the gun hadn't been fired in years –' he paused – 'and the pathologist has decided that death was due in part to a hand being clamped over Lorraine's mouth and nose.'

'So she was suffocated?'

'Not quite as simple as that.' He paused again to drink some mineral water and I felt my impatience rise.

'She choked on her own vomit,' I suggested, 'with the murderer's hand covering her mouth.'

'That was only a contributory factor.'

The waiter appeared then to remove David's plate and I made headway with my second glass of wine. 'You don't have to drink the whole bottle,' said David. I had a feeling he was testing me – perhaps he thought I had no moral fibre or was verging on dipsomania. Neither of which was true, of course, but I didn't want to waste good wine and my moral fibre was no concern of his – yet.

'Contributory factor to what?' I asked.

'It seems the vodka she was drinking was Russian and nearly fifty per cent proof.'

That was the stuff I'd been drinking too!

'That would have dulled the pain,' he continued, 'from an ectopic miscarriage. She died of a combination of factors. Inhaling vomit due to the vodka plus shock.'

I sat in silence. I could only think sadly of the irony of her longed-for pregnancy playing its part in her death.

'The pathologist thought the hand pressure wasn't particularly violent,' David informed me, but I was only half listening. 'Are you all right, Kate?' he asked.

'Fine,' I said, 'just pondering on the unfairness of life and dreams not coming true.'

'Don't start getting depressed on me, Kate, or I shall be forced to give you a bear hug.'

I smiled but then drank more wine, knowing it would make me feel even worse. 'So if she hadn't been drinking – if *we* hadn't been drinking – that night, she might have survived.'

'That's about the size of it.'

I pushed my wine glass away, the taste sour in my mouth. Straightforward murder would have been easier to cope with. Now I felt it really was my fault . . . If I hadn't drunk the vodka I would have woken; maybe she'd cried out in pain or surprise at the intruder. Sober, I would have heard. I could have called an ambulance – she might have survived.

When my main course appeared my appetite had gone and I stared at the plate, feeling slightly sick. 'Don't upset yourself, Kate,' said David as he tucked into his own meal. 'You didn't force the vodka down her throat and you didn't make her pregnant.'

'She thought she was infertile,' I said. 'But she wasn't. She was just very unlucky.'

I picked up my fork and then put it down again.

'Forget Lorraine,' he said. 'Eat up. There's nothing you can do for her. All the guilt in the world won't change the event.'

No one could argue with that, but it didn't make me feel any better and my eating or not eating being observed didn't help either.

'Someone, it seems, *was* trying to incriminate Jenkins,' he said, obviously changing the subject.

'So what do you do now?' I asked.

'We search for the body of Paula Jenkins.'

'You don't sound very hopeful.'

He shrugged. 'Eat your food, Kate. It's not your case any more – let's forget it.'

I struggled with a morsel of chicken and swallowed it. 'Lorraine's husband wants to employ me. He thinks Ian's guilty.'

'As I said, it's over. You're way out of your depth.'

I didn't argue. There was no point. I'd been floundering from day one and yet I knew I couldn't let it go.

'I'm sure you're right,' I said to mollify him. 'What happens if the body isn't found?'

David flashed me a confident smile. 'We'll find it. Jenkins won't get away with it. Did you know he stands to inherit quite a bit? Paula's first husband died in a car accident. He was well insured and she got compensation.'

I hadn't known Paula had been married before but I didn't want David to know that. 'Is everyone married more than once these days?' I asked, not expecting an answer.

'Seems to be two camps,' said David. 'Serial weddings or serial live-in partners.'

At that point I longed to ask him about his sexual/ romantic background but I didn't. I told him about mine instead, which didn't take long. He didn't volunteer any information so I didn't ask. Sometimes it's better not to know.

'Is Paula's ex-husband a suspect, then?'

'Stop fishing, Kate. We haven't even spoken to him yet.'

David drove me back to Farley Wood, which I thought was a better bet than Humberstones, because I might, just might, want to ask him in and I didn't want Hubert's beady eye on me.

Most men seem a lot more attractive after two or three glasses of wine and David Todman was no exception. 'Do you want a coffee?' I asked, hoping I didn't sound too eager. The truth was I couldn't even remember the last time a man had crossed this threshold with only me in mind.

He smiled, looking pleased, but said, 'I need an early night, Kate. I'm shattered.'

I was peeved and instead of appearing cool I muttered, 'I suppose you've got a headache too.' I didn't wait for a response, just said, 'Good luck on the case.'

'Goodnight, Kate—'

If he was going to add anything I didn't give him a chance. The front door was firmly closed in his face.

I watched him drive away. Lucky escape, I thought. I might have done something I regretted. It was only later, in bed, that I wondered who the hell I was kidding. Sometimes you *need* to regret things, otherwise you're not living life to the full.

It was two days later that Ian Jenkins contacted me. 'I'll come to your office,' he said.

He appeared an hour later, looking baggy-eyed and pale. 'I can't sleep, I can't eat. It's only a question of time before they arrest me again.'

'Sit down,' I said. 'I'll make you some coffee.'

He slumped in the swivel chair and stared at the floor, only looking up when I handed him a mug of coffee. 'What's the next step?' he asked.

'From your point of view or mine?'

'From yours, of course. There's nothing I can do. The police are watching my every move.' From his jacket pocket he bought out a wad of notes. 'Here,' he said. 'Take it – it's a thousand quid.'

I'd never seen so much paper money in my life. I took it and placed it on my desk. 'Before I put it away,' I said, 'I need a few straight answers.'

'Fire away.'

'Why all the caginess about knowing the Farnforths?'

He shrugged. 'I didn't know I was being cagey. But money, jealousy, ambition – all a part. What can I add to that?'

'Not sex?'

He shook his head. 'Carl was my best friend – a childhood friend. We went to Shefford University in 1976 – we were both eighteen, both doing engineering. We shared a lot of beer and a lot of laughs. We graduated; I got a first, he got a third. For three years we worked together, mostly on the design side of the business. His interest lay in weapons, mine in surgical instruments, but anyway we planned to set up in business together. Money was our only problem.'

'You were living in Harrow then?'

'No. We rented a house in Manchester. Had parties, shagged girls, got drunk, but we still worked bloody hard.

'When the Falklands War broke out it fuelled Carl's militaristic tendencies. He wanted his own war. He became a mercenary. He was away for two years fighting in Africa or anywhere there was a civil war going on.'

'Did he make any money?'

'Being a mercenary pays peanuts. The money wasn't an issue; he wanted the adventure. The chance to fire a gun.'

'And you married while he was away?'

'A quickie marriage and a quickie divorce.'

'What about Carl's love life?'

'Women loved Carl,' he said. I tried to read his expression. Was he jealous of his friend's success with women? 'He looked and acted the tough guy,' he continued, 'but he was soft where women were concerned.'

'When did he meet Lorraine?'

'Early nineties. She'd been married twice before and she had money. We were planning to go into business together.'

'So he put capital into the venture?'

Ian shook his head. 'No. My father died and I took over his factory in Longborough.'

'And that was a problem for Carl?'

'He was jealous, of course. I had enough money to do what I wanted – and that was to make surgical instruments. I didn't offer him a partnership. The workers need to be very skilled and the wage bill is high. I didn't think he'd be an asset.'

'Wasn't he a good engineer?'

Ian laughed dryly. 'He was more interested in handguns. And he was a hopeless businessman. He spent money like water and Lorraine spent what was left over funding useless fertility treatments. He resented that. I don't think he even wanted a family. He took various jobs in the Middle East designing weapons. Just as she was obsessed with having babies, his obsession was to have the perfect handgun named after him – so instead of Smith and Wesson or Colt or Luger it would be Farnforth.'

'So you ceased being friends?'

'That's about it. The two women were great friends at first, but as soon as Paula became pregnant all that changed. I have a suspicion Lorraine wanted my wife to be a surrogate mum. But they fell out big time and never spoke to each other again.'

'Strange then that you should all land up in Longborough.'

'We were here first.' It was the first time he'd sounded defensive.

'But why would they follow you?'

'I had no idea they *were* living here until a year ago when I met Lorraine in the High Street.'

'You talked to her?'

'Of course.'

'What explanation did she give?'

'The house in Harrow fetched a great price,' he said, 'and there was a brand new fertility clinic ten miles from here.'

'Did she say anything else?'

'She asked after Paula.'

'Nothing else?'

'What would you expect?' He was beginning to sound a little irritable.

'Did she mention Carl?'

'She said he was well and working in Saudi.'

'Did she mention his work on the perfect handgun?'

Ian frowned. 'What do you mean? What would she know about the gun?'

'So he has designed it?'

'I've no idea.'

He was lying. I was sure of that but I didn't challenge him. Instead I changed tack.

'Who do you suspect?' I asked.

His shoulders visibly relaxed. 'Of murdering my wife?'

'Yes.'

'I've been thinking about that. I reckon Carl arranged for a hitman to do it.'

'Why? What possible motive could he have?'

'Revenge.'

'For what?'

'He needed my help to make a prototype gun. I refused him.'

'Surely he could have done that in Saudi – in house. Anyway, why not kill *you*? Why kill Paula?'

'Who knows. I told you he was obsessive. His weapons work in Saudi was concentrated on large weapons. Any interest in handguns by the company would have been minimal.'

What I knew about weapons was also minimal and the only pistol I'd ever fired was a water pistol. So I dropped the weapons tack and asked about Paula.

'She was a good mother, very kind and reliable – a steady sort.'

'So you weren't in love with her?'

'I didn't say that.'

'You didn't have to.'

Previously he'd given me a different impression. Be more like a proper detective, I told myself – believe nothing until it can be verified.

Ian began muttering then about 'bloody mind-reading women' and I sat silently until he declared, 'Talking to you is worse than being interviewed by the police.'

'Thanks for the compliment,' I said, 'but I can't do any investigating until you tell me everything, and I mean everything.'

'I'm trying to do just that,' he snapped back. 'I respected my wife. We weren't on our honeymoon, were we? She was taken up with looking after the kids. I often worked late – when you're your own boss you have to put the hours in.'

'You felt guilty about that?'

'I didn't then, but I do now. I'm knackered trying to look after the kids and run the house. Paula made life easier.'

'I'm sure she did.'

My tone riled him.

'Just because I wasn't madly in love with my wife doesn't mean I'd go to the other extreme and kill her.' Then he added quietly, 'I needed her – I really did.'

It was the most honest thing he'd said, and I felt it best to leave it on a positive note. After all, I needed to believe most of what he said to justify my working for him. Honour among PIs and all that.

'Have the police verified your alibi for the time of your wife's death?'

'Yes. I was working in my office. The cleaner saw me.'

My planned trip to his factory now didn't seem worth pursuing. The police, after all, were the professionals and life was too short to over-investigate – it was on a par with frying chips twice.

'One more question, Ian,' I said. 'If you found out your wife was having an affair, what would you do?'

'She wouldn't. She wasn't the type.'

'You're sure of that?'

'Positive.'

'She did walk out on you on a few occasions.'

'I've told you about that before,' he said, irritated. 'Two kids and a husband working long hours, she got a bit down and stressed, but for the most part she was happy.'

'Did you ask her if she was happy?'

'No. I didn't need to. She seemed happy to me.'

When he'd gone I sat facing my blank computer screen, thinking about his last remark. I'd known a few people who'd suffered real misery and yet outwardly they showed only signs of cheerfulness. Hubert often *looked* miserable, but then he didn't expect life to be happy – he just knew it was fragile and short, so you had to make the best of it. Had Paula merely been making the best of things? Getting away from time to time to recharge her batteries, or to escape from Ian who admitted not love, but need? I no longer felt sorry for him but I still didn't think he'd killed his wife.

I was still staring at the computer screen when Hubert returned from a funeral.

'It helps if you switch on,' he said, handing me a sandwich and a jam doughnut.

'I've been thinking,' I said.

'That's a start. But you'll think better with sarnies inside you.'

I started to open the packet. 'It's odd, isn't it? My two prime suspects want to hire me to find the killer.'

'They want to do the right thing?' suggested Hubert.

'No, that's not it – they want to *appear* to be doing the right thing.' I ate my sandwich slowly. 'Do you know what I suspect?'

'Surprise me.'

'They've hired me because they think I won't know what I'm doing.'

'Well, they got that right, anyway.'

'Thanks, Hubert, for that vote of support.'

'I was only joking.'

'I may not be Sherlock bloody Holmes but I am dogged and determined.'

'Of course you are – so what's next?'

I shrugged. 'I'm not sure. Probably my jam doughnut.'

'What's the link between the two couples?' asked Hubert, looking at me disapprovingly.

'Initially friendship. And location. They lived in Harrow and then they moved here.'

'So who followed whom?'

A little click in my brain flashed. The fertility clinic wasn't a reason – London had its fair share. 'You are brilliant, Hubert.'

'What did I say?'

'You've just made it clear that the Farnforths *did* follow the Jenkinses and that it wasn't for friendship's sake, it was because Ian had something Carl wanted.'

'His woman?'

'No, something more valuable to him than that.'

'What?'

'I'm not sure, but I reckon it comes from their shared past – when they were students.'

'So you know what you're doing now?'

I bit into my jam doughnut to find a goodly amount of jam in the middle. I savoured the moment. 'Of course I do. I'm going to Shefford University.'

Eleven

For once my old jeans and flat shoes didn't look out of place. I hadn't decided quite what mission I was pretending to be on, so I followed a straggle of students into the union bar and ordered a pint of lager. I sat on a stool next to a nerdy-looking guy wearing glasses and a grey sweater fraying at the sleeves. I was struggling to find a way to start up a conversation with him when he said, 'Fucking prices in here are a fucking disgrace.'

I could see the vocabulary wasn't going to be a problem. 'You're fucking right,' I said.

He stared into his glass. 'Three years surviving on pasta and baked beans and what the fuck do you get at the end of it?'

I guessed this wasn't a philosophical question. 'A crap job?' I suggested.

He looked up at me with slightly bloodshot eyes. 'Not just a crap job – you have a student fucking loan that staggers on to become a huge fucking student debt.'

'Would you like another lager?' I asked, wondering how I'd managed to find the uni's biggest piss artist.

'Why not,' he said, 'I'm rat-arsed anyway.' It was one thirty p.m.

When I returned, he took the lager and muttered, 'What's your name? I'm Simon.'

'Hi, Simon – I'm Kate.'

'Have you got a lecture this afternoon?'

I shook my head.

'We could go to my place for a shag,' he said.

'That's a great idea,' I replied, 'but I'm working.'

'Essay?'

'No. I'm not a student.' He slid his glasses to the end of his nose and focussed on me with only slight difficulty. 'Don't tell anyone,' I said, 'but I'm a private investigator.'

'Are you checking bar prices? They're on the fiddle, you know.'

'I think Weights and Measures do that.'

'You don't look like a private dick to me.'

'I like to blend.'

'You've done that all right. You look like one of us – a fucking pauper.'

I resolved there and then to smarten up my act. After all, there comes a time when looking like a student in your thirties smacks of immaturity.

'Simon, how about if I buy you a decent meal?' I said. 'And then I tell you about my investigation and perhaps you can help me with it.'

'Not Mission Impossible, is it?'

'Nope,' I said, adding in a whisper that I hoped would add a degree of gravity, 'I want you to find out about two students doing an engineering degree in the mid-seventies.' Then I added, for good measure, 'It's a murder enquiry.'

He thought about the proposition for all of twenty seconds. 'Okay. But no pasta – and how about throwing in a shag?'

Once he was on his feet, he towered above me and insisted on holding my hand. 'Never argue with a drunk' was one maxim I tried to live by, so off we went. I wasn't quite old enough to be his mother but I felt that old, especially when his long strides had me trotting to keep up.

Outside of the university I asked Simon what he fancied

– Indian, Thai, Chinese, Mexican? 'What I really fancy is roast beef and all the trimmings,' he said.

'Just like Mother used to make.'

He laughed. 'My mother needed Delia Smith to tell her how to boil water.'

'What does she do?'

'She's a lawyer.'

'You shouldn't be too short of money then.'

'Haven't you noticed?' he said, swaying a bit as the fresh air hit him. 'Those with the most money are the tightest. Anyway, she's washed her hands of me.'

'Why?'

'I was expelled from two public schools,' he said, with a tinge of pride, 'and I had to resit my first year here due to an excess of wining, dining and shagging.' He wasn't wearing a coat but he seemed unaware that it had begun to rain. 'She stopped my fucking allowance and told me not to darken her doorstep again until I knew how to manage my money and mind my language.'

'Did it work?'

'Nah. I haven't seen her for a year.'

Simon eventually found a pub with a carvery and a policy of self-serving as many vegetables as can be crammed on the smallest of plates. He managed to create a small mountain on his plate and he ate as though someone might snatch it away at any moment. I found myself adding to his plate my Yorkshire pudding and half of my beef. He merely grunted in gratitude. He was so obviously hungry that even *my* appetite deserted me and I found myself pushing food around the plate like a fragile member of the royal family. At this rate, I told myself, a size twelve, once the impossible dream, could, with enough off-putting moments, become a reality.

Conversation between us was impossible. Simon was far too preoccupied with eating. 'Dessert?' I queried.

'Why stop now?' he said. 'Apple pie and ice cream would be great.'

Eventually he did stop.

'What degree are you reading for?' I asked.

'Pornography and the Economics of the Sex Industry,' he said, straight-faced.

'Let me guess – English Lit.'

'Wrong – actually I'm reading Philosophy and Political Science.'

'What do you want to do when you finish?'

'Doss.'

I didn't take that too seriously. If he'd been expelled twice and still managed to get to university he was probably very bright. 'I think you'll become a politician,' I said. 'Possibly Chancellor of the Exchequer.'

'Is that because my brilliance shows through?'

'No. You'll do it just to prove how wrong your mother could be.'

He slipped his glasses back on. 'Right, Kate, buy me a pint and I'll ransack the dean's office if you want.'

'I'd prefer it if you asked someone senior in the faculty if they remember your "uncle" – Carl Farnforth – and his friend Ian Jenkins. Don't take any chances – you don't want to be sent down, do you?'

He shrugged. 'It wouldn't bother me.'

'It would bother *me.* This is confidential, you know.'

He nodded and a fine dusting of dandruff settled on his shoulders. 'I've seen one old tutor in the engineering faculty,' he said, draining his pint. 'But most of them wouldn't have been around twenty years ago. All student records are on computer now, anyway.'

'Are you computer literate?' I asked.

He smiled, his teeth slightly crooked. 'I'm a fucking genius.'

The wisdom of choosing Simon caused me some fretting.

I'd chosen him purely on a whim – he looked like a loner. Loners talked little and gossiped less. And he looked intelligent, in spite of his shambling appearance.

I'd booked into a B&B because I didn't know how long it would take and I didn't want to be seen any more than necessary at the university. Now I lay on a sagging bed and worried about the wisdom of sending Simon on his risky venture. I'd found that, for many people, PIs induced suspicion bordering on paranoia. Men with secrets were the worst – assuming that their wives had tracked down their mistresses or secret love child or forays to the betting shop. A vanload of uniformed police with dogs wouldn't have caused them so much consternation. That was my justification.

The hours ticked by, punctuated by a two-finger Kit-Kat, three throat sweets with soft centres and *Countdown*, where I failed miserably. I'd given Simon my mobile phone number and said I would wait for his call. But why should he bother? He'd been fed and watered and I hadn't offered him any inducements. Why the hell should he do anything at all?

I spent a long evening switching the TV on and off, leaving the screen blank when I wanted to think. Both Lorraine and Carl had lied, Ian had been evasive and I wondered if even David had withheld information – after all, he was a cop. Now I'd put my trust in a drunken student. The only solution, if I didn't see him again, was to find someone else and this time offer deferred gratification. Pub grub just wasn't going to be enough.

When my mobile did ring at midnight it was Hubert. 'Where are you?' he asked, as if I should report my every move.

'I'm in bed,' I replied, 'and looking forward to sleep.'

'There's a development,' said Hubert, in the tone of voice he reserved for imparting surprise information.

I sat up in bed as though preparing myself. 'What's happened? Has Ian been arrested again?'

'The police have started digging up his garden.'

'Oh,' I muttered, because what else was there to say?

There was silence from Hubert's end and I sensed his disappointment as if it were emanating from the phone's receiver.

'Was your trip worthwhile?' he asked, obviously deciding to change tack.

'Of course it was.'

'So what have you found out?'

'Nothing yet – I've delegated.'

'You're good at that.'

'Trust me. I know what I'm doing.'

He had the cheek to laugh but my resolve, like superglue, took a few seconds to stick. Simon would come up trumps. I just knew he would.

My breakfast at the Primrose Guest House was the climax of my morning. I sat with an elderly couple who regaled me with their B&B holiday highlights from around Great Britain. I learnt it was essential always to travel with a flask of hot tea, a plastic box of sandwiches, a selection of boiled sweets and an emergency supply of tea bags and dried milk.

'You get ripped off at these service stations,' said Bill, a robust little man with white hair and pink cheeks. 'But they don't catch us now, do they, Marjorie?'

Marjorie, equally robust, dressed in horizontal yellow and black stripes, reminded me of a round humbug. 'No, dear,' she agreed. 'We've got our little trips down to a fine art. We've never stayed here before but we'd come again just for the breakfast, wouldn't we?'

I smiled and nodded in agreement. Breakfast at the Primrose was worth three meals in one. 'And,' added Marjorie, 'they keep a lovely stock of tea bags in the room and nice cups and saucers.'

I told them I too was impressed. I was trying to eat my last slice of toast when my mobile rang. It was David. 'We need to talk to you again about the shooting,' he said. There wasn't a 'how are you' or 'it was fun' or 'looking forward to seeing you again'. I may not have been particularly interested in him but I was peeved that he wasn't *slightly* besotted.

'Is that a royal *we* or a collective term for half the CID?'

'Could be just me if you play your cards right.'

'What time?'

'This morning?'

'I can't make it until late afternoon.'

'Why not?'

'I'm not in Longborough.'

'Fair enough. Ring me when you get back.' I noticed *he* hadn't wanted to know my whereabouts, which again was a slight disappointment.

Bill and Marjorie sat watching me with interest, tinged with suspicion. 'I have to dash – don't want to keep my men waiting, do I?'

Marjorie murmured, 'Bye, dear, nice to meet you.' Bill ignored my cheerful goodbye wave. He was too busy collecting unopened butter pats and wrapping his leftover toast in a paper napkin. What a bundle of fun he must have been on England's highways and byways.

In my room I cleaned my teeth and packed my overnight bag, which in all took five minutes, and then switched on the TV. I had to vacate my room by eleven and by now it was nine forty-five. I could recce the shops or stay put for a while.

It was raining heavily so I decided to sample the delights of daytime television. I quickly got into a confessions-type show entitled 'I Stole My Mother's Lover' and began to enjoy in true voyeuristic fashion the various reactions of daughters to their mothers' treachery.

My own mother thought flirting with any man, mine or not, was her duty and mission in life. I hoped that, if she *did* snatch my man, I'd be grateful rather than upset because the man would have been a complete arsehole and would have wrecked my life. He would have cheated on me with someone else, I reasoned, if not my mother.

I was just leaving the Primrose Guest House in pouring rain and making my way to the car when my mobile rang. I sprinted down the steps to the car park, struggled to find my car keys and then, once in the dry haven of my car, the damn thing stopped ringing. 'Unanswered Call' came up on my mobile and as I didn't know how to find out who had rung I pressed a few buttons at random to no effect. Then, deciding simply to wait for the caller to ring back, I clutched the phone in my hand. Thankfully it rang twenty minutes later.

'I've got the info you wanted,' said Simon. 'Where shall we meet?'

'Outside the university? The main entrance?'

'Okay, in about twenty minutes – I've got a meeting with my fucking tutor.'

I'd found the university easily enough the day before but now I was lost, traffic was heavy and I took several wrong turns until, eventually, I saw Simon huddling under a tree near the university entrance. He wore a denim jacket that was already soaked through.

Once in the car he handed me several sheets of computer printout. 'This has been an eye-opener,' he said. 'Orwell's *1984* wasn't just a work of fiction.'

'I hope you didn't take any risks?'

He laughed. 'Nope, but I managed to look at my own psychological profile and I rewrote the fucking thing.'

'You mean this,' I said, waving the sheets of paper, 'contains psychological profiles? Is that legal?'

'Was storing children's organs without parental permission legal?' he asked. 'There's always some pseudo-scientist looking for glory. You've done us a favour, Kate.'

'How come?'

'Some of the claptrap in our personal files needs trashing. It could wreck lives – and the bloke doing it in the seventies is still at it now.'

'Be careful, Simon – if you get caught –' I paused. His face was pale, his lips tight.

'I don't give a toss. The bastard has to be stopped.'

Whatever Simon had read had genuinely upset him. I fished fifty pounds from my purse and pressed it into his hand. 'There's no need,' he said, trying to force the money back into my hand. 'If I hadn't seen my own profile,' he said, 'I'd be lucky to get a job stacking shelves.'

'Take the money,' I said. 'Go and see your mother. Convince her you're a reformed character. Buy her some flowers and don't swear in her presence.'

Simon smiled. 'That may not be such a bad idea. She believes in justice, or says she does; maybe this is her opportunity to prove it.' His eyes flicked to the money that I was now proffering again. 'Phone a friend or take the money?' he said with a grin. 'I'll take the cash.'

I kissed his cheek as he left. 'Is it okay if I ring you?' he asked.

I nodded. 'Let me know how you get on.'

'Yeah,' he said. 'I'll do that.'

Twelve

It was late afternoon when I got back to Longborough. The bad weather hadn't been confined to Shefford. Longborough could boast more torrential rain and in the near-dark the puddles in Humberstones' car park looked like embryonic ponds.

Hubert's lights were on and I went straight up to his flat. Jasper ran to greet me like a long-lost pack member and Hubert, viewing my rain-soaked hair and face, asked, 'Is it raining?'

I declined to answer. 'I've got to go straight out,' I said. 'DCI Todman wants to give me the third degree again.'

'You're not going out like *that*?'

'I don't care what I look like,' I said. 'I'm not interested in him and you can forget any romantic notions you might have. He just doesn't light my fire.'

'Too straight for you, is he?'

'If by that, Hubert, you mean strait-laced – boring, even – the answer is yes. I just don't trust a man who has no obvious weaknesses.'

Hubert shrugged. 'I think you just make excuses not to find a man.'

'It's my business,' I snapped. He looked crestfallen, so I added, 'How would you like it if I began matchmaking for you?'

'When can you start?'

He made me a cup of tea and produced chocolate biscuits.

I ate three, having decided that since I'd forsaken my search for an intrepid man I might as well continue with my one vice – food.

From the inside pocket of my jacket I produced the profiles on Farnforth and Jenkins and handed them to Hubert, who looked suitably impressed. 'How did you swing this?'

'It must be my charm.'

Hubert began reading immediately. 'I haven't read them yet,' I said.

'You're going out – if you like I'll get them on computer for you.'

Since I'd had visions of shoving them in a drawer it was my turn to be impressed. 'Thanks, Hubert. I'll stay here tonight and read through them.'

'You haven't asked about the dig.'

'How's it going?'

'I heard it had been abandoned,' he said. 'Because of the rain.'

'It's not like your line of work,' I said, as I hastily swallowed the last of my tea. 'Gravediggers work in all weathers.'

'You've never said a truer word, Kate. The funeral business in this country is one of the most efficient, reliable services we have. When did an undertaker last go on strike?'

'I wouldn't know,' I said. 'They don't go broke either. I'm glad to be associated with such a profession.'

'Sarky madam,' he said good-naturedly.

I blew him a kiss and left.

The rain hadn't abated and the legs of my jeans became spattered with mud. By the time I arrived at the station I felt as attractive as an old sock but, with my new resolve, vanity was no longer in my list of failings.

I was directed to an interview room straight away and

prepared myself for a long wait. DCI Todman, however, turned up within minutes. 'You look cold and damp,' he said. 'Fancy a cuppa?'

'Great. Thanks.'

When he returned with the tea, he said, 'This is all very informal, Kate – nothing taped, nothing taken down in writing.'

'Is that because as hearsay evidence it's inadmissible in court?'

He gave me a sharp look. 'Let's not get technical, Kate. Ian Jenkins is still prime suspect for killing his wife. The more we find out about him the more likely it looks. We just can't nail him yet.'

'Does he have an alibi for the night Lorraine was found?'

David frowned. 'No. He was alone in the house with the kids. Trouble is, we have no forensic to link him with the break-in.'

Was he really the type to leave his children to either terrorise or kill a woman who was once a friend? I looked up to find David smiling at me. 'You look puzzled,' he said.

'I was wondering about motive. Silencing Lorraine seems to be the only one.'

'That's strong enough, surely.'

'Yes,' I murmured, unconvinced. 'Strange, isn't it,' I said, 'that Lorraine turns up at the very moment he decides to shoot his wife.'

'We had thought of that,' he said, sounding a little put out.

'And?'

'We're not jumping to any conclusions.'

'You sound like a politician,' I said. 'And I think you *have* been jumping to conclusions. You decided from day one Ian Jenkins was the prime suspect – all you had to do then was find Paula's body.'

David Todman's facial expression showed I'd hit a raw

spot. 'A great deal of time and attention to detail,' he declared, 'has already been extended on this case.' He paused and stared at me. 'Let's not forget you were the one withholding information.'

'Point taken,' I murmured grudgingly, trying to look suitably chastened.

'Good.'

There was another pause before he said, 'Is there anything you've thought of since you first met Lorraine that might provide a clue – anything, however slight?'

I guessed this was my chance to mention Dr Reece Gardener but the words just stuck in my throat. 'She told me she'd been seeing a friend but I think she was seeing . . . a lover.'

'What makes you think that – intuition?'

'No, merely the fact she wouldn't give me the address.' That wasn't a lie. She *hadn't* given me the address.

'Anything else?' he asked.

I racked my brain. 'The vodka.'

'What about it?'

'Supermarkets and off licences don't sell vodka that strong. At least, I've never noticed it.'

'I'm not exactly an expert on alcohol, but I get your point,' he said. 'We found three other bottles with the same label at her place. It could be from a job lot or a present.'

'Or deliberately planted on her? After all, I can't imagine that she checked the proof.'

He nodded, 'Yeah, that's a possibility. *Why* isn't so easy to answer.'

An uncomfortable silence followed in which he seemed to be staring at my damp hair. I flicked a strand away from my right eye and foraged for something to say. 'Have you found out anything about the red beret and scarf?' I asked.

He passed a hand wearily over his face and I noticed for the first time how tired he looked. 'There were no labels to check out,' he said, 'so we sent it to forensic. It's hand-knitted but the wool can be bought anywhere. We're checking out the wool shop in Longborough and nearby towns that do still have wool shops.'

'Knitting is a dying art,' I murmured. I couldn't knit. Plain and purl could have been two girls from Essex for all the knowledge I had. So I changed the subject.

'What about Carl? Has he told you why he moved back here?'

David sat back in his chair and crossed his legs. His pose was relaxed but irritation showed on his face. 'Who the hell is asking the questions here? You're showing a lot of interest for someone who's no longer involved.'

'I *am* still involved.'

'Who's employing you? Don't answer that. It could only be Ian Jenkins.'

I resented his tone. 'I'm not going to tread on your toes.'

'You already have.'

At this point I thought he'd finished and I slung my handbag on my shoulder and shifted in my chair.

He laughed briefly. 'You don't get away as easily as that. Tell me again what Lorraine said about the shooting.'

Sounding like a uniformed plod I recapped Lorraine's witness account. 'Lorraine Farnforth was returning to her vehicle on the evening of Friday 12th January. The car was parked near the picnic area by the river. From a distance –' I hesitated.

'What distance?'

'I don't know.'

'Ten yards – fifty yards – a hundred yards?'

'I don't know.'

'You mean you didn't ask her?'

'Okay, charge me for failing to ascertain distance.' Then I

added, by way of apology, 'Women aren't as good at judging length as men.'

David raised his eyebrows, which I judged to be a mute comment on women's failings in general, but perhaps I was being hypersensitive.

'She told me her car was parked facing the river; the only other car was the murderer's.'

'Were the couple at the driver's side or the passenger side?'

'They were –' I hesitated, trying desperately to remember Lorraine's actual words.

'You don't know, do you?'

'Just give me a chance,' I snapped. 'I did make notes at the time. For God's sake, I thought I had time to ask her more questions. I'm not psychic – I—'

'Calm down.'

'I am calm.'

'Would you rather we continued in the pub?' he asked, smiling.

'No. I wouldn't. I'm trying to be as helpful as I can. My interview was only a preliminary one – time was on my side – then.'

'You don't have to apologise.'

'I'm not!'

'Let me get you another cup of tea.'

I nodded but I didn't think a vatful of tea would help my memory.

While he was out I rummaged in my bag for my notebook. My notes told me nothing new or enlightening. Anyway, I reasoned, they were Lorraine's observations and not mine. I knew two people seeing the same thing would focus on different objects and have different recollections. I didn't know if that applied to a murder, especially when a gun was being brandished and your own life was in danger. Self-preservation, I reasoned, concentrates on escape rather than the detailed account you might live to tell. So do as the man says, I told myself, and calm down.

David, placing the plastic cup in front of me, seemed to have had a change of heart. 'We do have another witness,' he said.

'That's great.'

'Not that great,' he said. 'A drunk old boy returning to his bedsit said he saw a couple rowing near the river.'

'What's wrong with that?'

'He's stone deaf – he didn't hear the shot or see the gun.'

'What about the make of car?'

'He said he was a pushbike man and he took no interest in cars.'

'Did anyone else hear the shot?'

'No, and worse still he wasn't sure it was even the right day.'

I could sense he was trying not to laugh, but I carried on. 'Did you find anything in the area?'

'A few lager cans, several fag ends and some dog shit. I wish I could say we found the odd bullet but we didn't.'

'What about the gun?' I asked.

'The river's been partially dragged but no joy.'

'Have you dug up the Jenkinses' garden yet?'

'The lads started but the rain was too heavy for them to continue. We're getting tarpaulins set up and Jenkins and the kids are planning to move in with his mother. She's not too happy about that but she doesn't have much choice, does she?'

'I didn't know his mother lived locally.'

'She lives out past Dunmore,' he said. 'In one of those thatched cottages set back from the main road. Nice but a bit small for an extra three people.'

'You're not much further forward then.'

'We're making steady progress,' he said, sounding like

a politician defending a cock-up. 'The Jenkins factory is having its books looked at. Profits seem to be down this year.'

'Is that significant?'

'It is if he expects to benefit from his wife's death.'

'He won't benefit until her body's found, will he?'

'No. So if Chummy thinks he's planned the perfect murder, the sooner the body is found the better.'

'He doesn't seem that devious to me,' I said, feeling that as he was my client I had to publicly defend him. 'His body language was okay.'

David grinned at me but I didn't smile back: sometimes you just know when someone is going to best you. A bit like putting one foot in a quagmire.

'Ian looked you straight in the eye, Kate, did he? Didn't fidget or cover his mouth? Not totally devastated but just upset enough for you to think he's being honest and not trying to bullshit you?'

I didn't answer. It was soapbox time and he was going to make the most of it. 'I've interviewed killers,' he continued, 'who were more convincing than a clergyman. They'll swear on their children's lives that they're innocent. Even as the evidence piles up against them they'll not only protest their innocence, they'll act innocent too. How do you think the Yorkshire Ripper or Fred West got away with their crimes for so long? If you don't have a conscience you don't have guilt and you can lie convincingly.'

'I can't argue with that,' I said. 'All I can say about Ian Jenkins is he doesn't seem like a violent man and he seems to have a forgiving nature.'

'You mean forgiving Paula for going AWOL before?' he asked.

I nodded.

David wasn't going to agree and I knew my argument in Ian's favour was based purely on instinct.

'Maybe this time,' he said, 'he sussed she was off again and it was the straw that broke the camel's back. That night he was trying to persuade her not to go, so he threatened her with a gun, thinking she would back down, and in the struggle he pulled the trigger.'

'A crime of passion, then?' I suggested. That made more sense to me.

'Not exactly. There was malice intended – why have a gun in the first place? They hung Ruth Ellis for being armed and prepared.'

'Obviously a male judge,' I said. 'Denying a woman a crime of passion plea because of his own prejudices.'

I'd expected an argument but none came. 'I agree with you,' he said. 'I think women can get a raw deal.'

I felt quite deflated. 'How about that drink?' he said, glancing at his watch.

I hesitated.

'And a bite to eat?' he added.

I'd had breakfast, a few biscuits and that was all. The evening was wearing on and I was in calorie deficit. 'Why not?' I said casually, not wanting him to think the food had swung it for him.

'Only one proviso,' he said. 'We don't talk about the case.'

'There is one thing,' I said, 'I've been wanting to ask you.'

'Fire away.'

'You don't belong to some happy-clappy church, do you?'

'No. Why should you think I do?'

'No reason,' I lied, looking him straight in the eye.

Thirteen

Benito's Italian restaurant, five miles away in the small town of Luxton, offered more than 'a bite to eat', and I couldn't see an empty table in the shimmer of the red candles. The atmosphere was loud and the wine had obviously been flowing freely. David had a quiet word with a waiter and, whatever he said, it worked.

We were allocated a table for two in a corner niche and I had a good view of the other diners between a red candle and a slim vase of red carnations. Part of eating out, I think, is guessing who the groups are and what, if anything, they are celebrating. One table of six had a gran in tow who wore a badge saying '80 Today'. Another table, four women and two men, seemed a little over-excited, as if they didn't get out often, and I thought they were probably teachers.

'Wine list, sir?' said a young waiter with slicked-back hair and teeth as white and even as a box of candles.

I looked across at David who said, 'Enjoy yourself. I'm driving.'

After much deliberation a whole bottle of anything seemed a bit optimistic so I ordered a half-carafe of the house red. David drank mineral water and we both ordered melon and Parma ham to start. Without discussing the case I wondered what on earth we would have to say, but David talked about his sisters for a while and about the joys of living alone unaccompanied by tales of lost tights, borrowed clothes and monthly moods.

'Best of all,' he said, 'the bathroom is always free.'

I was an only child so I'd never experienced any real contrast. I'd always seemed to be alone. I was regaling him with stories of various disasters I'd encountered during my nursing training, which he didn't think were so funny, when I looked up to see a couple arriving. A waiter approached them, checked his watch, smiled, nodded in the direction of one of the tables and the couple sat down in the small reception area.

'What's wrong?' asked David. 'Is the wine okay?'

'It's fine,' I said. 'I was just watching that couple.'

He shrugged and turned his head. 'They look pretty ordinary to me. Do you know them?'

'I was just wondering if they were a married couple.'

'Why?'

'I think they're sitting a little too close together, and she keeps looking straight into his eyes.'

'And married couples don't do that?'

'Not if they've been married a few years.'

The couple continued to be engrossed in each other and I kept watching them.

'Are you doing it on purpose, Kate?'

'What?'

'You've spent more time eyeballing the punters than eating.'

'Sorry,' I murmured. I tried to eat my Neapolitan spaghetti and avoid a messy chin but my concentration was still on the couple.

'Do you have a five-year plan? he asked.

'A what?'

'A plan of ambition. Where you hope to be in five years?'

My mind was still fixed on the couple. She was petite, small-boned, probably size-three feet. Could have been what we called in the trade an AA – Anxious Anorexic. From where I was sitting she looked a size eight with room to spare. I guessed she was in her late twenties. Every so often he touched her hand as if he couldn't believe his luck.

'Life plan?' he repeated.

I apologised again. 'Oh yes,' I said, struggling to gather a few ambitions together. 'In five years I hope to have a pension plan, a few thousand in a high-interest account and an agency big enough to need two paid assistants.'

'Car?'

'A neat little sports model. And you?' I asked. 'What about your five-year plan?'

'At least chief inspector. Wife, two kids, and a place in the country.'

'You're a very traditional type, aren't you?' I said with a smile.

'What you really mean is I'm a boring old fart.'

'You're not old.'

He laughed. 'You really know how to wound a man's ego, don't you?'

'It's not deliberate.'

'No, but it works just the same.'

I was definitely warming to DCI Todman. He was a nice guy and sometimes the nice guys should win the day.

'That couple over there waiting for a table,' I said, with a slight jerk of my head.

'Yes?'

'He's Dr Reece Gardener and that woman isn't his wife.'

Grinning, he said, 'Do you want me to arrest him?'

'I think you should talk to him.'

'Tell him the error of his ways?'

'No. Ask him about Lorraine Farnforth. They were having an affair.'

David lost his grip on his forkful of pasta. 'Why the hell didn't you tell me before?'

'I thought he was okay. He told me he'd been in love with her. And I'm apt to believe that sort of thing. He was most convincing.'

'And this other woman has made you change your mind?'

'He's obviously a complete bastard. And a rotten doctor to boot.'

'Lorraine was his patient?'

'Yes. He said he was supplying her with the contraceptive pill.'

'And *she* said something else?'

'Not exactly. She was getting the prescriptions but not getting them filled.'

'Why not?'

'She was trying get pregnant.'

'By him?'

'Yes.'

'Christ almighty, woman. Why tell me now? Why not just keep me bloody guessing?'

'I thought it would complicate the issue . . . I believed him.' I knew it sounded lame.

He took a deep breath, trying to control his temper. 'That's as maybe,' he said, through gritted teeth. 'But if this Reece Gardener is such a womaniser – and you seem pretty sure he's not with his wife tonight – then maybe there's a connection with Paula. I suppose you hadn't thought to check if Paula was also a patient?'

I had to admit then that it hadn't crossed my mind.

'It's just as well,' he said. 'I already knew she was on his list.'

'Oh shit,' I murmured.

'Yes, and it's fan time for the doc.'

Our resolve not to talk about the case had vanished in the presence of Dr Reece Gardener. Not only had he cheated on his wife, he'd cheated on his lover. He couldn't just have one affair, he had to have two.

'He's a greedy sod,' murmured David.

'Agreed. But that doesn't make him a murderer.' A cold look was his only response to that so I followed up with, 'I've heard some men, especially public schoolboys, need to have two women – one to mother them and the other to slake their carnal lusts.'

'Sounds like hell to me,' he said. 'Too much trouble for most blokes. They can't take the guilt.'

'I don't think guilt is a problem with Gardener,' I said, observing him stroking AA's wrist as though handling the Holy Grail.

Two customers began noisily pushing their chairs back and gathering their belongings. As they left a waiter guided Gardener and partner to the vacated table so that now they were only a few yards away. Although he hadn't seen me yet it could only be a few minutes before he did. I was longing to observe his disquiet when that happened.

I was probably overreacting by feeling betrayed, but I did. A little bit of me wanted revenge for all betrayed women. Which is why, I suppose, women friends pour such scorn on cheating men or men who won't commit. 'He's a bastard' and 'You're better off without him' are meant to be words of comfort. But of course they're not. Women suffer by proxy. Someone dumps you and your friends fear for their relationships – it's misery and insecurity all round. Men, are less empathetic; when one of their number gets the push, they view him as returning to the clan and true manliness. A few nights getting legless will be all that he needs. It isn't, of course; no severe wound heals that quickly. Women happily debride their wounds and then pick at the scab until eventually healing is complete—

'Are you still with me, Kate?'

I smiled apologetically. David may not have been the most dynamic bloke in the world but I was supposed to be on a date. 'I was just thinking,' I said, 'about the difference between males and females on the cheating front.'

He removed a crumb from the tablecloth and placed it on his empty plate before saying, 'Having seen my sisters in action, they can be the most heartless little bitches. They duck and dive in their love lives like members of MI5.'

'Maybe they're just learning male ways.'

David didn't look convinced. 'I think they have no regard for male emotion, thinking if we don't show it we don't feel it.'

'You could be right,' I conceded, 'but the Reece Gardeners of this world are so shallow, their emotions are fully contained in their Y-fronts.'

'He's got to you, hasn't he?'

I shrugged, realising that now was the time to tell all. 'He duped me.'

'You haven't?' he said, sounding shocked.

'Haven't what?'

'Slept with him.'

Now it was my turn to be shocked. 'Of course I haven't,' I said. 'That's a ridiculous idea.'

'He seems to have a way with women.'

We both stopped to take in the view of the couple, engrossed now in eating and eye contact. Gardener must have sensed someone was watching him, for he looked up and saw me. He held my glance for a moment and then smiled, a confident, cocky smile.

I scowled back and sipped more wine. 'When I said he duped me, David, I'd better tell you what happened.'

I told him how I'd been followed to Farley Wood, how he'd barged into my house and admitted he'd falsified records, so that in effect only his partner had seen Lorraine.

If David was angry he hid it well, although when he asked, 'What about the staff?' I noticed he'd clenched his hands and his knuckles were turning pale.

'Maybe he holds sway with all women,' I said. 'He convinced me he genuinely cared about Lorraine and his wife.'

'You're a liability, Kate,' he said coldly. 'If you want to keep your agency I suggest you learn to trust no one until they've proved themselves.'

There was nothing I could say to that. Of course he was right. So I kept quiet and ate the chocolate concoction I'd chosen from the dessert trolley.

'He's blatant about this woman,' said David, as he relaxed his hands and flexed his fingers. 'Strange he should fall into a panic about Lorraine. Unless, of course, he found the body – but why not enter by the front door?'

I didn't have an answer to that either.

Abruptly David stood up. 'I won't be long.'

I assumed he was going to the loo but ten minutes later I began to think that I'd been abandoned. When he eventually returned he looked more cheerful.

'You had me convinced,' he said.

'About what?'

'How couples behave,' he said. 'I've been talking to Benito, the owner. The doc lives just down the road. He's a regular and for the past year he's eaten here once or twice a week – always alone.'

'And the punchline?'

'She *is* his wife,' he said, with a hint of triumph in his tone. Clever cop versus smartarse PI – cop wins. 'For a year she's been in a private psychiatric clinic being treated for post-natal depression and anorexia. They're celebrating her release and improved health. At one point she weighed only five stone and it was thought she wouldn't survive. Explains his panic – she only left hospital recently. The last thing he'd want is for her to be greeted by news of his infidelity.'

I didn't have much to say after that. I was willing to

concede that Dr Gardener may have had a tiny excuse, that maybe he'd been weak and lonely rather than an out-and-out bastard. But I still wouldn't trust him with any ailment of mine.

'I'll still need to talk to him,' said David, as he paused to signal to a waiter for the bill. 'But I'll be discreet after all. I don't want to be responsible for a family break-up. Now, I think we've done enough guesswork for one evening.'

I offered to go Dutch but he refused, telling me I could pay next time. So there would be a next time. That *did* surprise me. Once in the car, however, he remained silent and I began to get a little paranoid that he was simply keeping tabs on me.

Once more I was planning to sleep in my own home, and I debated about asking him in. It was one of those times when my sexual urges were curtailed by not having made my bed, not having something glamorous to wear, but most of all not being sure if I even half fancied him. For me a man has to have the right smell and so far his hadn't penetrated my nasal passages.

He parked the car and switched off the ignition. 'It's been an interesting evening,' he said, with a hand placed on my knee. I murmured in agreement and kissed him. 'Pity about the garlic,' he said. 'Are you going to offer me a coffee?'

I hesitated, slightly tempted, but I'd run out of mouthwash and I was looking for an excuse. 'I'm—'

The ringing of my mobile phone was all I needed. It was Hubert.

'I've got a surprise for you, Kate.'

'At this time of night?'

'Yes.'

'Don't keep me in suspense.'

'You'll have to come over.'

'I'm with someone and I've had a drink.' By now I was annoyed. Hubert had introduced us and whilst David was never going to be the love of my life he was MPA – male, presentable and available. And at my age perhaps that was all I could hope for. But I did at least want the *option* of turning him down.

'Let me talk to David,' said Hubert.

'Is it about the case?' I asked.

'Kate, give him the phone.'

I sighed and handed my mobile to David. I couldn't hear what Hubert was saying but already there was an answer. 'Okay. No problem. We're on our way.'

'What the hell is going on?' I asked.

'I'm driving you back to Longborough – that's all I know. Hubert says it's important.'

Hubert stood under the security light in the car park waiting for us. He didn't look at ease but he managed a half-smile when he saw me. 'Don't tell me,' I said. 'Let me guess – your lottery numbers have come up – the Co-op wants to buy you out for five million – or, failing that, you're going to get married to a woman you haven't had the decency to let me meet.'

'Stop being silly, Kate. Come inside and I'll tell you.'

Fourteen

'It's nothing to worry about,' said Hubert, coming up the stairs behind me. It wasn't until he'd sat me down in my office swivel chair that he announced, 'It's your mother.'

'What about her? Is she ill? Has she got married?'

'Calm down, Kate. It's nothing like that. She's here.'

Aghast, I looked round the room. 'What do you mean, she's here?'

'She's in my guest room.'

Gormlessly I asked, 'What's she doing there?'

'She's kipping. Clapped out. Jet-lagged and in the land of nod.'

I was in shock. If I wasn't careful I'd hyperventilate. Finally I said, 'I expect she's run out of money. Why else would she come back?'

'I don't know why you're so anti. She's a lovely woman.'

'Don't you dare, Hubert – don't you dare.'

'Dare what?'

'Start ogling my mother's feet.'

'She's got good legs and—'

'Stop it.'

He shrugged. 'You're getting spinsterish ways as you get older.'

'Good!'

Inside I was worried sick. My mother had the habit of making situations a whole lot worse. She could be blunt to the point of rudeness and all with a big smile. She was useless with money, helpless around the house and would flirt with anyone from the window cleaner to her bank manager. Worse, she was often successful, at least in the short run.

'Where's Jasper?' I asked, suddenly missing his wet nose and friendly fawning.

'He's lying on the bed curled up with your mother.'

Somehow that was the final straw. I wanted to cry on my own. 'You'd better go,' I said.

Hubert looked crestfallen. 'What have I done? I couldn't let her walk the streets, could I? I could have sent her over to Farley Wood but I thought that might be too much of a shock.'

'It's a shock anyway.'

'She may have plans – she might only stay a few nights.'

I stared at Hubert. 'You don't know her – she meets people all over the place and, being polite, they say "If you're passing do call in" and that's what she does. Last time she was passing it was somewhere in Manitoba, Canada – she stayed for three weeks. Another time it was Madrid – that was a two-week stay . . .'

'Marrakesh next then,' said Hubert, trying to be jaunty. I wasn't in the mood.

'It's not funny. She's an embarrassment. She's the sort who goes topless in your back garden.'

'There's no garden here so don't go off at a tangent. Wait until you've seen her in the morning. You can talk.'

'Talking with my mother is as easy as promoting New Labour to Margaret Thatcher.'

'She's mellowed in her old age.'

'Not that much and my mother doesn't mellow, she just gets more outrageous.'

'I think you're over-reacting. Just wait and see.'

By now I didn't feel quite so tearful, but I did feel a

sense of foreboding. In many ways I loved Mum – her name's Marilyn, a name she's been trying to live up to, on the glamour front anyway – but it's less a mother-daughter relationship than daughter-ageing adolescent, and I resent having a mother incapable of mothering. I suppose I should have grown out of the need but it's still there. I had to face the fact that Hubert had become mother and father to me. And I didn't want Marilyn rocking any boats – or coffins, in this case.

In the morning I peeped into the guest room. She was just emerging from the shower, wrapped in a white towel, brown as a nutmeg. Jasper sat on the bed wagging his tail. 'Kate,' she called out excitedly. 'Come on in. Let me give you a kiss.' She hugged me. 'You've lost weight,' she said, patting my arms and giving them a squeeze as if I was a prize cow. 'I expect you're surprised to see me.' She threw off her towel, allowing it to fall to the floor, and picked up a pair of white lacy briefs from the bed. 'Your landlord tells me you're doing really well – a murder case and everything.'

'Missing person at the moment.'

I watched in silence as she blow-dried her hair. 'Won't be a sec, dear.'

'I'll go,' I said, making for the door, knowing that she always underestimated.

She switched off the hairdryer. 'No, wait. I won't be long,' she said, pointing the hairdryer at me and managing to look plaintive. 'If I could just stay at your place for a few days I'll get myself sorted.'

She'd never been *sorted* in her life and I couldn't see her changing now. She finished drying her hair and, mesmerised, I watched as she applied various cosmetic mulches and fertilisers to her face. Jasper hadn't yet moved from the bed so I guessed he too was fascinated. 'I won't be any trouble,' she said. 'My skin is as dry as a camel's back – the flight was so long – I tried to stay off the pop – but you know me.'

'Only too well.'

She gave me a searching look. 'I've decided to settle down,' she said. 'Perhaps find a little housekeeping job.'

I managed to keep a straight face. 'Marilyn, you have trouble loading a dishwasher. Who would employ you?'

A slight shrug of her shoulders indicated she didn't want to hear my opinions and she began a reconstruction job on her face. She carried more make-up with her than an Avon lady and more brushes than an artist. Once she'd finished she gave herself a fine misting from a water spray to set the look and muttered into the mirror. 'Not too bad for a forty-eight-year-old.' It had been her little joke for five years – but now I think she believed it herself.

Hubert had invited us for breakfast and when she appeared wearing well-polished black court shoes with four-inch heels his pupils dilated faster than a camera shutter. Her black skirt, which came to just above the knee, was quite smart but she'd topped it with a pink sleeveless T-shirt with white butterflies on it. I wanted to say to Hubert 'Take that stupid look off your face', but I bit my tongue.

Marilyn smiled coyly at Hubert as he served our breakfast of scrambled eggs. 'You're wonderful,' she said. I'd heard that sort of thing before, seen her in action many times. With some men it didn't work, not many, but some. Hubert was in the majority. His face flushed an unnatural pink. I could see in his face that he wouldn't walk over hot coals for her. He'd crawl on hands and knees.

Unusually for my mother, she was relishing her breakfast, whilst Hubert danced attendance, providing more toast than anyone could eat and fresh coffee because Marilyn preferred it. I ate a slice of toast and made my terse excuse, 'Got to go – very busy.'

'Bye, dear – see you later.'

Not if I can help it, I thought, and if she mentions going clubbing I'll lose the will to live.

I sat in my car, took some deep breaths and began reading the profiles of Ian and Carl. I tried to put my mother out of my mind but my eyes failed to refer to my brain. Instead I thought about the loss of my house. It might only be temporary, I consoled myself, and at least I still had a base. With any luck I need only see her once a week. That settled, I decided it was Hubert I was worried about. He needed to be warned. She'd have him ensnared as surely as Jasper had done and in the state I was now in, any sort of relationship between the two of them seemed to border on incest. A friend and one's mother should be banned in law. Somehow I had to curtail progress between them.

I resumed reading the profiles. Work was the answer, I told myself. If I had to work eighty hours a week, it would be eighty hours without time to worry about my mother.

The initial pages on Ian were the results of several psychological tests – the usual: verbal reasoning, spatial, mathematical ability and general knowledge. Plus an IQ test that gave his score as 160 – well above the norm. Thereafter there were sections on all aspects of his life: Family, Health, Education, Achievements, Ambitions, Social Life et cetera. It seemed to me the only thing that the report didn't cover was his bowel movements.

Mrs Dorothy Jenkins answered the door. There was no mistaking that she was Ian's mother, even if the likeness was only in the colour of her eyes and the way she held her head.

'Come in,' she said flatly, after I'd introduced myself and told her I was working on Ian's behalf. She walked stiffly but with an upright back. The hair at the back of her head had flattened and I could see grey roots amongst a brown tint.

'Sit down,' she said. I sat on a brown leather sofa and she eased herself into a recliner chair. The room was permeated by the heady smell of the hyacinths that lined the window sill. A large mock-coal fire roared comfortingly. Bookshelves filled one wall and on a round table by the side of her chair there was a pile of newspapers. There was no television.

'I don't know why you've come here,' she said. 'There's nothing I can tell you. The police have been here already.'

'Were you able to be of any help?' I asked.

'Help?' she snapped. 'A lot of stupid questions. Was my daughter-in-law the flighty sort? Did she and Ian row? How did I get on with her?'

I changed tack. 'What do you think has happened to Paula?'

'It doesn't matter what I think, does it? There are maniacs everywhere.' She jabbed at the pile of newspapers. 'You've only got to read those to know that.'

I nodded in agreement. 'So you think Paula was killed at random?'

She picked up a pair of spectacles from the table and slipped them on, the better to see me with. Her glance, filled with disdain, conveyed the fact that she thought I was stupid.

'Of course I think that. Paula was a respectable woman, a mother, for goodness' sake. Who could possibly want to kill her?'

'That's what I'm to trying to find out. Your son is the prime suspect.'

Her shoulders sagged. 'He wouldn't have harmed her. Ian is a very controlled man – very forgiving.'

'But they did have their problems?'

She was reluctant to agree but eventually muttered, 'What couple doesn't have problems these days?'

I tried to draw her out further on the subject but she stayed silent and tight-lipped, watching me flounder. Eventually she said, 'What help do you hope to give Ian by coming here?'

It was a good question and confirmed to me that I was wasting my time. 'I hoped,' I said lamely, 'that by finding out more about Ian I might help his case.'

She peered at me over the top of her glasses. 'I think, young lady, you'd be better off finding out more about Paula.'

'Is there anything you can tell me about her?'

She paused and said softly, 'What mother-in-law really understands her daughter-in-law?'

'Are you saying – ?'

'I'm saying no more on the matter. Try asking Paula's mother.'

Mrs Jenkins folded her arms and fixed me with a solid stare. It was time to go.

'Just one more question.'

She nodded. 'What is it?'

'About Thomas.' I'd found out from the profile that Ian had a younger brother.

'What did you say?'

'Thomas,' I repeated loudly. 'Ian's younger brother.'

'I know who he was,' she said.

Her eyes were bright and I noticed her lower lip trembling. 'I can't talk about him at the moment. All this is bringing back terrible memories. You'll have to leave.'

'I'm sorry. I didn't mean to upset you.'

She didn't answer. I stood up to go.

'See yourself out.' Then she murmured, 'You could always talk to Sidney. He lives in the cottage opposite.'

As I got to the door, I turned to see her hand at the side of her chair. She was removing a pair of knitting needles.

Fifteen

Outside I told myself that lots of women of her generation could knit. Maybe the police had already asked her if she'd knitted the hat and scarf. But why didn't Ian know? Or perhaps he did know. If she *was* the anonymous sender, it proved she knew Lorraine. I'd concentrated on Ian, being swayed in part by the university profile, when I should have looked at the whole picture – and the whole picture included Lorraine and Carl. All in all, I'd wasted a visit, but the day was still young. I was in the area and I could talk to Dorothy's nearest neighbour. Time away from the office also meant time away from Marilyn, which was, I thought, by far my best option.

Mr Sidney Picton in the cottage opposite was slightly stooped with a stick in one hand and a pipe in the other. He had a shock of white hair, straggly eyebrows and wore a grey cardigan over blue striped pyjama bottoms. 'You're not a reporter, are you?' he asked suspiciously, which I thought was a strange thing to ask. Why would a pensioner living in the middle of nowhere *expect* a reporter – unless the press had already called? I assured him I was working on Ian's behalf and he muttered, 'As long as you're not from a newspaper.'

Sidney's living room had paintwork in varying shades of brown with a fine coating of dust. The only thing that sparkled was the glass of whisky that sat on a table beside his high-backed chair. Weak rays of sun had slinked through the nicotine-tinted windows and given the glass centre stage. There was a television switched on but turned down low. Judging by the tobacco pouch, three pipes, four boxes of matches and an ashtray full of old shag, Sidney's day was spent filling, lighting, puffing on and emptying his pipes.

He placed his walking stick over the arm of his chair and sat down heavily with a slight groan. 'Blessed knees,' he said. 'They've been arthritic for years.'

He invited me to pour myself a drink and, when I declined, muttered, 'Can't get a blighter to drink with me these days – all flamin' mineral water now. Sit yourself down, dear.'

He had two chairs by a drop-leaf table, so I moved one close to him and sat down. I was surprised when he patted my knee but I pretended not to notice.

'Have you lived here a long time, Mr Picton?' I asked.

'Call me Sidney,' he said. 'I came here when I was seventeen. I thought I was a man then. I was lodging here with Mrs Harris. She was a widow in her sixties – I did odd jobs for her and she treated me like the son she never had. So much so she left me the house and a considerable sum of money. Set me up for life.'

I nodded and smiled. 'What about the Jenkinses?'

He checked his pipe and relit it, puffing on it until it smoked to his satisfaction. 'Newly married they were. Dorothy was a lovely girl – we became the best of friends.'

'What about her husband, Patrick?'

'Now that man *was* a worker,' he said admiringly. 'He started his factory in a lock-up and by God he put the hours in to make it a success.'

'And Ian?'

'He was born at home five years after they married. Middle of winter it was – worst snow in years. Midwife couldn't get through, so Dorothy called across to me and I was the one who delivered him. Lovely little fellow he was

– always smiling.' He paused to sip more whisky. 'Always a happy lad,' he murmured, 'until . . .'

'Until what?'

There was a slight shoulder shrug and then silence. I changed tack. 'Did you ever meet Paula?' I asked.

'Oh yes. Plenty of times. Lovely girl – she was the making of Ian. He really settled down once he'd met her.'

'A bit wild, was he, as a teenager?'

'I wouldn't say that,' said Sidney, defensively. 'When he was sixteen he got depressed. He could have worked harder at school but he was bright enough not to need to put in too much effort.'

'Why did he get depressed?'

Sidney gulped on his whisky. 'You'll find out soon enough – it's common knowledge round here . . .'

'What is?'

'His brother Thomas. I'm surprised you haven't heard.'

'Heard what?'

'He disappeared. It was in all the papers – searching night and day – no trace of him was ever found.'

'He didn't just run away?'

'He didn't take anything with him,' Sidney replied bluntly.

'What happened?'

Sidney gazed at me sadly for a moment. 'The three lads went out on their bikes . . . it was a smashing summer's day. They cycled to Dasset Lake, nearly ten miles from here. Not much traffic then, of course. Anyway, it seems Thomas left his bike and wandered off. Being lads they didn't get worried for a while. God knows how long he was missing before they even noticed. Then, of course, they did start looking for him. They searched until it grew dark, then they biked home to raise the alarm. The police dragged the lake the next day but there was no sign. His mother had a bit of a breakdown – she's never really been the same since.'

'Who was the third boy?' I asked.

'Carl Farnforth. I thought he was a bad influence.'

Surprises were now coming thick and fast. 'In what way?'

Sidney shook his head thoughtfully. 'Just something about him. He and Ian knew each other from junior school. More like brothers than friends. Thomas was always the odd one out.'

'Do you think Thomas is still alive?'

'No . . . no, I don't think so. The lads heard a car pulling up before Thomas disappeared. I reckon some pervert took him and he's buried miles away.'

'Poor kid,' I muttered. Somehow children being abducted seems a more modern crime – this would have occurred twenty-seven years ago. Not that long after the swinging sixties. And yet of course there had been the horror of Hindley and Brady.

I tried again with my question. 'So you thought Carl was a bad influence?'

'He was a cocky little sod – always keen on guns. Ian seemed a bit in awe of him – know what I mean?'

I nodded. 'And you didn't approve of his interest in guns?'

'I wouldn't say that. Country people do take an interest in guns – but for shooting vermin or a few birds or scaring off foxes. Carl was interested in guns like boys used to collect stamps. He started his collection at the age of twelve – mostly replicas.'

'Ian didn't share his interest?'

'I never said that either. Ian was fascinated by guns, but he didn't want to make it his life's work.'

'They remained friends?'

'As far as I know, although when Carl went to work in the Middle East that caused a rift.'

'Why was that?'

'Ian hoped Carl would be his partner at the factory, but I reckon Carl wanted fast money and he was a bloke who enjoyed the social life out there on the base.'

I sighed inwardly. Everyone had an angle and an opinion. But who was I to believe?

'What about their wives?' I asked 'Were they still friendly?'

Sidney looked puzzled and stared at the amber liquid in his glass. 'I think the husbands warned them off good and proper, because they were good friends *before* Carl went abroad.'

'Do you think Carl might have been responsible in some way for Paula's . . . disappearance?'

Sidney's forehead creased into deep lines. 'I heard there had been a shooting . . . but I can't think of any reason why Carl would harm Paula. Anyway, he wasn't even in the country, was he?'

'That's true,' I said. 'I was thinking of a hitman.'

'You don't get many of them in these parts,' he said, with a hint of a smile.

Of course he was right and I was obviously barking up the wrong tree in the wrong forest.

'I reckon,' said Sidney, 'Paula was approached by a man, tried to fight him off and got shot. He could have come from anywhere.'

'Strange that Lorraine should just have arrived on the scene.'

'Coincidences do happen.'

I didn't comment on that. I wasn't convinced it was a coincidence. Changing the subject completely, I asked if Sidney had any children. He smiled. 'Never been married, dear. Mind you, I had my chances. I was a good-looking man in my younger days. I'll show you a photo, shall I?'

My heart sank. There is no such thing as *one* photo. There

are albums and loose photos in boxes. I guessed his were the loose variety.

He rummaged for a while in another room then returned, carrying with him a large tin box. I prepared myself for a long stay. We sat at the drop-leaf table that he opened out to accommodate the photos he must have taken by the kilo. 'Most of them taken with a box camera,' he said proudly. 'Now, this is me when I was twenty-one.' The photograph before me showed a handsome strapping young man in swimming trunks. I murmured my approval at regular intervals. 'This is Ian on his first day at school' progressed to, 'This is Ian on the day he graduated'. There were plenty of photos of Ian and his mother at family events but none of his father and only two of Thomas. It was as if Thomas had never really belonged to the family.

'Strange that two people in one family should go missing,' I murmured.

'Just another horrible coincidence,' he replied. 'And Paula isn't missing like Thomas – she's dead.'

'But you think Thomas is dead too – so that makes two deaths.'

'Nothing to do with me,' he said sharply.

Odd how a denial can sound like an admission. Of one thing I was now sure: Sidney Picton knew something he didn't want me to know.

Just before I left I asked one more question. 'Did you know Lorraine Farnforth?'

He shook his head. 'Never met her. After Ian finished university I didn't see much of Carl again.'

He paused and stared into space. 'Come to think of it,' he said slowly, 'I haven't seen him in years. I miss the lads, I really do.'

For some reason when I left Sidney Picton I felt compelled to drive to Dasset Lake. It was well signposted and as I drove along a gravel path towards the lake I tried to imagine what it might have been like on a warm sunny day. It took all my powers of imagination. The day was cold and the earlier thin sunshine had disappeared to leave thick murky clouds. In the woodland clearings picnic tables had been placed – they looked new and forlornly empty. The lake itself, surrounded by grass and pine trees, reflected the dull leaden colour of the sky. I stopped in the car and stared at the lake. On a warm day surely there would have been families picnicking and, assuming it was school holidays, other teenagers. Had there been predators there too, perhaps posing as fishermen? Maybe Carl and Ian had ignored the younger boy, deliberately leaving him alone, vulnerable to the friendly attention of strangers.

I sucked a Polo mint, scanned the horizon and counted four 'No swimming' notices. The lake was obviously deep and twenty-seven years ago police divers had searched the lake for young Thomas's body. But had the lake been dragged *this* time in the search for Paula's body? The police excuse would be that they couldn't afford police divers for every stretch of water unless they had a good reason to suppose there was a body there. Were a long-missing brother and a missing wife a good enough reason to drag Dasset Lake again? I thought it was, but would David Todman agree?

If Ian Jenkins *was* more than capable of killing his wife – *how* did he do it? He had the factory cleaner's alibi, and it looked as if someone else had tried to incriminate him – or was that too part of the plan? Could Carl have helped him in some way? Perhaps by supplying the gun. The perfect double murder or even triple murder. Even though I now suspected Ian of being implicated in his wife's murder, it seemed doubtful that he had had a hand in Thomas's disappearance – disposing of a body isn't easy and anyway, the boys had been on bikes.

Sucking two more mints didn't help. The only way

forward, I reasoned, was the idea of a contract killer – unlikely, but it did happen. Hadn't Carl been a mercenary for a while? He could have met men during that time willing to kill their grandmothers for the right price. The only fault with that idea was why would Carl want Paula dead? The bond between the men seemed to have broken years ago – unless they had lied about that too.

Feeling more dynamic, or at least telling myself I felt more dynamic, which works nearly as well, I drove from Dasset Lake to Longborough and the Jenkins factory.

The same security guard sat in his glass box drinking tea from a thermos flask. 'No dog this time?' he said, as he lifted his window.

It was time to come clean about who I was and why I was bothering him.

'I've never met a private detective before,' he said. 'I thought you lot snooped on husbands who played away.'

'I'm versatile,' I said.

'I bet you are,' he said, with the suggestion of a leer.

'I wondered if you could help me?'

'What can I do for you? Now your boyfriend doesn't want a job here.'

'Sorry about that – lies are essential in my job.'

He raised an eyebrow waiting for my question.

'Have the police talked to you?'

'They certainly have,' he said. 'They wanted to know if Mr Jenkins had left the factory before seven thirty on the night of the twelfth.'

'And had he?'

'I didn't see his car drive through.'

'You'd always notice it, then?'

He shrugged. 'Unless . . .'

'Unless what?' I asked, adding conspiratorially, 'I won't tell anybody.'

He looked around as if his glass booth had ears. 'I may

have been looking the other way,' he said. 'You see, my relief should have turned up by seven but he has another job during the day and if he's late I cover for him.'

'So that night he was late?'

'He didn't turn up until about eight. I was dying for a jimmy riddle and a smoke so I sneaked over to the gents. I could have been gone ten minutes. The boss's car was still here – it wouldn't do for his car to be nicked, would it?'

'Why didn't you tell the police this?'

'So I lose my job and a mate's? Anyway, I don't reckon Jenkins did it. She was a good wife by all accounts, two lovely kids. I mean, neither of them seems the kind to have a bit on the side. Jenkins was always here, anyway – sometimes he left as late as ten o'clock.'

'Why do you trust me not to tell the police now?'

His big face creased into a smile. 'Me and me mate have got new jobs.'

'Good for you,' I said. 'Just one more question, if you don't mind.'

'My pleasure – this job is as bloody fascinating as watching paint dry.'

'Do you know that bit of river past the shops in Longborough?'

He nodded. 'More of a stream, I'd call that.'

'How long would it take you to walk there and back?'

'Ten minutes, I suppose, give or take.'

'So your boss could have walked there and back in, say, just over ten minutes.'

'Now look 'ere. I said ten minutes and I meant ten minutes. If Edna the cleaner said he was in his office, he was there all right. Edna is a stickler for time and detail. She'd have given the police a minute-by-minute account. Nothing gets past her and that includes the boss.'

Okay, I thought, the gospel according to St Edna was that

Ian didn't leave that evening to shoot his wife. Disposal of the body was therefore purely academic.

'You've been a great help,' I said.

'Have I, love?' he answered in surprise.

Back in my office I was disappointed that Hubert wasn't around. Jasper was nowhere to be seen either. I made myself a cup of coffee and wondered if Marilyn was now firmly ensconced in my house. There was only one consolation. I couldn't see her being happy in Farley Wood. The village population's idea of an exciting event is the yearly fête when the local vicar has wet sponges thrown at him as he sits in the stocks. Amongst the legion things my mother hadn't accomplished in her life was driving a car. Without a vehicle there was no escape from the village and I couldn't see Marilyn becoming a leading light at the church sewing hassocks and arranging flowers. All in all, I reasoned, there was no need to get upset – she wouldn't be staying long.

With that thought uppermost I continued reading the university profiles. Simon had been outraged by something he'd read but so far it all looked fairly innocuous to me. Carl's tests were nowhere near Ian's standard and his IQ was judged at 120. He was the only child of a widowed mother. The point of real interest came in the small section devoted to the friendship between Ian and Carl. Although it contained more jargon and long words than the *Nursing Mirror* – and that tries hard enough – the gist seemed to be that their relationship bordered on homosexual, especially on Ian's part. The author felt that Ian's hero-worship of and dependence on Carl verged on the erotic. His final personal comment was: 'If these two ever committed murder they could use the defence folie à deux, even though they are unusually of the same sex.'

It was an interesting statement but I needed the dictionary.

Folie à deux: *a delusion shared by two emotionally associated persons*, folie itself meaning insanity. That certainly gave me something to think about.

I could see why Simon was upset but from my point of view it was vaguely reassuring. Their relationship, past and present, was, to put it mildly, an extremely odd one. Had they both shared a sense of guilt that they had lost Thomas? I searched the text for more information. There were few references to Thomas, though one was interesting.

> Ian feels that Thomas is a cuckoo in the nest, not a true sibling but a mere half-brother. But for some reason his father prefers Thomas. Ian admits to hating both his father and his 'so-called' brother.

It was obvious from this that Ian, far from telling the truth, had not told the psychologist of Thomas being missing. Someone else had also kept that fact quiet. I rang that someone straight away.

'Kate, I was about to ring you – you must be telepathic.'

'No, David – I'm mad.'

'What have I done?'

'Not done in this case. Why the hell didn't you tell me Ian's brother had gone missing?'

'I didn't think it was relevant. Paedophiles didn't emerge with the Internet, you know. I've looked up the file and everything was done that could be done – widespread searches, dragging Dasset Lake – hauling in local sex offenders – there were several suspects but, as you presumably know, no body and no forensic evidence.'

'What about Ian and Carl?'

'They were questioned but they were obviously very upset and blamed themselves. Apart from hearing the car they saw and heard nothing.'

'I think Carl and Ian did murder their wives.'

'Do you? That's a quick change of mind.'

'I'm beginning to think they wanted to hire me to muddy the waters.'

'How do you mean?'

'I haven't worked it all out yet.'

'Have a drink with me and we'll talk it through.'

'There's something sinister,' I said, 'about a man who invites a woman for a drink and yet doesn't drink himself.'

David laughed. 'Does that make me more interesting?'

'I'm reserving judgement on that one.'

'See you at nine or thereabouts.'

I wondered as I put the phone down if CID knew about the university profiles. Should I say anything? If they didn't know the files existed yet, and then found out that I had copies and hadn't disclosed the fact, it would hardly result in a brownie point. All things considered, I decided to delete the file from my computer and consign the paper to a mini-bonfire.

But only once I was quite sure I'd missed nothing.

Sixteen

I felt quite practised now in getting myself dressed up and by eight thirty I was wearing a long black skirt, black boots and a red blouse to offset my black jacket. Copying Marilyn, my warpaint had been fixed with a light misting of mineral water and I'd dabbed perfume on all the pulse spots magazines recommend. I was game for more than a mere gin and tonic. In fact, in absentia, I was feeling pretty hyped up towards David Todman. He lived, he breathed, he smelled good and he was a decent type. Surely tonight we could manage *something* between us.

I sat in Hubert's lounge and watched television for a while. Not that I could concentrate. Being ready to go out and waiting is only marginally better than waiting for a delayed train. I felt as twitchy and nervous as an arachnophobic in therapy about to be confronted by a plastic spider, except that nothing happened. No spider – no man.

Nine p.m. crept slowly towards ten. I was tempted to strip off, stamp my feet and go to bed. I didn't. Instead I rang Jem, apologised for ringing so late and wondered if he was at a loose end and whether he would like to go out for a drink. It seemed that he would and we arranged to meet at a wine bar in town – one that attracted the slightly younger element.

I was dressed up and I wanted to be seen, or at least seen with Jem. I didn't want Todman thinking he was the only guy in my world.

Jem was waiting for me outside the Quill and Pen, a wine bar for office workers who lunched there and, if single, migrated there for a few hours in the evening. Hubert had told me it was the favoured haunt of the young and single. But it was a shock to see how young they were – most were early twenties, and Jem took one look at the clientele and said, 'Come on, let's make for the Frog and Fiddler.'

Once a proper pub with men who propped up the bar, the Frog and Fiddler was now more a restaurant with chalkboard menu and, as a concession to being upmarket, courgettes served with its chips.

Jem was as handsome as I remembered and attentive, wanting to know why I hadn't rung him sooner. 'You look great,' he said, air-kissing me on both cheeks. 'I had to go back to Aldershot or I would have been wining and dining you.'

I drank gin and tonic, not wanting to appear naff by ordering lager. Anyway, I guessed gin was Jem's favourite drink.

'What have you been up to?' he asked. Being nosy, I wanted to know the same of him but I told him a little about the enquiry and the dubious post-mortem results. I didn't tell him about my trip to Shefford University. Even though David had stood me up I still thought it was police information and not for Jem, however devastating his looks.

'The only other news in my life at the moment,' I said, 'is that my prodigal mother has returned.'

'And have you killed the fatted calf?'

I shook my head. 'No. But I'm allowing her to stay in my cottage.'

'What a shame,' he said, sounding either concerned or disappointed. I hoped he was disappointed because that might mean he had designs on my body. By the time I'd drunk two G&Ts I was particularly enamoured with his eyes.

We talked about our school days. Jem volunteered the information that he joined the army to escape from Longborough. Travel was his main joy and he'd either held army posts abroad or spent his holidays in exotic places. But he hadn't been to New Zealand and he was happy for me to regale him with scenic descriptions. I was telling him about the sea view from my bedroom window in Plimmerton, near Wellington, when the pub door opened and a noisy group of men walked in – headed by David Todman.

I had to admit the man had balls. He murmured something to his companions, who made their way to the bar, and then came straight over to me and apologised. 'Sorry, Kate,' he said with a disarming smile. 'I did ring you on the land line and tried your mobile but you obviously didn't wait long.'

I was at a disadvantage, but I smiled and introduced him to Jem. 'We have met,' said David. 'What are you both drinking?'

'I'll get them,' said Jem.

David shook his head. 'Not for me, thanks. I can't stay.'

While Jem was waiting to be served, David sat down beside me. 'I couldn't get away,' he said. 'Something cropped up.'

'To do with the case?'

He nodded. 'Ian Jenkins tried to top himself this evening. We've been keeping him under surveillance. He took his kids to his mother and then slashed his wrists.'

'Is he okay?'

'He did a good job, lost a lot of blood, but he's in hospital now.'

'Did he say why?'

'He claims he can't go on without Paula.'

'There is something else—' I began, but I didn't finish because Jem had appeared with the drinks.

'I'll ring you tomorrow,' said David.

'What was that about?' asked Jem as he placed a double

gin and tonic in front of me. I wondered then if I had struck lucky; after all, he was plying me with drinks.

'It seems Ian Jenkins has slashed his wrists – he's in hospital.'

'Guilty conscience?'

'Could be,' I agreed. 'Although his alibi seems watertight and what the motive could be for killing a friend of his wife's as well, I don't know.'

'A lover?'

'I thought of that, but the children would be a drawback and in Longborough, if you talk to the milkman everybody knows. Anyway, it still doesn't explain how he could be in his office, shooting Paula and disposing of the body at the same time.'

'He had an accomplice?'

'I thought of that too. A hitman does seem the most likely explanation. But how easy are they to find in Longborough?'

Jem shrugged. 'Perhaps he was recruited elsewhere. It's easy enough if you've got the money.'

'Elsewhere . . .'I murmured. 'Like the Middle East?'

'Exactly.'

Carl remained the prime suspect on the recruiting front – but how friendly had they remained? And why deny that friendship? Was it the two women who had come between the 'brothers'? Another possibility struck me. Carl had another woman. Lorraine confessed she'd been drinking that afternoon. It was dark at the time and a tallish hooded figure could have been a woman – maybe a hitwoman, or should it be hitperson? – at least from a vodka-addled viewpoint. But why kill Paula? Unless the red beret and scarf had meant to signpost Lorraine and not Paula. Carl's other woman would have been unlikely to know Lorraine's taste. I thought there was a few yards, if not mileage, in that idea. All I had to do was find the 'other woman'.

When the pub bell rang for closing time, Jem said, 'You

seem preoccupied, Kate. Is there anything you want to talk about?'

I shook my head. The gin was already beginning to numb my upper lip and I wasn't in talking mood. He held my hand as we walked back to Humberstones. All the lights bar the neon Funeral Home sign were off, so I assumed Hubert was out – he rarely went to bed early. As we got to the side door, without any preamble at all, Jem kissed me – and after we emerged for air he even nibbled at my neck. I fought the temptation to drag him upstairs and managed to murmur, 'Fancy a coffee?'

'I fancy *you*,' he said. 'But –'

The 'but' was ominous. I held my breath. 'I'm involved with someone else,' he said, 'and although I'd like nothing more – it wouldn't be fair.'

I felt like shouting that I didn't care if he had a harem full of women – I was here now ready, willing and hot! In the event I said nothing. I was totally dignified. Kissed his cheek and pushed him gently on his way.

Upstairs in the dark I bawled my eyes out. It was about an hour later that Hubert returned, looking smug. He stood in the doorway of my office peering at me as I sat by the light of my computer screen.

'What's wrong with you? Have you been in a chat room?'

'Nothing's wrong. I've just been updating my file.'

He stood silently watching me. I tried to ignore him.

'I know you well enough by now, Kate. Someone's upset you. It's not David, is it?'

I shook my head. I didn't want him to be nice to me. I might start bawling again and, after all, a missed night of passion isn't a great trauma in life, is it? Well, not compared to losing an arm or a leg.

'Kate – imagine I've asked you what's wrong three times already. And now you're getting ready for the big breakthrough – you're going to tell old Uncle Hube all about it.'

This time I managed to smile. 'I'm okay now. It was only a disappointment in lust.'

'Thank God for that. I thought it might be serious. Was it David?'

'No, it wasn't – it was Jem Harrison.'

'The galloping major,' said Hubert, raising an eyebrow. 'He's as smooth as a dollop of cream and just as slippery.'

'How do you know?'

'I asked the right people – the milkman, the postman and the gasman. They say Harrison is a real ladies' man.'

'They're all *persons* now.'

'Not in Longborough they're not.'

'He told me he was involved with someone, so at least he's honest.'

'Can't count, though, can he?'

'Leave me alone, Hubert. Let me wallow in self-pity.' By now I felt worse than before. One other woman was a perfectly acceptable excuse. But if he *was* as promiscuous as the tradesmen's gossip seemed to suggest, how come he didn't want to bed me? Suddenly his chivalrous excuse seemed like an insult. Bastard!

'How's the investigation going?' asked Hubert, as if everything was suddenly back to normal because he'd put me straight about a womanising male . . . trollop!

'It's not going anywhere at the moment – except that Ian Jenkins has slashed his wrists.'

'Oh. Do you think that means he's guilty?'

'Hubert,' I said, crisply, 'at the moment I feel all men are guilty of something.'

He ignored that remark. 'Do you want to know where I've been tonight?'

'No.'

'I'll tell you anyway.'

Before I could shut him up he said, 'I've been out with your mother.'

Just as you think things can't get worse – they do.

The following morning I left early. I couldn't bring myself to speak to Hubert and I thought it best to keep busy and avoid dwelling on any dire possibilities – such as Marilyn and Hubert becoming an item.

The weather was as grey as my mood and as I drove, the sky opened up to produce a downfall so fierce my windscreen wipers could hardly cope. I arrived in Aspen Gardens and sat in my car waiting for a let-up in the torrential rain. I wanted to talk to Carl. It was after nine but there was only the porch light on, which might have been for security purposes.

The lights were on next door at Jem's aunt's and through the onslaught of water hitting my windscreen I thought I saw a female shape outlined behind a drawn curtain. I switched on the car engine and flicked on the wipers at full pelt. The light remained on but the figure was gone.

Eventually I braved the rain, head down, collar up and at a run. But there was no reply at Carl's door. Drenched, I got back in the car and drove to the hospital.

At the nurse's station I professed to be Ian's legal adviser. Dawn, the nurse in charge, said I could visit if Ian wished to see me. I waited for about ten minutes and she returned, saying that he would like to see me but could I please not upset him. I said, 'I'll do my best.' She gave me a look which suggested legal advisers are not what they were and bustled away.

Ian was lying in bed in a bay of four with his eyes closed. The three other patients were either asleep or semi-comatose. One was in the process of receiving a blood transfusion and had a monitor, which was as high-tech as it got; in general the ward had a look of benign neglect.

I sat beside Ian's bed and noted stale bloodstains on the floor.

He opened one eye and peered at me. 'I keep my eyes closed,' he said. 'I can't bear to look around.'

'How are you feeling?' I asked. A bog-standard dumb question, but what else can you say?

Without opening his eyes he said, 'I only nicked one radial artery – sod's law that the police turned up like the cavalry and staunched the flow.'

'If you had died, what about your children?'

'They'd be better off without me.'

'Who would look after them? Your mother isn't a young woman. What about Paula's mother – could she take them on?'

He didn't answer; just turned his face to the wall.

I sat for some time watching the other patients, automatically noting their breathing, colour and position in the bed. Then I took to watching the slow drip of the blood transfusion. Eventually I said, 'If you give me the address of Paula's mother I'll go and see her.'

There was no answer and I was about to give up when he muttered, 'What good will that do? She hates me. She never wanted me to marry her daughter.'

'She might be able to shed some light on Paula's killer.'

'I don't see how. Paula didn't have any enemies.'

'What about her friends?'

'She only had one or two acquaintances locally. Her old friends are still working in Saudi.'

'Working in Saudi?' I queried, in surprise. 'You didn't tell me that before.'

'Didn't I? Well, it's not important; she only worked there for a year before we were married.'

'Was she happy there?'

'Paula enjoyed nursing,' he mumbled, as though half

asleep. 'She loved the children, but they weren't the be-all and end-all of her life.'

I wondered, hearing the slight slur in his voice, if he were either sedated or had been given anti-depressants. 'Give me your mother-in-law's address and I'll see what I can find out.'

He seemed to doze off at that crucial point but after a few minutes he stirred and gave me the address – a village called Bozeat in Northamptonshire – The Old Bakehouse – Bakehouse Road.

He curled himself into the foetal position, ignoring my, 'Hope you feel better soon.' I left, stopping only for a Coca-Cola from a vending machine on the way out of the hospital.

The heavens were still on open vent, and after a few minutes with the car's heating on, I began to steam and smell like wet washing does after being left for a few days in the washing machine. By the time I reached Bozeat, after a stop for lunch, I had dried out but the rain still hadn't stopped.

I'd taken a chance that Mrs Clarke would actually be in, but I could see someone moving about in the front window of the Old Bakehouse so I felt vindicated.

Paula's mother, Catherine, actually seemed pleased to see me. She was a small woman in her late fifties, wearing a grey pleated skirt, grey jumper and white blouse – a small red crest indicated it was a building society uniform. 'I've just come in from work,' she explained. 'Do sit down.'

The room's focal point was an inglenook fireplace with a wood fire that was just beginning to burn. Two deep armchairs sat facing the fire. I chose the one nearer the fire. With the rain beating against the bow window and a standard lamp behind me shedding a comforting glow, I only needed crumpets and tea and I would have been reluctant to leave.

Catherine didn't offer me tea. She wanted to talk about Paula. 'I'll never believe she's dead until I see her body,' she said, as she rearranged a smouldering log with a pair of tongs.

'Have the police talked to you?'

'Oh yes,' she said, wearily. 'At length.'

'Tell me about your daughter,' I said. 'Was she happy with Ian?'

The response was immediate. 'No.' Then she added, 'Maybe at first, when they lived in Harrow. I didn't see her much then, but once they moved to Longborough she *told* me she was unhappy.'

'Did she give a reason?'

'Ian has no interests other than his work. He's not a loving person, if you know what I mean. It's as if he's obsessed. He takes his business very seriously – to the exclusion of everything else.'

'Did Paula have interests of her own?'

Catherine shrugged. 'She didn't have much time to herself. I know she wanted to go back to work, but at every turn Ian made it difficult for her.'

'What was Ian's relationship like with the children?'

'I can sum that up in one word,' Catherine said. 'Cool.'

'Was he jealous of them?'

'I think he was,' she said slowly, as she stared into the fire that had come alive and now crackled noisily. She continued to stare into the flames and I noticed the tears dripping down her face. She made no attempt to wipe her face; it was as if the tears were too minor an irritation to bother about.

After a while I said, 'Would you like me to go?'

She shook her head. 'I just miss her so much,' she said, her voice croaky. 'We used to talk on the phone every day.'

'Is it possible . . .' I began tentatively, 'that Paula was seeing someone?'

I expected a quick denial but none came. This time she

wiped her face with the back of her hand. 'I'm not sure about her *seeing* someone but I think she was in contact with someone she knew before she married Ian, and . . .'

She was frowning now, looking anxious. 'And what, Mrs Clarke?'

'I lied to the police.'

'What about?'

'I don't know why I didn't tell them,' she said, 'but it seemed disloyal. Now Paula's . . .'

I'd already guessed what she was going to say, but I waited as she took a deep breath.

'I lied to Ian and the police. When Paula left him on those occasions she didn't come to me, but sometimes she left the children. I don't know where she did go. She tried to reassure me, but she couldn't hide the fact she was frightened of Ian, and it was best he thought she was staying with me.'

'Could it have been Carl Farnforth she stayed with?'

'I never met Carl, although I knew of him, of course. Paula said she didn't entirely trust him. She knew, for instance, that he had a woman friend in Scotland and that each leave he would stay with her for a week, so I don't think it could have been him.'

'Do the police know this?'

'I'm not sure. Why, would it be important?'

'If Carl was in the country before he said he was then he might have had the opportunity to kill Paula.'

'Why would he kill my daughter? What possible reason could he have?'

I raced through a mental list of motives for murder – money, jealousy, revenge, rejection – and then I thought of Lorraine's words: 'He *has* to silence me.' Suddenly I knew why Paula had been murdered, the same reason Lorraine had to die – to silence them because they had guessed the secret their husbands shared.

'What's the matter?' asked Catherine. 'You look worried.'

'It's nothing,' I said, hoping she wouldn't pursue the matter.

'I'll make some tea,' she murmured, wearily. 'I haven't had a cup yet.'

While she was in the kitchen I glanced at the family photos arranged on a shelf to the right of the fireplace. To do so I had to pass by Catherine's chair, and on the arm, I noticed a tiny piece of red fluff. My interest in the photos disappeared as I looked around for any other signs that Catherine Clarke could knit. I wondered if I dared risk opening the Welsh dresser. I'd just decided to have a peep when she returned with a tray of tea and biscuits.

'Can you knit, Mrs Clarke?' I asked.

She nodded. 'I know what this is about. The police asked me the same thing. Yes, I did knit the red beret and scarf for Paula. And yes, I sent her two of each. It was like a little joke between us. She was always losing gloves and scarves and umbrellas. So I knitted her two of each. My daughter looked good in red—' She burst into tears.

I drank my tea, nibbled distractedly on a biscuit and felt totally confused. Had Paula sent Lorraine the beret and scarf and if so, why? It wasn't Lorraine's style and Paula must have known it would worry her . . . or was that the idea? Red for danger. Be on your guard.

Seventeen

Some days I can feel quite paranoid. Both Hubert and David were obviously avoiding me. I'd rung Longborough Police to be told by a nasal voice that, 'DCI Todman isn't in his office, madam – would you like to leave a message?' I declined and rang Carl Farnforth instead. There was no reply. Hubert was nowhere in sight and although the day was still young, I had a feeling it didn't hold much promise.

For a while I updated my notes on the computer. The mystery of the red beret had been partially solved. At least I now knew the identity of the phantom knitter, though no doubt CID had known for ages. They must have known too that Carl Farnforth could have been around to shoot Paula. The why still remained a mystery. My theory, that the two men might have jointly wanted their women silenced, was still a contender. But, of course, plain old sex may have been at the core. Paula, who'd once worked in the Middle East, could easily have been having an affair with Carl and, perhaps, she'd threatened to tell his wife. He had admitted affairs, so why not with his ex-best friend's wife? But affairs aside, it seemed he had wanted to keep his marriage going. Perhaps he was the sort of man to react murderously to rejection.

Somehow I didn't find that angle convincing. Another angle interested me more – Carl wanted what Ian had. Pure jealousy. All along, Ian had the advantages denied to Carl.

He'd had a legal father as well as 'Uncle' Sidney Picton, a brother, was brighter, had a better degree and a more stable wife. He'd inherited a factory, changed its manufacturing base, and increased turnover dramatically. He'd fulfilled his youthful ambition and he had children. Carl, in contrast, had been denied all of this. Carl remained my main suspect.

I reread Ian's profile and, although there were assumptions made, I realised the psychologist had only judged Ian on the information he'd had. I'd never quite understood what the quasi-psychological term 'sociopath' means, but it implies someone who fails to have 'normal' emotional responses. Ian Jenkins, according to the profile, was a borderline psychopath, who functioned in the world as a sociopath and was unable to be empathetic or understand other people's feelings. The final lines were perhaps the most revealing.

> Somewhere in Ian's childhood his emotional growth and maturity became stunted. He is not a man to be trusted with decisions that might affect people's lives.

Just as well he's not a politician, I thought. But I could see why Simon was upset. If these sorts of sweeping generalisations were being made on every student, and being used as the basis for references, then some of them would be turned down for jobs and never know the reason why.

Carl's profile, in contrast, although finding him a bit of a 'Jack the lad', judged him to be 'an extrovert with leadership qualities'.

I didn't hear Hubert coming up the back stairs, but he did manage to give a little cough to let me know he'd arrived.

'I'm glad you've come,' I said. 'There have been a few developments.'

'I thought maybe I was persona non grata,' he said, moving into the room like a silent black shadow. He'd obviously just come from a traditional funeral. He was wearing a black suit and wing collar. And if death itself had a smell, something emanated, corpselike, from Hubert. 'What on earth is that smell?' I asked.

He looked hurt, but sniffed at himself. 'I like that smell. It's Dingle-Dangles – they're discs you hang in the wardrobe to keep your clothes smelling fresh.'

'Dingle-Dangles!' I repeated in disbelief. 'Your old mothballs smelled better.'

'Mothballs worked,' he declared. 'When did you last see a moth in any of my wardrobes?'

'That's an interesting question, but I need a listening ear. Have you got time?'

He nodded. 'Let me get changed and we can go to the pub.'

In the Mermaid I drank coffee and Hubert had a pint of shandy. We were the only customers. I was miffed to find Hubert knew that Ian had been discharged from hospital and that both he and Carl were once more 'helping the police with their enquiries'.

At that moment I'd never felt so despondent about being a private investigator. What the hell was I doing? My fears that I'd only been employed because they wanted to appear innocent came flooding back.

'What's wrong?' asked Hubert. 'You look as if someone's just asked you to eat a sheep's eyeball.'

'I did think both of them might be innocent at first,' I said, 'but now I've changed my mind. They're as guilty as sin.'

'You're being emotional. Have they paid you?'

'Yes.'

'Well, then,' said Hubert, patting my hand. 'You can get some retail therapy and put all this behind you.'

His patronising irritated me. 'I can't put "all this" behind me,' I said. 'They haven't found Paula's body yet.'

'Just a question of time,' he murmured, in the soothing funereal tone he reserved for the bereaved.

'Really?' I replied, unimpressed.

'I've heard,' he said, 'that the police are planning to dig up the Farnforth garden.'

I thought about that for a moment. Was that the reason Lorraine was so scared?

Who wouldn't be, if they suspected their husband had buried a body in the garden? The body of a woman who had once been a friend.

'It's the friendship that worries me,' I said.

'What are you talking about?'

'Four one-time close friends. In Harrow they socialise – they follow each other back to their roots – male roots at least – but at some point their friendship dissolves.'

'Attagirl,' said Hubert, raising his glass.

'What's that supposed to mean?'

'You can't let it go, can you?'

I smiled. 'No, I suppose not. But I feel I could go old and grey –' I paused. That little phrase 'old and grey' ticked away in my brain, trying to tell me something.

'What is it?' asked Hubert. 'Is it one of those sharp pains up the bum or have you thought of something?'

'I'll keep it to myself if you don't mind.'

'I've got some spare time,' said Hubert eagerly.

'Could you go to the *Longborough News* office and see if they have any back copies – circa 1974?'

'Could be on microfiche. What are you looking for?'

'Details of Thomas Jenkins's disappearance.'

'I remember that,' said Hubert. 'As if—'

'It were yesterday,' I finished for him. 'Why didn't you tell me?'

'You didn't ask. It was in all the papers. We had reporters here for weeks.'

'If you remembered it so well, how come you didn't at least admit you'd heard the name Farnforth before?'

Hubert shrugged and looked uncomfortable. 'I wanted you to get back in the swing. I would have told you in the end.'

I felt Hubert had let me down, but there was no point in harbouring a grudge. I just hoped it wasn't going to become a trend.

'I think my mother is addling your brain,' I said.

A faint trace of pink highlighted his cheekbones, like phantom blusher. 'You've got a wonderful mother,' he said, shyly.

I wanted to puke. Hubert was as lovesick as a sixteen-year-old – and over my mother! 'She'll let you down. She's as tough as a tractor's tyre, and—'

'I don't want to hear any more,' he said, looking pained. 'You should be ashamed of yourself.'

He downed his shandy quickly. 'I'll be off, then,' he said, 'to get those newspaper reports.'

I sat alone in the pub with the middle-aged barmaid observing me. I had a feeling she thought Hubert was my sugar daddy and we'd just had a lover's tiff. I ordered another coffee and she muttered, 'Men, huh!'

She obviously wanted to engage in conversation, and I was about to say 'That's no man, that's my landlord' when my mobile rang. I delved into my shoulder bag for the usual scrum around and eventually collared it.

It was Ian. 'I've been released,' he said. 'I want to see you.'

'Now?'

'Yes. As soon as possible.'

'Where are you?'

'At home.'

A few minutes later I found him there, unshaven and looking exhausted. He poured himself a whisky and then sat slumped at the kitchen table, one hand propping up his head. 'The bastard did it, you know,' he said.

'Did what?'

'Farnforth, the devious bastard – he killed my wife.'

'Are you sure?'

'Of course I'm sure. He was always jealous of me. He always wanted what I had.'

'What do you mean?'

'When we were kids. He was an only child; his mother was a single parent. I had a proper family and Sidney, who was twice the man my father was. Carl often stayed with us, said it was the happiest time of his life – until . . .'

'Until Thomas disappeared?'

He looked at me sharply. 'I suppose it's common knowledge I had a bad couple of years after that, but university was great – it helped me forget, and Carl and I were still friends then. He was more like a brother. Even my mum looked on him as a son.'

'What changed things?'

'The gun. That's what changed things. We were in competition. I came up with a design that he knew was superior to his.'

'Where did you make it?'

'Near my mother's place.'

'You mean at Sidney Picton's?'

'Yes. He's got a workshop at the back of the house with a lathe and all the necessary gear.'

'He's a useful man to know.'

'Part of my life – like an uncle. My father was always working. Sidney even used to take my mother dancing.'

'Almost a ménage à trois?'

Ian grimaced. 'They're a bit old for that sort of thing.'

'They weren't always old and grey.'

'What's that supposed to mean?'

'Only that when Thomas disappeared Sidney was a comparatively young man.'

'What are you getting at?

'I'm sure Sidney was a great comfort to you and your parents at such a terrible time.'

Ian shrugged. 'Look, I don't know what you're talking about. I wasn't heartbroken about Thomas. He was a little sod most of the time. Anyway, he was the cuckoo in the nest.'

'I beg your pardon?'

'You heard. He wasn't a true brother. He looked nothing like Dad or me.' He paused and stared at me. 'I reckon Sidney was his father.'

I didn't allow myself to show any surprise. 'How did you feel about that?'

'I didn't really care. Sidney was always good to me. My father was a workaholic – it was Sidney who taught me to read and Sidney who turned up at sports days. And I know, even if Thomas was his son, it was me he preferred.'

'Did your father have any suspicions?'

'If he did he didn't say.'

'The day Thomas disappeared—'

'I don't want to talk about that.'

'Did you feel responsible for what happened?'

'No; why should I?' Ian's voice had changed. Before he'd been on safe ground, telling the truth I was sure, but now there was a brittle quality to his tone, as if, pushed too far, he'd explode.

'I just thought as the older brother you may have felt a degree of responsibility.'

'Thomas wasn't a baby. He was fourteen. He thought he was old enough.'

'Old enough for what?' I queried.

'Old enough to be with us.'

'You resented that?'

'Of course I did. Everywhere I went he had to tag along too. He was like a bloody shadow.'

'He's still a shadow,' I said softly. 'Isn't he?'

Ian smiled slyly. 'It's you and the police who talk about him. I never give him a thought.'

'Does Carl?'

'How the hell would I know? All I know is – he killed my wife.'

'You say he's jealous?'

'He's jealous all right. He hadn't got the facilities or the talent to make a new-style handgun.'

'And you think because you made the gun and he didn't, that was sufficient motive to kill his wife and yours.'

He stared at me through slightly bloodshot eyes. 'Put like that it doesn't sound likely, but I *know* him and what he's capable of.'

I stayed silent and after a few seconds Ian said, quietly, 'I've got nothing to lose now.' He lifted the sleeves of his sweater to show me the bandages. 'The bastards took me straight from hospital to the cop shop. I suppose they thought I'd be weak and confess, but I've done nothing I'm ashamed of.'

'What about Thomas?'

'Why do you keep harping on about him? I told you I've done nothing to be ashamed of.'

He was getting agitated again. Beads of sweat had broken out on his forehead and he'd begun clenching and unclenching his fists. 'Have you got any plans?' I asked.

He laughed dryly and mimicked me, 'Have you got any plans?' Then he leaned forward and whispered, 'I'm going to kill the bastard.'

I felt a creeping sensation sneak up my back, but I managed to avoid a full-blown shiver. 'Why are you telling me?' I asked, trying to keep my voice even. 'Do you want me to stop you?'

'How the bloody hell would you do that? Go straight to the police and say I'd become deranged?'

Before I had time to respond, he'd taken hold of my wrist and pulled me towards him. I could smell the whisky on his breath. 'I'd deny everything,' he said. 'I won't do anything today or tomorrow. I'll bide my time. I'll plan it. And remember, you're supposed to be working for me. You find proof of Farnforth's guilt and I won't need to kill him, will I?'

I didn't answer. 'Will I?' he repeated.

'I can only do my best.'

He let go of my wrist and said with a sneer, 'Your best is a joke but not much worse than the professionals provide. They couldn't find Thomas's body and now they can't find Paula's. You're useless – you stupid bitch!'

Being called a stupid bitch isn't so bad, but it does depend on the tone of voice. And I didn't like his. I stood up to go. 'Don't forget to earn your money and keep in touch,' he said, in the same tone he'd called me a bitch.

Outside in the fresh air I took a few deep breaths, partly in sheer relief and partly to steady myself. I reasoned my next move was to find David and warn him of Ian's mood. The last thing he needed was a *High Noon* situation.

I rang the station but he wasn't there. I tried his mobile. There was no reply, so I drove to Aspen Gardens, hoping he might be watching the excavation of the Farnforth property. The road was blocked off, and tarpaulins had been thrown across the front and back gardens, uniformed men were milling around and men with spades dressed in white boiler suits were toing and froing.

I asked one of the uniformed PCs if DCI Todman was inside. He said he didn't know who was inside the house, but if he saw him he'd say I was looking for him. In the meantime I decided Jem's house was as good a vantage point as any and I might get offered a cup of tea.

I knocked on the door several times and was about to walk away when his aunt opened the door a fraction on a safety chain. 'Hello, Kate dear. Come on in.'

I followed her along the hall. Progress was slow, but nothing stopped her talking. 'I *am* pleased to see you, dear. I haven't spoken to a soul in ages – well, not someone who talks sense anyway. And there's been so much going on outside. I haven't seen so many handsome young blokes in a long while.'

Her body might have shrunk over the years, but her voice certainly hadn't.

'You go and sit down, dear, and I'll make us a nice drink,' she said, directing me to an armchair by the window.

'I can do that,' I said. 'I'm good at making tea.'

'I'm sure you are,' she said, 'but I have to keep doing things, otherwise I'll land up in a home. So it's best if I do it.'

The tea and biscuits turned out to be a protracted affair, but finally she sat down in her chair by the window and I was allowed to pour.

'It's a shame Jem isn't here, but I do like to meet his girlfriends.'

I laughed, somewhat embarrassed. 'I wouldn't call myself that.'

'Pity. Did you know I was the spinster of the family? Don't have spinsters now, do they? Only singles. I wasn't single for lack of chances, mind you. If I'd found a man even halfway promising I could have done something with him – improved him, if you know what I mean – but it wasn't to be: no-hopers, all of them.'

'I haven't had much luck either,' I said.

She peered at me. 'Pity Jem's heart is elsewhere. I like the look of you.'

I wanted to change the subject, but Jem was obviously a much-loved nephew and I had to admit I was intrigued. 'He's got a steady girlfriend, has he?'

'I don't know about steady,' she chuckled. 'But I think he's serious about her, because he's not mentioned her. That's a sure sign with Jem. He gets a bit secretive. I just can't understand why he isn't married yet.'

'How old is he?' I asked, casually.

'He's forty – doesn't look it, does he?'

'He certainly doesn't.'

'Do you know he came to live with me when he was five? His mum – my sister – and his dad died in a car crash. I haven't regretted a minute of it. He's been like a son and he still is. He's made my life complete.'

'He was my knight in shining armour,' I said, 'the night of the intruder at Lorraine's.'

'She was an unlucky girl. That husband of hers – Medallion Man, I call him – was hardly ever there. It's no wonder she turned to drink.'

'Did you see her drinking?'

'Not exactly. Jem told me and I could hear the bottles chinking as she threw them in her wheelie bin.'

'Did you ever talk to her?'

'Of course I did, dear. I talk to everyone. Very pleasant she was, too. Always willing to do a bit of shopping for me. She did go away from time to time – said she was going to stay with friends. Men friends, more like.'

'Did she have male callers?'

Aunt Emily paused to nibble on a biscuit. 'I don't sit by the window all day and I draw the curtains as soon as it gets dark, but a car would sometimes pull up quite late.'

'What about female friends?'

'That woman who's missing, she used to visit; sometimes they went out together.'

'Have you told the police this?'

A puzzled look crossed her face. 'I don't remember if they asked me, dear. My memory isn't what it was. It was mostly questions about the night she died.'

The sound of another car drawing up caused us both to gaze out of the window. 'They're coming and going like ants,' she said. 'I don't mind, though; it gives me something to watch.'

'That's the man I want to see,' I said, as David emerged from his car.

'I can't see his face,' she said, 'but he looks all right from the back.'

'I'll have to dash,' I said. 'Thanks for your help.'

'You'll have to come back when Jem's here.'

'When will that be?'

'I'm not sure. He goes down to his own place more and more these days.'

'I didn't know he had his own house.'

'Lovely cottage he's got in Devon. Near Seaton, it is,' she said proudly. 'A place in the middle of nowhere. He's called it Hope Cottage – that's quaint, isn't it? Now that he's leaving the army, I suppose he'll be spending more and more time there . . .'

She was still talking as I tried to make a hasty exit, and by the time I got outside David was already in the house. All I could do was wait.

Eighteen

David emerged half an hour later. 'What are you doing here, Kate?' He sounded irritated and looked harassed.

'I'm not sightseeing. I've been waiting for you.'

'I can't talk now,' he said. 'This is turning into a bloody fiasco. The lads have dug almost to the inner core and still nothing.'

'It's important – I think Jenkins is planning to kill Farnforth.'

'What do you want me to do? Arrest him for *thinking* about murder?' Already David was walking fast towards his car. 'Look, my career's on the line. This case is costing a fortune. We've dragged lakes and rivers and dug up gardens and allotments. It's over. The bosses are winding down the investigation.'

'They can't do that!'

'They can and they have. All we can do now is work on the two of them and hope one of them cracks.'

'They haven't so far.'

'Exactly.'

He was in his car and giving me a brief wave within seconds. I stood on the pavement feeling like a bride left at the altar.

What the hell next? It was then I turned to see Carl in running gear talking to a uniformed constable. I waited until he'd finished before I approached him. If the police weren't interested in murder threats at least the intended victim might be.

'I'm going for a run,' he said.

'Could I have a quick word?'

'You can run with me if you want and if you're up to it.'

Of course I didn't want to, but I was willing to try and wanted to prove that I could. He jogged slowly at first and I had no problem. I could even speak. 'Ian thinks you're guilty of killing his wife.'

'I know.'

'Did you also know he wants to kill you?'

'I guessed he might.'

'It doesn't worry you?'

'He's not good on stealth tactics. By the time he gets round to taking a potshot at me, I'll be back in the Middle East.'

'You think he'll *shoot* you? A bit obvious, don't you think?'

He speeded up and I began struggling to keep up. 'Ian can be a law unto himself,' he said, without a trace of breathlessness. Luckily an old lady with a dog was ahead of us. I intended to slow down, but I had to stop, gasping. After a few moments' rest I managed to speed up and catch him but I was soon lagging behind again.

Eventually he stopped. 'You're not very fit, are you?'

I shook my head. I didn't have the breath for any words.

'I'll be ready for him,' said Carl, stopping to flex his legs and run on the spot. 'He had a hand in my wife's death. I know he did, but I'm prepared to wait for vengeance. However long it takes.'

'Ian said the same thing.'

'Did he? Well, we'll both be minding our backs then, won't we?' He increased his running on the spot. 'I've got to have a proper run,' he said. 'You concentrate your efforts on proving Jenkins is a murderer.'

I watched him speed away and slowly walked back to my car. My chest felt sore and tight, but otherwise I felt fine. In fact, although my performance was abysmal, I felt quite exhilarated – until the young copper standing guard outside the Farnforths' house commented dourly, 'Not exactly fit, are you?'

'I'm getting fitter all the time,' I replied archly.

'You'll suffer tomorrow,' countered PC Knowall.

He was right. The next morning the only muscles I wasn't aware of were the muscles in my hands. I thought frequent walks with Jasper might help my general fitness but Hubert had already gone walkies to the local park. So I decided to go there anyway. Walking for the sake of it always seems odd to me, whereas walking a dog has real purpose and you get to stop frequently while trees are sniffed and watered. I found Hubert huddled in a black overcoat on a park bench while Jasper explored the bushes by the path.

'Is everything all right?' he asked, hardly glancing at me.

'I'm walking more to keep fit.'

'It won't last.'

It was then that I noticed how miserable Hubert seemed. 'What's up?' I asked. 'You look like a stockbroker about to take the high jump.'

'Your mother went out with another bloke last night.'

Two thoughts crossed my mind. One, how does she do it? And the second was, Bitch!

'I'm sorry, Hubert. I really am. Don't take it too personally. She treats everyone like that. Once she was quite respectable – it was only when . . . never mind. It's too cold to sit here discussing my mother's shortcomings.'

He called Jasper, who came running instantly, tail wagging, happy to be reunited. 'Stick to Jasper,' I said. 'He won't let you down.'

Hubert said nothing most of the way back but as we neared Humberstones, he told me he'd got the newspaper reports I wanted.

In my office I began reading the cuttings and Hubert sat opposite me on my grey swivel chair, looking less animated than setting custard.

'BOY DISAPPEARS ON DAY OUT' was one headline. Another read 'VANISHED'. The report quoted Ian and Carl as saying they'd cycled the ten miles to Dasset Lake, where they'd had a picnic. It was so hot they'd taken off their shirts, put on swimming trunks, had a swim, then fallen asleep. When they woke up Thomas had gone. His bike was missing so they assumed he'd gone home. Later, when they found his bike in bushes near the lake, they began to get really worried. Carl had even dived in the lake to see if Thomas had fallen in.

'Have you read this?' I asked Hubert.

Hubert nodded and I continued reading. One eyewitness was mentioned, a fisherman called Harry Goodman, who'd joined in the search. 'Hubert, I know you're in the doldrums, but I'd be grateful for your help.'

'Fire away.'

'Look up this Harry Goodman in the phone book.'

'That's a long shot, isn't it? Lost interest in real murder, have you?'

'This *is* real murder,' I said. 'I think Ian and Carl murdered Thomas that day. I don't know how they did it, but somehow they disposed of his body. All these years that's been their bond and their nightmare. Either one could give the other away.'

Hubert's face showed no expression as he searched the telephone directory and when he reported there were two H. Goodmans listed, his eyes were still dull.

'Hubert, how about you and I go out as a team. You could be a Chief Inspector from the Met – as long as they haven't used you in the past – and I'll say I'm part of the investigating team.'

He shrugged. 'I'm not busy today. The embalmer's in but one of the staff can pay him.'

Hubert drove the Daimler at funereal pace and we drove to the first H. Goodman's address. There was no answer, so we progressed to the second address on a council estate on the edge of town. The house itself had peeling paint, greying net curtains and an overgrown front garden. As the door opened there was no doubt that the occupant was a fisherman. There were rods and baskets and muddy wellies filling the hallway.

'Mr Harry Goodman?' I queried, thinking that, although his house more than suggested 'fisherman', his appearance didn't. He was in his sixties, with a paunch that was barely encased in a threadbare green jumper, and his face had a moonlike quality, exaggerated by the fact that he had no hair. 'We're the investigating team, newly re-formed, gathering information about the disappearance of Thomas Jenkins. This is Chief Inspector –' I hesitated, looked at Hubert's face and said, 'Jolly, and I'm Kate.'

'Well, well,' he exclaimed. 'That *was* a long time ago. You'd better come in.'

His living room smelt foetid. The remains of a fish and chip supper were still on the table along with empty lager cans and a loaf of bread. 'Sit yerselves down,' he urged us.

Hubert imperceptibly shook his head – the two armchairs looked none too clean – but I sat down because I'm not as squeamish as Hubert, a strange trait for a man professionally committed to the care of cadavers.

'You were a witness at Dasset Lake, Mr Goodman?' said Hubert, sounding every inch the Chief Inspector. 'Interviewed by the local paper?'

Harry Goodman smiled like a happy Teletubby. 'I was a

bit disappointed they didn't take me photo, but I got me name in the paper and the reporter bought me a drink.'

'So you remember the day well?' queried Hubert.

'I've never forgotten it,' said Harry. 'It was as hot as hell and I never caught a thing.'

'I meant did you remember anything about the missing boy,' said Hubert, sounding severe.

'I know what you meant, squire, but I'm telling you I remember that day very well.'

'What time did you get to the lake?'

'About five thirty. Lovely morning – all still and quiet it was. Not a soul there but me. Warm, but not hot. Just how I like it. I took my camping stove and cooked meself eggs and bacon. Got all me gear organised and then sat back for a day's fishing. Heaven it was – bloody heaven.'

'Did you see the boys arrive?'

He shrugged. 'Them and quite a few others. A couple of other fishermen arrived and we passed the time of day.'

'What were the boys doing?'

'Riding round on their bikes at first. I told the reporter I wasn't sure when they arrived but I saw them first about twelve. When you're fishing, you keep your eye on yer float or yer line and they were behind me so I can't say I saw that much of 'em.'

'When exactly did you see them?' asked Hubert.

'I went for a jimmy riddle about 'alf past one. They were 'aving a picnic.'

'Was that the last time you saw them?'

I had to admit I was quite impressed with Hubert as Chief Inspector Jolly. I enjoyed sitting back and letting him ask the questions, and at least it kept him from thinking about my fickle mother.

'No. It wasn't the last time,' said Harry thoughtfully. 'I'd 'ad a little nap, sort of nodded off where I was sitting. I still 'adn't caught nothing so I 'ad a little wander around. The lads were queuing for an ice cream – that was about four thirty. I didn't see them again till I was packing up to come 'ome about eight o'clock.'

'What were they doing then?'

'They were just sitting throwing stones into the lake.'

'Was anyone else around?'

Harry shook his head, 'Nah. The mums and kids were long gone. Just a few couples snogging and walking about 'and in 'and.'

'And the boys just sat there?'

'Yeah.'

'The three of them?'

Harry looked quizzically at Hubert. 'I tried to tell the police and the reporter but no one seemed to take any notice of me.'

'Notice of what?'

'I only ever did see the two lads – the older ones. I never saw that Thomas.'

Hubert's mouth dropped a little. 'What about the other witnesses?'

'I dunno – one or two saw 'im, or said they did, but I can only say what I saw for meself and that was just the two lads. But I don't 'ave eyes in the back of me 'ead, so others could 'ave seen him. I didn't.'

'Did you see Ian and Carl searching for Thomas?' asked Hubert, as he glanced at me with a 'What the hell is going on?' expression on his face.

'They didn't look to me like they was searching, but they told the police they didn't get worried till they found 'is bike. They thought 'e'd gone 'ome. Anyway, I reckon they were scared to go 'ome once they'd found 'is bike.'

'Did you see his bike?'

'No. Well, I wasn't looking for it, was I?'

'So the boys were still by the lake when you left?'

'Yeah. I left around 'alf past eight. Sun had long gone in

then, but it was the sort of day you don't want to end. Of course, I didn't know then that a lad was missing. I would 'ave 'elped search for 'im if I'd known.'

'The search was started next day, was it?'

'Lovely day like that,' mused Harry. 'But it started raining about midnight and it rained all the next day. I went back and joined in the search, but the police didn't find any clues, even though they dragged the lake and everything. It seems 'e'd just disappeared off the face of the earth.'

'Or he was never there in the first place,' muttered Hubert.

Harry looked puzzled. 'You mean the boys' story was a bit iffy?'

'Fishy would be the word I'd use,' said Hubert.

There was a short pause whilst Harry thought about the implications.

'Come off it, squire,' he said, red-faced. 'Us fishermen 'ad nothing to do with it. We was all seen by the police.'

'It was just a figure of speech, Mr Goodman. You've been extremely helpful.'

Harry's face faded to mere pink. 'My pleasure, Chief. Always willing to 'elp the police.'

As we left I felt a sense of elation. At long last there seemed to be a breakthrough of sorts. 'You were brilliant, Hubert – as a Chief Inspector you have real presence.'

'I'll stick to undertaking,' he said, dourly. 'You know where you are with corpses.'

He was about to drive off when I asked, 'From what you know of Ian and Carl, who do you think is the weakest link?'

'They're not the only two in the chain, are they?'

'No.'

'I don't think you'll crack them, Kate,' he said, as he started the engine. 'They're both cold as marble slabs and they have too much to lose. But someone else must have suspicions about Thomas's disappearance.'

'Who else but his mother?' I was excited now. Once we'd found out what happened to Thomas I was convinced we would also know who killed Lorraine and Paula. No longer was the motive in doubt, either. Both women must have found out their husbands were responsible, and they had to be silenced.

Somewhere out by Dasset Lake lay the body of Thomas Jenkins and maybe also the body of Paula Jenkins. But it would take more than just my suspicions for the police to start another search. They would have to know the *exact* position of the graves – and who would tell us that?

Nineteen

I knocked several times on Dorothy Jenkins's door but there was no reply. Looking across the courtyard to Sidney Picton's cottage, I saw that a light was on. Sidney answered the door immediately; he smiled at me, but not at Hubert.

The Chief Inspector angle might not work with Sidney, so I decided to play safe. 'We were in the area and I told Dorothy I'd call back – my friend here, Hubert, is an expert reflexologist. I thought a spot of reflexology might help her . . . aches and pains.'

'She's got the flu,' he said.

'Some reflexology might do her good,' I persisted.

Sidney shook his head. 'Couple of days' time, maybe.'

'Have you called the doctor?' I asked.

'Of course I have,' he said. 'Plenty of drinks and paracetamol. That's the only treatment.'

'We'll come back, then.'

Sidney glanced at Hubert with deep suspicion, smiled at me, then briskly closed his front door.

As we drove away I looked back at the Jenkins cottage and for some reason I shivered. I was of course disappointed and at a loss.

'What do we do now, Hubert?'

'Nothing much we can do, is there?' he said. 'The only thing *you* could do is try your feminine wiles on David.'

'They haven't worked so far.'

'Your mother could give you lessons.'

I was about to snap back when I glanced at Hubert's expression. He looked bereft, almost in pain. So I changed the subject. 'I might get more of a result with David if I could persuade him to take a trip out with me to Dasset Lake. After all, he wasn't around twenty-seven years ago – he'd see things with a fresh eye. As long as I don't mention graves and digging he might just listen.'

'It's worth a try,' he said dully.

'Hubert, come on,' I said. 'This isn't like you. I admit I didn't like the idea of you and Marilyn being friends, but that's only because I can't bear the way she treats people and you're very special to me.'

'Am I?'

'Of course you are. And, just to prove it, I'll have a word with her and find out what she's up to.'

'Will that help?' he asked, obviously unconvinced.

'Would you feel *better* if I did that?'

'I suppose I would.'

That made two of us who were unsure, but I wasn't going to let her steal my home and then break the heart of my best friend without having a showdown.

'Consider it done, Hubert,' I said, full of resolve. 'Drop me off in Farley Wood and I'll see what I can do.'

He drove at a snail's pace and I had the pure joy of planning my own scenario with her. How to start? Would I use Plan A or Plan B?

Plan A had no preamble, merely: *Now look, you raddled old slapper. How dare you treat Hubert in this way. He's worth ten of you – it's about time you stopped being a promiscuous old tart – blah blah blah.*

Plan B was more conservative. *Mum, I know you've had some difficulties in life, but you can't treat people, and especially Hubert, like a doormat – you insatiable old trollop!*

Life, of course, never turns out quite as you plan it and this was no exception. When I entered my own domain, without knocking or hesitating, I found my mother on my sofa sobbing her heart out. All my ire and resolve disappeared to be replaced by worry. She looked old and careworn, her make-up streaked, her hair not brushed. 'Oh, Kate, my life is such a mess,' she cried, not seeming surprised I'd appeared from nowhere.

'What's happened? What's the matter?'

She carried on crying and I let her continue while I patted her back. She edged closer to me until her head was on my shoulder. Eventually, after several minutes, she quietened a little and began gulping and sniffing instead. She tried to wipe her face with a tiny screwed-up piece of tissue, so I dug a few tissues from my pocket and handed her those. 'I don't know what's wrong with me,' she wailed. 'I'm forty-eight. I've got no money, no home, no job, no real friends and my daughter hates me.'

'I don't hate you, Marilyn,' I responded. 'And you are *not* forty-eight.'

She went on in the same vein for some time. She'd also wasted her life, she was too fat, made bad choices in men and allowed the sun to shrivel her skin. 'Come off it,' I said. 'Your skin isn't shrivelled. It's just lost its bloom.'

She looked at me incredulously. 'So you agree with me. I *am* a mess.'

'I didn't say that. Perhaps all you need is a job and some HRT.'

'So you think I'm menopausal?' she asked, as if I'd suggested she'd decided to gender-bend.

'What else could it be?' I said, thinking to myself that she was the only woman I knew who had taken ten years to get through the menopause.

It was some time before she muttered, 'Maybe it's only a mid-life crisis.'

I was mystified. Was my mother suffering from a largely unknown condition – *menopause denial*? Should I ring a TV company?

'A job,' she said. 'I'd love to find a job, perhaps in a beauty salon or a fitness centre.'

I stayed silent, not wanting to point out that, although Longborough had one beauty salon and a fitness centre that boasted a set of weights, one rowing machine and two exercise bikes, neither place employed anyone over the age of twenty-five.

'Most daughters would have offered me a brandy by now,' she said, in perked-up mode.

'Have you left me any?' I asked.

I keep my alcohol at the back of the kitchen cupboard, but I hadn't done a stocktake since I'd come back from New Zealand. No wonder she'd asked for brandy. It was the only bottle left. I made her a coffee and added a generous measure.

She'd drunk half of it when I brought up the subject of Hubert. 'He's a lovely man, Kate. He really is, and I know he fancies me, but I can't get his job out of my mind.'

'We all need the services of men like Hubert one day,' I said. 'And after all, he is a businessman. He doesn't do the nasty stuff – I mean, he's not a gravedigger or an embalmer.'

'I suppose that's a consolation,' she said, unconvinced. 'But going out with an undertaker does bring your own mortality into focus.'

'Personally I'd say it was a damn sight better than going out with a gynaecologist or a bowel specialist – your haemorrhoids would never be your own, would they?'

'I haven't got haemorrhoids,' she said.

'That's a blessing, then,' I replied. I thought she might laugh, but I could see I was on a loser. My mother never did have much of a humorous streak.

'Anyway, as I was going to say – I'd rather you weren't friendly with Hubert if all you're going to do is hurt him. He says you've been seeing someone else – is that true?'

'It was true,' she said, 'but not any more. I found out he was sixty-five and his idea of a good night out was playing dominoes in his local.'

'Well, there you are then. Hubert's a well-respected man in the town and he'd love to take you to exotic places, I'm sure.'

'Would he take me to the Dome?'

'If that's your idea of exotic and it was still open, then I'm sure he would.' I didn't add that if she wore high heels he'd probably take her to the Taj Mahal.

'I'll give him a ring then, shall I?'

Now she'd cheered up a bit, I wondered if I'd done the right thing. I was even more concerned when she said, 'Are you sure I couldn't help you in your work?'

'No,' I snapped. 'No way.'

'It was worth a try,' she said. Then she smiled sweetly at me. 'You're a good girl, Kate.' My momentary basking in her rare praise ended abruptly as she added, 'Could you lend me twenty quid?'

Handing over the money left me with two pounds fifty in my purse. I'd lost count of the money I'd 'lent' her in the past. If she ever paid me back I'd be a rich woman, but at least I'd done my bit to help Hubert, although I had a feeling I'd live to regret my intervention.

In fact, as I drove away, I realised how quickly she'd suggested ringing him. House, money, landlord, even a job with me – she wanted the lot and I'd succumbed.

By the time I got to Longborough Police Station I wasn't in the mood to be fobbed off. David Todman might be a rare breed as a teetotal man and a nice guy but he wasn't the only CID officer. Anyone who would listen to me would do.

I marched in feeling assertive. The desk sergeant obviously noticed, because when I asked for DCI Todman, he told me to go straight up to the office.

David was waiting for me in the corridor. 'I saw you arrive,' he said. 'I rang down to make sure you weren't kept waiting.'

So much for feeling assertive.

'Come on. There's an interview room free. I've even ordered tea.'

'I want to talk about the disappearance of Thomas Jenkins,' I said. 'I haven't come to drink tea.'

'Fair enough,' he said, as he opened the door and sat me down. He sat forward, elbows on the table. 'I'm all ears.'

'Don't take the piss.'

'I'm not, Kate, but you look so belligerent I can't resist it.'

'I'm trying to be assertive and I want you to take me seriously.'

He tried hard not to smirk, but my confidence was beginning to shrivel as fast as my mother's suntanned skin. 'The day Thomas went missing, the boys biked ten miles. According to one witness they were first seen around twelve. According to the press report they left home at nine a.m. Three hours seems a long time to cycle ten miles—'

'Hold on, Kate,' he said, with his hand raised as he stood up. 'I've got the police reports on my desk. Just hang on.'

I wanted desperately to convince him my theory had substance and the interruption unnerved me. No doubt he'd return saying I'd got it all wrong.

He was back within minutes with a thick folder. 'You carry on,' he said. 'I'm still listening.'

For once I realised he meant it. He *was* taking me seriously. 'This is pure conjecture,' I said. 'But I think something like this happened. The three boys start out from the Jenkins house at nine o'clock cycling towards

Dasset Lake. They stop somewhere along the way – one of them might want to pee – whatever – they come off the road. Some sort of fight breaks out. Thomas is killed. They don't know what to do. They panic. They hide his body and the bike nearby and go on to the lake as if nothing has happened. Once there, they try to act normally, but as the day goes on they realise the body might be found and that they need help. Ian turns to the person he's always turned to in good times and bad – his neighbour Sidney Picton. Sidney—'

'Hold on a minute. You're saying Thomas was never at Dasset Lake – that's impossible.'

'Not according to one of the fishermen.'

'One fisherman's account doesn't make a case.'

'No but I have a feeling—'

'Feelings are not evidence, Kate.'

'I realise that, but sometimes people see what others expect them to see or they fail to notice.'

David opened the file and began reading. I watched him, hoping something might catch his eye. I had, after all, spoken to only one witness.

After a few minutes he looked up. 'I'll have to do this in my own time. As far as the bosses are concerned, finding the body of Paula Jenkins is the immediate priority and without real evidence, they won't allow us to excavate any more of Longborough or surrounding districts. Have you any idea how much it costs?'

Of course I hadn't. And to be honest I didn't care. I wanted to say something about justice and truth being more important than mere money, but he wanted a practical approach, not a philosophical one. Bribery might work, though. 'I know you're busy, David, but if we could spend an evening going through Thomas's file I'd cook you a wonderful meal – your choice.'

He closed the file. 'Tonight?'

I paused. I might have to bribe Hubert too. After all, I wanted to use his kitchen. 'Fine. About eight?'

'You know I can't promise an exact time. Better make it a casserole.'

'Beef?'

'With dumplings?'

'Of course.' I'd never made dumplings in my life, but I could always read a recipe.

'Apple pie and custard for dessert?'

'Don't push it, David.'

He grinned. 'See you.'

Later that day Hubert came up to my office with a bunch of carnations and a big smile. 'Whatever you said, Kate – it worked. We've had a long chat on the phone and she's seeing me tonight.'

I didn't want to burst his bubble by telling him that he was preferable to a sixty-five-year-old who played dominoes. 'Thanks for the carnations – they're not funeral flowers, I hope?'

'Certainly not.'

'If you're going out, Hubert, would you be a dear and let me use your kitchen? I've promised David a casserole.'

'Is that all you've promised him?'

'He's not interested in my body, just my dumplings.'

Hubert gave me an old-fashioned look. 'I've promised him beef stew,' I explained.

'He's not a new man as far as food goes, then?'

'He doesn't watch cookery programmes,' I said, 'so red wine sauces and sautéed fennel are not on his menu. He's still a Bisto or an Oxo man. And he wants dumplings with his beef casserole, but I can't do them.'

'You've done me a favour with Marilyn,' he said, 'So you go out sleuthing and I'll do the cooking.'

I didn't need telling twice. I wanted to drive from the Jenkins house to Dasset Lake to find the spot where the boys may have stopped. I had to have some idea, some way of convincing David that the key to all three murders lay in the first – and the first, like Paula's, still with no body. Perhaps the murderer thought the burial place so safe Paula was buried there too. Surely, I thought, finding *two* bodies would be police money well spent?

The sky was grey with low clouds, but the forecast was for rain overnight and for some reason I believed the weather man. By the time I reached the Jenkins place, however, it was raining steadily. Sidney Picton's lights were on; so too were Dorothy's. I was tempted to knock on her door, but knew that Sidney would do his guard dog act. I carried on driving.

The narrow road was waterlogged in parts, but there was little traffic and I drove slowly as I tried to gauge the sort of place young boys would stop. I reasoned that at the start of their day they'd be energetic and cycle quite fast. Any gradients might tire them, make them want to stop and rest.

When I was the only car on the road I decreased my speed even more so that I could give my full attention to the roadside, hoping I could spot any breaks in the bushes or tracks that might have seemed interesting or inviting to boys on bikes. But after twenty-seven years no doubt the landscape had changed.

It began to rain more heavily and I failed to notice the car behind me. As I looked towards the horizon, I caught a glimpse of what the boys must have seen that day.

I felt a surge of excitement – I'd found the place. In my overhead mirror I caught a flash of red. The driver behind me wore a cap. That was all I could see. The road ahead was straight and clear, so I slowed for him to overtake me. Instead he drew closer. I wasn't going to speed up. He could overtake me if he wanted to. I tried to ignore him. But he was refusing to be ignored. He was practically on my bumper. I wound down the window and gave him a hand signal. When he ignored that I decided to speed up. He too speeded up. The bastard began ramming me. I saw the 'SLOW' sign a fraction too late. I took the bend too fast.

I had run out of road. 'Oh, shit,' I breathed as I fought to control the car.

Twenty

It was dark and silent and, wherever I was, it took me several moments to work it out. I finally realised I was on my side in my car and I could feel my right foot was trapped. I was wearing boots, but when I looked down I could see neither boot nor foot. Oh God, I need that foot, I thought. Where is it? I also needed light and, although I managed to locate the light between the visors, it didn't come on. I closed my eyes. This was just a bad dream, I told myself, and when I woke up it would all be over. Or at least someone would be there to get me out – maybe a handsome fireman.

When I did open my eyes again, I was aware my face felt sticky and my head ached. Now I could smell my own blood and the pain in my foot was as though it was being squeezed in a vice. What frightened me most was that I couldn't remember what had happened and that I was perished with cold. How long had I been here? I stared at my watch but couldn't see the hands. I listened for sounds of passing cars but all I heard was the sound of rain hitting the car.

Some situations are hopeless and I was beginning to realise this was one of them. Again and again I tried to remove my foot; I even found the top of the boot zip but with one hand I couldn't even unzip an inch or two. I began to shiver and pray at the same time. I mustn't lose heart. Someone would miss me – Hubert would miss me. Then

I remembered that Hubert was seeing my mother and that would probably mean they would go back to my place in Farley Wood. David would think I was getting my own back by not being at Humberstones and, anyway, nobody knew where I'd planned to go. If I wasn't found till morning I was sure that I'd die from hypothermia.

I drifted off again. For how long I couldn't guess. A repetitive ringing noise woke me. My mobile phone. It rang and rang but wherever it was ringing from, and it sounded as if it were under the back seat, there was no way I could reach it. Every few minutes it rang again. *Please don't give up – please don't give up.*

I desperately wanted to go to sleep, but sleep could be an enemy and if I slept, I might lose the will to live. I decided to set myself mental tasks; remembering old boyfriends seemed a challenge. I started with Neil, my first love – we were both six. I loved him for two years, fascinated by the fact that his dad lived in a shed at the bottom of the garden. I tried to imagine him as Neil the teacher or Neil the accountant. Then I remembered he'd wanted to be a sailor – or was it a pirate? I imagined him in the tropics wearing a white and gold uniform, bronzed by the sun and incredibly handsome. My fantasy was short-lived because I remembered why I fell for Andy Openshaw instead. Andy Openshaw didn't have a runny nose. Neil had been adenoidal and his ears stuck out. At eight years old I grew fussy – flat ears and a dry nose being vital components in the attractiveness stakes.

The sound of a car driving past halted my mental parade. Silence fell again until I heard another car engine – not passing, but stopping. 'Help! Help!' I yelled as loudly as I could, banging on the window at the same time.

And then the miracle of light. A torch shone straight in my face and, joy of joys, Hubert's face pressed up to the window.

'Don't move,' he mouthed at me. I managed to smile – *move*? If only I could!

The next face I saw was David's. He'd managed to open the passenger door and was covering me with a blanket. I don't remember much after that. I vaguely saw a fireman and remember him calling me 'sweetheart'.

My boot, my *expensive* boot, was cut from my leg in Longborough General Hospital's A&E department. My foot was black and blue but the fractures were only minor, at least according to the X-ray. They didn't seem minor to me. The wound on my head was sutured and luckily wouldn't show under my hair, at least when the patch they'd shaved off grew again. I had one or two bruises, and I knew I was lucky to be alive. Although I was told I couldn't bear any weight, I could go home the next day.

The casualty officer had a strong Liverpudlian accent and half of what he said I couldn't understand. Through Hubert and David acting as interpreters he did ask me what had happened. I feigned ignorance. I knew *why*, I was on the road, but couldn't remember much other than the image of a cloth cap. I didn't want to say anyway. I wanted to sort things out in my addled brain – then perhaps I could talk sense.

My guardian angels hovered in the background and came with me to settle me into the ward for the rest of the night. It was a shock to realise it was midnight and I'd been in A&E for hours.

'I'll be out tomorrow,' I muttered, between dry lips and in spite of a raging headache. Again I struggled to stay awake, not willing yet to give in to the desire to sleep. 'I think I know,' I said, 'what the boys would have stopped for.'

'What did happen on the road?' Hubert asked.

I opened my mouth to reply, but I couldn't remember. The only thing I remembered was the cloth cap. 'Oh God, I'm brain-damaged.'

'Don't be daft,' said Hubert, patting my hand. 'You'll remember in the morning – you were concussed.'

He and David both kissed me on the cheek and then I was left in the dim ward with the sounds of others stirring, moaning and coughing, but I was more than grateful. Even when my pupils were checked every half an hour I didn't mind, because, although the accident was a big blur, one image had stayed with me. I knew where the boys had stopped that day.

Late the next day Hubert and David came to collect me. I'd been practising on my elbow crutches and was managing to hobble around, but I had to leave in a wheelchair. I wondered why they had both come, but it dawned on me as we approached Humberstones – it would take two of them to carry me up the stairs.

The process was slow and embarrassing. Hubert grew red in the face with the effort and, between clenched teeth, muttered that I weighed a ton. David behaved stoically, but once I'd been deposited on Hubert's sofa, he sagged alongside me, unable to speak for some seconds. He declined the brandy Hubert offered, but I did notice a moment's hesitation.

Hubert gave me full credit for preparing the casserole and the apple pie before my 'accident', but I don't think David was convinced, especially as I saw Hubert wink at him. 'I thought you'd rather be here than with your mother,' said Hubert. 'But she does want to see you.'

'Oh, goodie.'

'Don't take that attitude, Kate. She cares about you.'

I would have liked to reply to that, but being incapacitated forces docility upon you, even if you don't feel it. So I smiled sweetly and kept quiet.

Once I'd been helped to rise from the sofa to the table to eat, David asked, 'Have you remembered what happened?'

I nodded. 'It wasn't an accident.'

Hubert placed a plate of steaming casserole in front of me. I felt reluctant to say anything more, in case I wasn't believed. With one leg raised on a footstool and still with a raging headache I didn't feel able to put up either fight or argument.

'This is serious,' said David. 'I need to know.'

'You weren't convinced about Thomas—' I began.

'You'll get no apple pie if you don't co-operate with the police,' said Hubert.

Suddenly I felt tearful and I had to struggle not to cry in front of both of them. 'If you must know, I was driving slowly. A red car came up behind me. I signalled for it to overtake but it wouldn't – so in the end I speeded up. Then I was rammed on the bend. And that's it, I thought. I'd had it.'

'Did you see the driver?' asked David. He'd already started on his food, but although I picked up my fork I didn't feel any inclination to eat.

I shook my head. 'I saw his cloth cap. It was raining hard.'

'But a man?'

'I couldn't swear to that on oath.'

'What about the car?'

'It was small and red.'

'Make?'

'I don't know – maybe a Fiat.'

David looked irritated.

'I can't help it if I don't know the exact make of the car that was lurking in my mirror,' I snapped. 'So many cars look the same.'

'Okay,' said David, sounding weary and pausing to eat more. 'Who do you think was driving?'

'I think it was Sidney Picton.'

'Why?'

'He must have followed me, and the cap, I suppose, made me think of him.'

David finished his casserole but I couldn't finish mine. I felt exhausted. 'I've got the file on Thomas for us to go through,' he said.

'You read it,' I said. 'My concentration's not up to much.'

Hubert, frowning, took away my still full plate of casserole and replaced it with a large slice of apple pie. 'It looks wonderful,' I said, 'but I can't eat it. Do you mind if I lie down on the sofa?'

A flicker of concern crossed his face and he rummaged in his pocket for the head injury card the hospital had provided.

'Do you feel sick?' he queried. 'Drowsy? Double vision? Headache?'

I denied all symptoms. 'I'll be fine. I just need to lie down.'

Once I was lying down the pain in my foot eased and I fell asleep to the sound of Hubert filling the dishwasher. When I woke David and Hubert were sitting at the table reading the file on Thomas. I couldn't help feeling peeved that Hubert was muscling in on my case. I felt like some lethargic harem woman waiting for her next bunch of grapes.

'I'm awake now,' I said, pointedly.

'You rest up, Kate,' said Hubert. 'We're making notes for you.'

'There's no need. I think I know where Thomas and Paula are buried.'

They both turned simultaneously to look at me. 'You do?' queried David.

'On my recce I was concentrating on the paths and roadside but when I looked instead at the horizon I saw what the boys would have seen.'

'Which was?' asked David, impatiently.

'The disused water tower.'

David began searching the file for any mention of the water tower. Silence reigned.

Eventually he looked up. 'I'll phone the water board in the morning. There's no mention in the reports.'

'There wouldn't be, would there?' I said. 'The boys didn't say they stopped along the way. The police would have concentrated their efforts around the lake and the immediate area. That water tower is only about four miles from Ian's home.'

David handed me a selection of witness reports to read. Only one woman said she had seen all three boys together, but she described a boy wearing different clothes and, on a subsequent day, failed to recognise a photo of Ian. I had a feeling David was embarrassed – he knew how witnesses could *want* to be helpful, especially in cases of missing children. And, of course, they didn't want to be thought stupid or not observant, so they related what they were supposed to have seen. So depending on how the question was put they might answer what they thought was expected of them. If a young PC asked 'What time did you see the three boys?' it would be easy enough to answer a time and add nothing. Some people, of course, might even deny seeing them at all, not wanting to get involved. It was school holidays and any mothers there would have been too busy watching their own offspring to notice what older boys were doing, especially if they attracted no attention to themselves.

'What do you think now, David?' I asked.

He smiled at me thoughtfully. 'I saw a video film not long ago,' he said, 'where a man dressed as a bear walked amongst a group of teenagers playing netball.' He paused. 'I didn't believe it then. No one noticed the bear. There was a scientific reason given – I don't remember the details, but it was something to do with the brain and eye seeing what they expect to see. *Now* I'm beginning to believe it.'

'So what do we do next?' I asked.

'You do absolutely nothing,' he said. 'You're temporarily crippled. I'm going to have a good look round that water tower.'

Hubert nodded in response, reminding me of those dogs sitting in the back of car windows. 'I'll make sure she doesn't go anywhere,' he said.

'Hang on a minute,' I burst out. 'If you two think I'm going to remain a prisoner here, you're mistaken.'

'What are you going to do? Clobber us with your walking sticks?' asked Hubert.

I wasn't best pleased and if I could have made a dignified exit I would have done, but two crutches and a lower extremity as big as a balloon don't qualify on the dignity stakes.

I hobbled off to bed early, reasoning that a long night with my leg raised on a pillow might mean I could walk in the morning. And if I could manage to persuade Hubert that I could easily get back upstairs on my bottom, then I was sure he'd drive me wherever I wanted to go. Failing that, I'd get a taxi.

I was just falling asleep when Marilyn appeared. 'If there's anything I can do, pet?'

I nearly said 'Give me back my twenty quid', but I didn't. Instead I murmured something about being very tired and I'd see her in the morning.

She tiptoed to my bedside and I couldn't fail to notice she was wearing platforms with six-inch heels. Hubert would be in shoe heaven and I resented that. A nasty thought crept into my mind – maybe she'd trip and break her ankle, thus ending her high-heel days. Maybe one day she'd be a proper mother; then again, that was as likely as the Queen Mother taking up skydiving.

She kissed me on the forehead, making me feel extra guilty – she hadn't kissed me in years.

'I must get some sleep. I'm exhausted,' I said, theatrically.

'Of course you are, dear. I'll see you in the morning.'

I opened one eye to watch her glide out. She was born to wear high heels, but was she born for Hubert? For his sake I hoped not.

Twenty-One

The following morning I didn't feel better. I felt worse. Worse still when I saw that Hubert, overnight, had been transmogrified into an evil gaoler. He provided breakfast in bed, but when I asked him to drive me out to see Dorothy Jenkins his face changed. 'I'll take your walking sticks away,' he threatened. His face had a horrible set look, so when he'd left the room I hastily slipped my crutches beside me in the bed.

A further shock awaited me in the bathroom. I had a black eye, matted hair with a bald patch and a huge bruise on my shoulder. Not only did I feel wrecked, I looked a wreck. I lurched back to bed feeling very sorry for myself. I certainly wasn't fit to be seen in public.

When Hubert collected my breakfast tray I thanked him profusely and he eyed me suspiciously. 'Not feeling too good?' he asked.

'I feel terrible. It's a miracle you found me.'

'A phone miracle. An anonymous call was put through to the station.'

'A man?'

'No, it was a woman.'

'In that case I think it was Dorothy Jenkins.'

'Why do you think that?' asked Hubert.

'Who else? I think she's either known all along what happened to Thomas or she's just found out.'

'I'm only a poor undertaker,' said Hubert, putting down

the tray and sitting on the edge of my bed. 'Explain it to me.'

'I'll ignore the "poor",' I said. 'This is only guesswork, but I think Sidney and Dorothy have been an item for years and years – probably still are. Ian was convinced Thomas was the cuckoo in the nest and hated his brother, probably because *he* would have preferred to be Sidney's son. Anyway, either Ian or Carl, or both, killed Thomas that day.'

'And you think they left the body near the water tower?'

'After dark, one of them – Ian, I would think – rode back and told Sidney. He took Ian back to the water tower and together they buried the body. Ian then rode back to the lake and joined Carl. Finally they rode home to raise the alarm.'

'What about Ian's father in all this?'

'I don't think he had any idea. Or he didn't want to know. He'd turned a blind eye most of his married life.'

By now I was feeling quite upbeat about solving the murders. Hubert's face, though, was full of doubt. 'It's only guesswork,' he said. 'There's not a scrap of evidence.'

'But there would be if I could get to Dorothy. She knows something, I'm sure, but she's not willing to face either the fact that her lover buried her son, or more crucially, that Ian murdered his brother. If I were in that position, I wouldn't want to face either possibility. Far better to believe her son had gone missing and would one day return.'

'What about Lorraine and Paula?'

'I think the gruesome threesome plotted that between them. Ian and Carl made sure they had alibis, leaving Sidney to do the dirty work.'

'Do you think Sidney was fit enough to do a spot of breaking and entering?' asked Hubert, with one eyebrow raised. I wasn't sure, so I gave Hubert a non-committal open-handed gesture and he smiled back smugly.

As he picked up the tray, he said, 'You could always try phoning Dorothy Jenkins to ask if she's recovered from the flu.'

I thought about that for a moment. If I was subtle I might, just might, get her to open up a little. 'Sometimes, Hubert, the things you say are inspirational.'

At the doorway he turned. 'And sometimes I wonder,' he said, 'why you're such a sarky madam.'

'I didn't mean it to sound that way,' I said, trying to be apologetic. 'By the way, is my mother back in her lair?'

'That's no way to talk,' he said crossly. 'She's in my flat having her breakfast. She'll be up to see you soon.'

Could anything be worse? The idea of my mother and Hubert sharing a bed under my roof filled me with horror. Not that I owned the roof, but my rent paid for a good few tiles. I couldn't bear to think about it. I would have to leave. Maybe go back to New Zealand. For the moment, though, the only thing to do was feign sleep. I skulked under the duvet and when I heard her footsteps I began breathing deeply. She called my name several times, peeled back the duvet and hovered over me. I carried on breathing deeply and steadily.

As soon as she'd gone I sat up and began gathering together my clothes – wide-legged jeans to cover the bandaging on my foot and a warm sweater. The bra I could do without. I slung my clothes over my shoulder and, with the aid of my sticks, made my way to my office. There I dressed and rang for a minicab. Telephone calls alone would not do in such circumstances.

With the aid of make-up and some careful hairdressing I looked reasonable. As I waited for the cab I rang Dorothy. Perhaps if she grew nervous about my visit she might give something away. There was no answer. I let it ring and ring but still no one picked up.

I managed to get down the stairs on my bottom quite easily and quietly. Easing myself into the minicab was difficult, but no worse than having sex in the back of a Mini, which was yet another life experience I wouldn't wish to repeat.

The driver, whippet thin and as silent as a deactivated robot, only spoke once as he helped me from the car. 'How long?' he asked.

'An hour.' It was a mere suggestion, made after seeing Dorothy had a light on.

He couldn't have looked more distraught had I told him he had an hour to live. 'I'll come back,' he said grimly. I paid him, giving him a pound tip, which I thought might cheer him up. It didn't, but he did manage a tight-lipped thank you.

Dorothy answered the door in her dressing gown. Her eyes were unnaturally bright and her cheeks had, as we say in the trade, a high malar flush. Her hair lay flat to her head, greasy with sweat. She ushered me in quickly and, in the hall, began to cough. The rasping dry noise sounded like sandpaper on stone and when she spoke her voice was barely more than a whisper. 'I don't want Sidney to see you.'

'Why not?'

'He's drinking more than ever. He's very upset about Ian.'

'Because Ian's under suspicion?'

'Yes.'

She didn't comment on my crutches, but her progress to the sitting room was slower than my swinging gait. I didn't think she had influenza. That might have been the origin but now I was pretty certain she had pneumonia. I could hear her chest wheezing and sense the real effort she had to make to move. She obviously had something important to say.

By the time she'd managed to sit down she could hardly breathe. 'I'm going to call an ambulance,' I said. 'You need to be in hospital.'

'No,' she gasped. 'No, please don't. I must . . . I must tell you.'

The idea of hospital had made her breathing more laboured, so I said, 'Just try and relax – I won't do anything you don't want me to do.'

That seemed to calm her a little.

After a few minutes and another coughing session she asked me for brandy. Once she'd taken a few sips she seemed more composed and her breathing, although shallow, was less laboured. 'I didn't want to talk to a policeman,' she said. 'I'll tell you and then you can tell them.'

I smiled encouragingly and waited for her to begin. 'I know I'm dying,' she said. I opened my mouth to disagree but she raised her hand. 'No, don't argue with me. I know it's true. If not this week then next. I don't want to go on but I want to tell you.'

I listened as she began slowly, sometimes having to catch her breath and sip the brandy. 'I was married at the age of twenty to Patrick. I didn't love him, but he seemed a good man and I wanted to leave home. We moved here and in the cottage lived Sidney all on his own.' She sighed. 'Oh, he was so handsome. It was love at first sight. I used to watch him all the time. I couldn't get him out of my mind. I'd make any excuse just to speak to him.'

'So Sidney didn't work?'

'He wasn't a lazy man, if that's what you're thinking. He did odd jobs all over the place – he could turn his hand to anything.' She sipped more brandy and stared into the middle distance. 'I saw a great deal of Sidney. He was always around to help me. Patrick was building up the business, working sixteen hours a day. For those first five years Patrick and I wanted children, but nothing happened and when I did fall pregnant I had my suspicions.'

'That Ian was Sidney's child?'

She nodded. 'Two years later, Thomas was born. I can't be sure, but he could have been my husband's child. I just don't know. Patrick was delighted to have sons – sons who would carry on the business. That's all he ever thought about. I think he knew I loved Sidney but he didn't care. In fact they got on together very well. It was as if he was pleased that the burden of being a husband and father was taken away from him.'

Dorothy began to cough and wheeze again and I began to feel guilty for stressing her even more. After a while she finished coughing and slumped back in her chair with her eyes closed.

'If this is too much for you, I'll leave,' I said, when she finally opened her eyes.

'No, don't go, please – there's so much I want to say. So much I haven't talked about before.'

'Fine,' I said. 'I'll stay until you ask me to leave. I know you don't want to go to hospital, but shall I call your own doctor?'

She shook her head wearily. 'I don't want to go on. Sidney knows that. He's been wonderful to me – he is a good man.'

I must have looked doubtful because she sat forward, her eyes wide and bright. 'He's only ever tried to help. When Thomas went missing . . . well, a mother knows, even though she may not want to admit it. I knew Ian was lying. He could lie well, but not to me. I lied to the police. I told them Thomas was always threatening to run away. They dragged the lake and searched the surrounding area but in the end they gave up the search.'

'When did you find out what really happened?'

She was about to answer when we both heard the click of the front door opening. 'It's Sidney,' she whispered. We listened as his footsteps approached and watched as the sitting-room door opened. He barely registered my presence but went immediately to sit by Dorothy's side. His eyes were red and when he spoke his voice was slightly slurred.

'Have you told her?' he asked.

'Yes, Sidney,' she said, patting his hand. 'It was time.'

They sat together, holding hands, the only sounds being the ticking of the mantel clock and the wheeze in Dorothy's lungs that sounded plaintive and far off. Sidney glanced across at me. 'You know what happened now. It's time you went.'

'I've got a minicab coming in a few minutes,' I explained. 'I'll be going then.'

'I haven't told her everything,' murmured Dorothy.

'There's no need,' said Sidney. 'They'll find out.'

'I *want* to tell her.' She began coughing again and Sidney flashed an angry look at me, as though I was responsible.

'She should be in hospital,' I said quietly.

'I know what's best for her,' he snapped. 'And I'll tell you what you want to know.'

'I wanted to know,' I said, 'when, exactly, she knew Thomas was dead.'

'Why would you want to know that? Does it matter when she knew?'

I paused, unable to think of an answer. It was Dorothy who managed a breathless response. 'Sidney told me straight away – my husband knew too. We had to pretend to the police and the press that we thought Thomas had run away.' The effort of speaking brought on more coughing.

'I'll do the talking, Dorothy,' he said. 'Don't you tire yourself any more.'

Sidney put the glass of brandy to her lips and then

refilled it from the bottle. He took several gulps before saying, 'Ian arrived here about eight o'clock that night. We were getting worried. He was in a terrible state. A row had broken out. Thomas was only fourteen, but he was as tall and heavy as Ian. It seems they stopped to look round the water tower – it was surrounded by barbed wire to keep kids out, but they managed it by standing on their bikes and jumping down. Anyway, it seems Thomas and Ian wanted a pee and Thomas made some remark about the fact that Ian wasn't very well endowed. A fight broke out and Ian got a kicking. It was then that Carl stepped in. Thomas got knocked down, hit his head on a stone and it killed him.' He paused. 'At least, that was what they told me.' He drank some more brandy and I noticed his words were less slurred the more he drank.

'So you went back with Ian to the water tower?'

He nodded and clutched Dorothy's hand. She closed her eyes and squeezed his hand in return. 'It was growing dark. I took blankets and a spade. I buried Thomas near a clump of bushes. Ian went back to the lake and then they rode home. We raised the alarm when I came back. It was too dark to start a search – that was started in the morning, but the boys reported seeing and hearing a car leave, so the police assumed he had been abducted.'

'And Dorothy knew all along?'

He nodded and smiled fondly at her. 'Poor love was heartbroken, but she couldn't risk losing her other son.'

'What about Carl?' I asked.

'What about him?'

'How was he affected?'

'He was upset, of course. Thomas was the most difficult of the three. Ian and Thomas didn't get on from the first. They were jealous of each other. I reckon Carl often got the two brothers at each other's throats. I don't think either of them meant to kill Thomas – it was an accident, but we doubted the police would see it that way.'

'That explains what happened to Thomas,' I said, 'but why did you have to kill Paula and Lorraine?'

Sidney's face registered surprise and he seemed lost for words. 'Well, I . . .'

Dorothy's eyes snapped open. 'Don't lie, please, dear, don't lie – we've told enough lies.'

'Let me have my say,' he said, gently. 'I didn't mean to kill Lorraine, and Paula had to die because she was threatening to expose Ian.' Dorothy's eyes grew wider still and she began gasping for air. Sidney flashed a look at me – a mixture of pleading and despair.

'Was it you who forced me off the road?' I asked.

Sidney was about to reply when Dorothy grabbed his arm. 'He hasn't driven a car in five years,' she gasped. 'He's lying about—'

At that moment car wheels sounded on the gravel outside. 'It's the police,' said Sidney, trying to disengage Dorothy's clutching hand.

'No, it isn't,' I said, but neither of them seemed to hear me.

I did hear Dorothy utter three words. Three words which, at that moment, meant nothing. Except that when I saw the flash of silver in Sidney's hand I realised she'd said, 'Do it now!' And with that realisation came the gunshot. He'd raised the gun to her left temple and shot her in one smooth, uninterrupted movement. I sat paralysed with shock. There'd been no warning. He hadn't seemed angry. He'd just been drunk.

Now there seemed to be blood in the air itself. I looked at the remains of Dorothy Jenkins's head and began to retch. Sidney had bent down and was kissing her hand and mumbling that he loved her. I tried to get to my feet, wanting to get out, wanting to breathe fresh air. But I forgot about my foot and fell back into the chair.

Hearing a noise behind me, Sidney stood up. He still held the gun. 'I had to do it,' he said. 'She would have found out.' My eyes were fixed on the barrel of the gun. I had stopped breathing – I waited, convinced he was going to shoot me. I closed my eyes – I had no thoughts at all. Even fear left me.

As the shot rang out my eyes sprang open. Sidney had shot himself in the mouth. One eye was missing and half his head was a bloody mash. I could feel my breathing revving like an engine.

I remembered my crutches and scrambled with my hands on the floor for them, unable to take my eyes from the corpses lest they should rise up, as in a horror film. I staggered out of the room, along the hallway, fumbled at the door and finally made it to God's good air outside.

The minicab driver was out of his car but using his car phone. 'Help! Police!' I called out. He looked at me with scared eyes, jumped into his car and drove off at speed.

I began walking. My head felt so much like cotton wool that no thoughts penetrated. I just concentrated on bearing my weight on the crutches. I heard the police sirens but the sound didn't halt my progress. Just keep walking, I told myself. Two police cars stopped alongside me but it didn't stop me. Left right, left right, left right, soon be home, don't stop, keep going, left right.

'Kate. Stand still.'

I stood still. Maybe they too had guns. 'Kate – David Todman.'

A blanket was put round me and I was helped into the back of a car. I felt so peculiar, as if I wasn't there at all. 'They're dead,' I said. 'Shot.'

I can't remember saying anything more. I was driven back to Humberstones and carried upstairs. Hubert muttered, 'Oh my God,' when he saw me and put his arms around me. My mother appeared, took one look at me and burst into tears.

I couldn't understand what was wrong. I hadn't been shot. I was fine. I told the doctor I was fine too, but he gave me an injection of something. And then all was quiet and peaceful.

Twenty-Two

Whatever the doctor gave me, it worked. When I woke up I felt groggy, but at least my brain functioned. It needed to, as I was sure the third degree would be order of the day. I seemed to have slept for hours, but when I came round I was still lying on Hubert's sofa and David was sitting opposite watching me.

'What time is it?' I asked him.

'It's six o'clock. How are you feeling?'

'Hung-over. I'd love some tea.'

'Do you remember what happened?'

I nodded. 'But a gallon of caffeine would definitely help.'

I drank the tea gratefully, which revived my throat and my thoughts. Once revived, I could see David was in DCI mode.

'Why did you go to the Jenkins place on your own?' There was no hint of friendliness in his voice and, since I had once considered spending the night with him, I felt a little peeved.

'Hubert wouldn't take me. Dorothy Jenkins, in my opinion, was the weakest link. She must have either known or had suspicions that Ian had killed his brother.'

'And did she know?'

'Yes. Sidney told her what had happened.'

'What did happen?'

I told him what Sidney had told me about the fight and how he had buried Thomas near the water tower.

'You didn't think to ask him where, exactly?'

'He didn't give me a map,' I said. 'But he did say it was near a clump of bushes. Seconds later the shooting started.'

'Surely he gave some indication?'

'It wasn't like in a film,' I said, irritated. 'He didn't come in brandishing a shotgun – it might have been less of a shock if he had.'

'So you had no idea?'

'Of course not. He wasn't wide-eyed and incoherent. He was drunk but rational.'

'You didn't suspect he was armed?'

'No,' I repeated. 'I didn't know.'

'What did Dorothy say?'

'She told me that she and Sidney had been an item since she was in her early twenties. She thinks her husband guessed, but he chose not to object – in fact she thought it suited him.'

'Is Ian Picton's son?'

'She was married for five years and didn't get pregnant so there's a strong likelihood.'

'Thomas could have been his son too,' said David, thoughtfully.

'Ian thought *he* was Patrick's son and that Thomas was the cuckoo in the nest.'

'DNA will solve that one,' he said, 'but it won't solve the murder of Paula and Lorraine.'

'Sidney confessed to that too.'

'How convenient.'

'What's that supposed to mean?'

David frowned. 'I don't like cases that are too neat. He was willing to dispose of a body for his son. Maybe he's also covering up for him. Why implicate his son when he was about to kill himself anyway?' I had to agree. Sidney's confession wouldn't have convinced anyone.

'So the case isn't closed?'

'By no means. Only when we find Paula's body will we be able to find her killer.'

'Maybe Paula is buried with Thomas.'

'That's what I'm hoping.'

'There was one other thing,' I said. 'Sidney admitted murdering both women but it wasn't him who ran me off the road. Dorothy said he hadn't driven for years.'

Silence fell then until David asked, 'Did you see the gun?'

'I saw it was a handgun with a silver-coloured barrel, but I was in shock – there was no warning and I didn't stop to inspect it after he'd shot himself with it.'

As I talked about the shooting, I began to relive what had happened, hear Dorothy's last words, see that sudden flash of silver, hear the blast and see the blood . . .

'What's wrong?' asked David. 'You've gone all pale and spaced out.'

'It's not every day I see two people shot,' I snapped. I could feel my breathing speeding up and hear ringing in my ears. It was some hours since the event and to pass out now would seem wimpish, so I took several deep breaths and tried to think of sunshine and beaches instead. It didn't work. There was blood in the sand.

'Did you get a flashback?' he asked.

I nodded. I'd remembered other incidents, but nothing as vivid as this. This was an instant replay and I didn't want it to happen again. I felt sick. I wanted David Todman to leave me alone. And where the hell was Hubert when I needed him?

As if reading my thoughts, David said, 'Hubert's driving your mother home so as soon as he gets back I'll get to work.'

'I'm perfectly all right to be left on my own,' I replied.

He ignored that and poured me another cup of tea. As he handed it to me, he said, 'Tomorrow, we'll check out the water tower – get a team in to do the digging and give the bill to the water board.'

I wondered if the water board would wear that, but I was past caring, especially about who paid for what. I was in self-pitying mode. I should have stayed in New Zealand where the newspapers had riveting headlines such as 'CAT UP TREE FOR THIRD DAY RUNNING'. I'd been back in the UK for less than a month – I'd lost my house, my car, nearly lost my life, plus my best friend was in love with a dog, or two dogs if you counted my mother. *That* thought almost made me smile and I closed my eyes.

When I woke Hubert was sitting in David's place. 'You should be in bed,' he said. 'You look like death.'

'You should know,' I replied as I gathered my strength and my crutches to make what now seemed a long journey to my bed.

That night my dreams were not filled with guns and blood, but with car chases. The driver chasing me kept changing – first it was Sidney, then Dorothy, then Ian. When I did wake my subconscious seemed to have worked something out for me. I didn't know the face of the person who had driven me off the road. But I realised it was most likely that someone driving back from the Dunmore area would have had business there. Whoever it was took a risk in ramming me and to take a risk like that you have to have a reason. Someone, and I didn't know who, wanted me out of action. But would they try again?

In the late evening, after a day spent drinking tea and coffee and e-mailing friends in New Zealand, I felt I was fast becoming a sad case. I'd hoped David would phone me with news of the excavation, but when darkness fell, I assumed the body of Thomas had not yet been found.

Hubert, meantime, kept me supplied with fattening nibbles and his repertoire of hometown homilies. At lunchtime, along with a chicken and mayo sandwich, came, 'It's not over till the fat lady sings.' Teatime produced a jam doughnut and, 'It's always darkest before the dawn,' and dinnertime, along with pasta, came a new one, the reported words of Mrs Thatcher: 'Never underestimate what can be achieved in ten minutes.' He'd obviously been reading my copy of the *Daily Mail*.

'I would try to live by that dictum,' I said, 'but I've achieved zilch in ten hours.'

'Tomorrow is another day,' he said, in chivvying tones. 'You should use this time to collate all your information.'

'I'd have trouble with a shopping list at the moment, Hubert. My brain feels as if it's been minced.'

'No change, then?'

'Ha, bloody ha.'

I noticed that my mother wasn't in evidence. Nor had Hubert mentioned her. Jasper had frisked around for most of the day and had now acquired all sorts of toys. Between meals I had watched his antics and now he slept, curled up next to Hubert on the sofa. 'No Marilyn tonight, then, Hubert?'

'She's got one of her migraines,' he said.

I gritted my teeth. She'd never had a migraine in her life. Plenty of hangovers, yes, but a multitude of migraines – no. Her motherly hint of concern hadn't lasted long, but at least she hadn't demanded Hubert's presence to soothe her brow.

At about ten I couldn't face the news on television and was about to slowly hobble off to bed when my doorbell rang. Hubert went off to answer it and returned with a defeated-looking David. 'Nothing,' he said, miserably. 'Looks as if Sidney Picton was prepared to go to his maker on a pack of lies.'

I felt somehow as if I was responsible. 'Why would he deliberately mislead me?'

'To protect his son?' suggested Hubert. 'If he was convicted without the body and with the story of a fight between brothers it would only be manslaughter.'

'The body would prove it was no accident,' muttered David. 'So Picton buried Thomas elsewhere – closer to home, maybe.'

I couldn't add anything to that. I felt genuinely sorry for David. 'I'm finished in Longborough CID,' he said, bleakly. 'I was told today this case has cost more than any other murder enquiry in Longborough's history.'

'None of it is your fault,' I said.

'That's no bloody consolation,' he snapped. 'I can see now why some police forces resort to plastic bags and rubber truncheons. Given half a chance I'd like to be left alone with Jenkins or Farnforth for half an hour. The bastards would soon change their tune.'

I was about to reply but Hubert gave me a warning glance. 'Do you fancy something to eat?' he asked David.

'Yeah. I wouldn't mind. I haven't eaten all day.'

Hubert returned within minutes with coffee and sandwiches and, while David ate and drank in morose silence, I tentatively broached the subject of my car ramming which seemed safer than mentioning bodies that refused to be unearthed. His response, between mouthfuls, was, 'Any nutter could have been responsible, or it could have been another of Picton's stunts.'

'I don't think it was him driving.'

'Why not?'

'Dorothy told me he hadn't been able to drive for five years, remember? I suppose it was his sight.'

David managed a half-smile. 'Being partially sighted doesn't stop a determined driver. Drunk, drugged, half blind, half asleep, half dead, banned or barmy – you name the condition, they're out there on the road.'

I couldn't be sure that my ramming hadn't been caused

by a homicidal maniac, but that didn't seem likely. 'When you interview the gruesome twosome,' I said, 'you'll find out if they have alibis for the time I was run off the road. It could have been Ian wearing a cap.'

'I'd already thought of that,' said David, irritated that I'd underestimated him. 'He was with his mother and his kids at the time, and Farnforth was at the gym.'

'So you think it was a rogue driver or a phantom?'

'I didn't say that.'

'My car didn't run itself off the road—'

He held up his hand. 'Say no more, Kate. I believe you.'

I paused for the follow-up. 'There is someone else in the equation,' he said, 'someone we've both overlooked.'

'Oh God, don't tell me,' I said, remembering. 'Dr Reece Gardener *was* an understudy of Dr Shipman.'

He smiled. 'No, we've eliminated him. At the moment we're investigating Jem Harrison.'

I was tempted to say he was far too good-looking and well-adjusted to commit attempted murder or indeed murder, but thankfully I kept my mouth shut. Ugliness and surliness do not a sinner make, I told myself, but I had yet to be convinced that I'd been such a poor judge of character. Although I did concede lust might have affected my thinking.

'What have you found out?' I asked.

'He and Paula were in Saudi together and they were reported to be very friendly.'

Suddenly there was a new perspective. Paula occasionally leaving Ian and lying about staying with her mother. Had Jem tried to persuade her to come away with him? Lorraine had said it looked like a domestic argument. That night, when he'd come to the rescue, was that mere coincidence? Had he come back and ended Lorraine's life? What was Lorraine's part in all this anyway? The only reason I could see for her being silenced was she knew Carl was involved in Thomas's death – both wives knew, but for how long, and were they threatening to talk? Sidney had admitted the killings, but was he lying to protect Ian? And why the elaborate set-up with the planted evidence in Jenkins's shed?

'Have you interviewed him yet?'

David continued to sound downbeat. 'Can't contact him at the moment – he's on army manoeuvres down south – but I don't think he's a major player at the moment.'

'What do you think he's guilty of,' I asked, 'other than being involved with Paula at some time in the past?'

'I didn't say he was guilty,' he said, adding more sugar to his coffee and stirring it so that the spoon chinked irritatingly in the cup, 'but I'd be interested to know why he lied about knowing Paula. It's just a loose end.'

'Like finding Paula's body?'

'I wouldn't call that a loose end, more the whole bloody ball of string.' Then he added, 'It's not your worry, Kate. All we can do is hope our two suspects give themselves away.'

It all sounded very negative. And my contribution wasn't exactly going to enhance my reputation.

Hubert, sitting silently with Jasper on his lap, stroked him thoughtfully.

'What are you thinking, Hubert?' I asked. It wasn't like him to be that silent.

'The male of the species is more aggressive,' he said, 'but less devious.'

'Is that your thought for today?' I asked. I supposed he'd been listening to Radio Four again, or it was in some way related to Marilyn.

It was only later, as I lay sleepless in bed, I realised that it might have meant something more pertinent to the case.

Twenty-Three

I was most surprised early the next morning to get a phone call from Ian Jenkins. 'I paid you to prove my innocence. So far you've done sod all.'

'Someone tried to run me off the road,' I explained. 'I'm on crutches.'

'I didn't kill my wife,' he yelled, 'and I didn't kill Lorraine. The police are trying to frame me.'

I held the phone away from my ear wondering if he was drunk or merely in high dudgeon.

'Perhaps if you came clean about the death of Thomas and tell the police where he's buried—'

He didn't let me finish, but at least he'd stopped yelling.

'I don't know what you're talking about,' he said, his voice at least two octaves lower. I did wonder for a moment if he knew about his mother's death, but after a short pause he said, 'My mother and Sid are dead because of that bastard.'

'You mean Carl?'

'Of course, who else?'

'Good old Sid,' I said. 'Even confessed to killing two women for your sake.'

Silence. 'No,' he said quietly. 'No – he wouldn't hurt a fly – he was like a father to me. He wouldn't have killed Paula.'

'If he *was* your father, would that have made a difference?'

'He was Thomas's father – he looked more like him than me.'

'Perhaps you were his son too.'

Again there was silence. Then came the sound of him clearing his throat. Finally he said, 'I've lost everyone.'

'You still have your children to think about.'

'Oh yes,' he said, bleakly, 'I still have them to think about.'

For a while, after that conversation, I sat wondering what to do with myself. I couldn't just sit around. Hubert had three funerals arranged. I had no car and even if I borrowed one of Hubert's my foot still wasn't brakeworthy. But then I decided I could let the train take the strain. I'd be in Devon in three or four hours – barring faulty tracks or missing drivers. And I wanted to get away from Longborough, if only for a day or two.

I knew the name of Jem's cottage and vaguely where it was. It was worth a try to find out why he'd lied or, at least, not told me he knew Paula. It would fill a day and I didn't see any other way to continue my investigation.

Filling a day was a minor point. It more than filled a day. The train was two hours late. I missed my connection and arrived so late in Seaton that I took a taxi and asked for the nearest B&B which, embarrassingly, was only two hundred yards from the station. At least now I could manage with just a walking stick, although I did need help from the taxi driver to carry my rucksack up the three steps and into the sanctuary of the Sea Shells Guest House.

The landlady, Doreen, a woman in her sixties with shining silver hair and a bosom as big as a shelf, hadn't heard of Hope Cottage, which wasn't surprising. She said she'd find out for me by asking around and by phoning other B&Bs and guest houses in the area. I offered to pay the phone bill but she wouldn't hear of it. She also insisted on carrying my rucksack to my room and explaining every feature of the room in great detail. Dinner was at six, she told me. I could eat out or have the best Irish stew I'd ever tasted. Since I hadn't had Irish stew in years there wouldn't be a great deal of competition. And after hours on a train with no buffet, even an egg sandwich would have tasted just fine.

I ate alone in a dining room of six small tables, all laid for breakfast, with an artificial rose in a clear glass vase on each one. With only the chink of my own cutlery for company it felt quite eerie, but I was pleased not to have to explain my limp or my bruises to other guests.

I crept up to my room just after six thirty. Doreen caught me just as I hit the stairs. 'Take this, dear,' she said, handing me a warm furry thing. 'You'll need it, it might snow tonight.'

A hot water bottle is a wondrous thing – comforting and portable. I snuggled into a bed that had sheets and blankets and an eiderdown. And now I had a hottie too. Life was definitely improving.

I switched on the television using the remote control and managed to stay awake for all of ten minutes.

I slept a dreamless sleep and awoke to the smell of bacon frying. My foot hurt less and for a moment I thought paradise was at hand. Then my mobile rang. It was of course Hubert – no one else seems to phone me, at least, not at seven thirty a.m.

'Kate – where are you?' asked Hubert, sounding annoyed.

'I did leave you a note on the reception desk,' I lied. 'I'm in Seaton in Devon, staying in a B&B.'

There was silence then apart from a little cough. 'Any reason you're there?' he said. 'Or am I being dim?'

'Planklike . . . and that's a joke, Hubert, in case you ever take me seriously.' He tutted and I said, 'Jem Harrison.'

Silence again. 'He's not in the same B&B, is he?'

'It's nice here,' I said, 'but not officer accommodation.'

'He left the army a week ago, Kate.'

'I knew he was going to.'

I wasn't sure where this conversation was going. Hubert had a worried edge to his voice.

'I'll be back tomorrow – trains willing.'

'I'm coming down,' said Hubert.

'I don't need nannying.'

'You need a driver.'

I couldn't argue with that. 'What about Marilyn?'

'What about her? I wasn't planning to bring her too.'

I breathed a sigh of relief.

'I'll get there mid-afternoon,' he said. 'What's the address?'

I told him and heard him laugh at the name. 'Is it on the seashore?' he asked, still amused. 'Just stay at the SS, Kate.'

At that moment nothing amused me. I lay back on the bed staring at the ceiling and wondering what exactly had brought me here. Jem Harrison had been too readily available the night Lorraine had been missing. The police must have checked him out. But why hadn't he admitted to having met Paula before? Another little niggle was why Lorraine should have visited the factory.

At eight thirty I sat alone in the dining room, drinking fresh orange juice and wondering if I was the only guest. 'Well, dear,' said Doreen, as she bustled about serving me a full 'English' breakfast. 'You're in luck. A friend of mine knows Hope Cottage. She wanted to buy it, but someone got to it first. Not even a local – she was most put out. It's about five miles from here – a mile or so from Little Neachem.'

I was delighted and thanked her profusely. Her breakfast was second to none and I made my way back to my room to recover from it.

I'd booked the room for two nights and I planned to hobble around the town and see the sea. But one glance from my window at a sky as grey as ash decided me. I crawled back under the bedclothes and within minutes I was asleep.

A knock at the door woke me. All sense of time seemed to have deserted me. I stared at my wristwatch. It was one p.m. 'Come in,' I called out, expecting it to be Hubert. It was Doreen.

'I don't normally do lunch, dear, but I'm having soup and sandwiches – thought you might like some.'

I thanked her, thinking Hubert would appreciate the sarnies, and told her I had a friend coming in the afternoon and that he might want a room for the night. She looked at me, a little puzzled. 'I've got plenty of spare rooms, dear – it's that time of year. He can have the one next to you.'

I managed the soup and left the piled plate of sandwiches for Hubert. Refreshed after my extra sleep, I now felt caged up and raring to go. What exactly I hoped to achieve at Hope Cottage I wasn't sure, but maybe Jem knew something. The arrest of Ian and Carl for the murder of Thomas was now only a matter of time. I was convinced the body was near the water tower – after all, why would Sidney Picton, on the verge of killing himself, lie about where he'd hidden the body?

Another little voice said why not lie? Maybe Sidney thought with no body there would be no case to answer. He was protecting his 'son' to the last.

At two thirty the internal phone rang. 'Your boyfriend's here, dear,' trilled Doreen. I didn't put her straight.

Hubert ate the sandwiches, complained at length about the traffic and finally said, 'What *are* you doing here, Kate?'

'Just call it a gut feeling,' I said. 'After all, *you* thought Jem Harrison was a tad suspicious.'

'Too confident by half.'

'And good-looking. Now, you could just be jealous –'

Hubert's eyebrows rose in defence. 'Don't be ridiculous. I haven't got a jealous bone in my body.'

Normally I would have managed some sort of riposte or argument, but this time I didn't reply. Somehow, still having to walk with a stick had made me lose confidence. I felt strangely vulnerable, but the wonderful thing about the Sea Shells Guest House was that I'd had hours and hours of uninterrupted sleep and not a single flashback.

'I am grateful to you for coming,' I said, smiling at him.

He looked at me quizzically. 'You're not quite the ticket, Kate – are you?'

'I'll be fine – it's just the last few days have been a bit traumatic.'

Hubert patted me awkwardly on the back. 'You don't have to go anywhere near that creep's place.'

'He's not a creep, and I know I don't *have* to, but I still don't know who killed Lorraine and Paula. And he might—'

'The police will find out sooner or later,' he interrupted me, as though afraid I would waffle on.

'It could well be later,' I said, 'but I reckon for all this suffering I need to know now.'

'In my opinion,' said Hubert, dourly, 'this trip is going to be a waste of time.'

The cottage was the type of place described in estate agents' jargon as 'nestling'. It really did nestle between all sorts of foliage, as if the cottage itself had grown naturally, like the trees. It blended with the surroundings from the earthy thatch to the creeping ivy that covered the walls. Inside, I imagined it as dark and cosy.

Jem answered the door. He was surprised, but seemed pleased enough to see us. 'Come on in,' he said. 'Come through to the kitchen. I'm making some scones.'

The kitchen itself looked out on to a walled garden and beyond that to trees and fields. 'Wonderful view, isn't it?'

he asked, taking off a plastic apron with 'CHEF' emblazoned on the front. It doesn't take much to put me off a man and I know there are men who can look sexy in the kitchen, but I like a man who can handle himself with a ladder and paintbrushes and a big box of tools. Even I could manage scones.

'Have you come on a mission?' he asked.

Hubert was staring out of the kitchen window and I got the impression he was embarrassed. 'Sort of – more a break really. There is some news from Longborough. Ian Jenkins's mother and neighbour are dead – shot.' The moment I spoke the word my mind gave me a full action replay – as vivid as the scene itself. My breathing began revving up and I felt faint and sick.

Jem muttered, 'Oh dear,' as he removed the over-brown scones from the oven.

Hubert noticed that I'd begun to sway and came to my rescue by holding on to my elbow.

'We'll have to go,' said Hubert. I didn't argue. Neither did Jem.

Once I was outside and walking, I no longer felt quite so faint, and in the fresh air I soon began to feel relatively normal.

Hubert had been driving away from Hope Cottage along the narrow winding road towards Seaton for about two miles when I realised. 'Could you find a lay-by?' I asked.

'Just don't be sick in my car,' said Hubert, speeding up. Half a mile later he saw a suitable stopping point and brought the car to a halt. 'Do you want to get out?' he asked, as he threw open the door.

'Actually, Hubert, I'm not feeling sick. I was thinking about those scones.'

'What about them? You can't want to go back and sample them?' he asked in amazement.

'Why would a man make scones?' I asked.

'Why not?'

'Scones should be eaten on the day they're made. So, he was expecting someone.'

'He could have a friend or two.'

'What if he was making scones to impress?'

Hubert shrugged. 'I wasn't impressed, they were burnt.'

'You make scones and cakes for children,' I said slowly, as if poor Hubert was slow-witted.

'Just tell me what you want me to do, Kate – you can explain it later.'

Hubert drove back to a lay-by nearer the cottage. The nearest place that we couldn't be seen from there. After five minutes he asked, 'How long have we got to sit here for?'

'As long as it takes. Sooner or later a car will drive past us, and then we'll know, won't we?'

Thankfully he didn't ask *who* we were waiting for, which was just as well, because if a carload of army chums turned up I was going to feel more incompetent than usual.

An hour later we'd finished a packet of extra strong mints. Hubert was beginning to get irritated and I was getting despondent. A few minutes later I heard a car approaching even before I saw it. 'Get down!' I said, as I lunged towards Hubert's feet. As it went past I looked up to see a small red car going towards Hope Cottage.

'Don't say it,' said Hubert. 'Let me. Follow that car!'

There was no hurry because the car could only be going to the cottage, but I wanted to catch a glimpse of its occupants before they actually went inside.

Hubert stopped the car some distance away, but produced from the glove compartment a pair of binoculars. Quickly I got the car in view.

'What can you see? Who is it?' asked Hubert, getting agitated.

Jem Harrison was at the door, all smiles and arms outstretched. And now I knew who his guests were, I handed the binoculars to Hubert.

'Strewth! Is that who I think it is?' he asked.

'Drive on, Jeeves. I think the fat lady is about to sing.'

Twenty-Four

First out of the car had stepped the driver – Carl Farnforth – followed by two excited children and a woman dressed in a black chador. Once they were in the cottage Hubert drove sedately in their direction.

'So far, so good,' said Hubert, parking the car on the gravel frontage. 'What do we do when we get there – knock on the door and ask for a scone?'

'I want an explanation.'

'They might give you more than that,' he warned.

I wasn't in the mood to listen to warnings. As far as I was concerned, the same red car had run me off the road and now it was my turn for both an explanation and an apology – and a few thousand in compensation would be great on a no win, no fee basis.

On the porch steps, with my hand poised to knock the door, Hubert took out his mobile. 'What are you doing?'

'Ringing the police.'

'Why?'

'Just in case,' he answered. While he mumbled on his mobile phone I banged on the door loudly.

It was some time before Jem answered. He ushered us into the living room, was charming and civilised, and even offered us tea.

'What's going on?' I asked.

'I'll make that tea,' he said. 'Won't be long.' He closed the door.

It took a few seconds for the penny to drop. I ran to the door but it was either locked or he'd put something against it. The sound of a car driving away made me rush to the window. They had all flown the coop and with only a glimpse of his head, it looked as if Jem was driving. I turned to Hubert, my feeling of disappointment replaced quickly by irritation when I saw he was smiling. 'I don't know why you're being so smug.'

'They won't get far,' he said, peering out of the window. 'Longborough CID patrol cars are just up the road. Someone must have tipped them off that Hope Cottage was worth a visit. They'll be backing up any second now.'

Sure enough, the car was reversing, forced back by a police car.

We were released from the front room and the cottage was suddenly full. The children, confused and miserable, began to cry. David Todman looked at me and said, 'Could you deal with the kids until a WPC gets here?'

Bloody cheek! I thought. Thankfully Hubert murmured in my ear that he'd look after the kids. They continued to grizzle and cling to the black-clad woman, who was now trying to disengage them and remove her chador at the same time.

With face uncovered it was obviously Paula. She'd dyed her hair black but I still recognised her from photos I'd seen at her mother's house. She sobbed quietly as Hubert took the children, who didn't protest, into the kitchen.

The two uniformed men were asked by David to wait outside. I'd thought a quick arrest was imminent, but David didn't seem to be in any hurry. Jem and Carl stood by Paula. Even then I wasn't sure which one was her lover. They both looked equally concerned about her.

'Sit down, Mrs Jenkins,' said David. 'We do know what's been going on, so there's no need to upset yourself any more. Your husband has been arrested for the murder of his brother Thomas and the manslaughter of Lorraine Farnforth.'

She looked up; her sobbing stopped in a breath. 'Thank God,' she murmured.

'Would someone mind tell me what's going on?' I asked.

David ignored me and spoke to Jem. 'Who's been a naughty boy, then?'

'Just doing an old friend a favour.'

I stood in total confusion. 'Who are you?' I asked Jem.

'Ex-Major Harrison – military intelligence,' he answered. Obviously taking pity on me, he began to explain. 'I met Carl in the Middle East. We got drunk together a few times and one night he told me what had gone on years before. The death of Thomas Jenkins.'

'But they didn't *mean* to kill him,' I protested.

Jem smiled grimly. 'Carl was there, but he wasn't involved. Ian Jenkins executed his brother with a shot to the back of the head.'

My mouth dropped open. 'The gun belonged to Sidney Picton,' he continued. 'He was responsible for Ian's fascination with weapons. Carl shared the interest. Ian had taken the handgun that day with the sole intention of killing his half-brother – at least, he assumed he was a half-brother.'

'But Sidney told me just before he shot himself that . . .' I trailed off, realising I really had been told a pack of lies.

'He told you the wrong burial site,' said Jem, 'hoping the police would eventually be forced to stop looking, in the same way the police gave up digging on the moors for the Brady/Hindley victims. Without a body, if charged, it would only be a charge of manslaughter – that is, if they stuck to the same story.'

I stared at Carl – cocky, confident Carl. 'Why didn't you tell the truth all those years ago?'

'I was just a kid,' he said. 'I was scared. I had a mother I didn't get on with, no dad. But I did have Ian and his family. I'd been a friend of Ian's since the age of eight. I'd always been in awe of him. He was very bright. He was the only reason I got to university. I was slightly dyslexic – he or Sidney helped with my homework. Ian helped me all the way through university. I felt indebted to him. I'd promised never to mention what really happened that day. He said my word was my bond and if I ever told anyone he'd kill me. And I believed him.'

My eyes strayed to Paula, whose head was in her hands. 'Did you know?' I asked.

She looked up at me, her face still tearstained. 'I always knew there was something. Ian was a violent man – the sort of man who gives you bruises that don't show. I also knew he had a hold over Carl. One day when Lorraine was drunk, she told me what that hold was. Finding out he'd shot his brother really scared me. Later on, when I asked for a divorce, Ian said that could never happen – first he would kill the children, then me and then himself. I didn't doubt that he'd do it.'

'So the shooting scenario was cooked up between the three of you?'

She nodded. 'I'd left Ian on a few occasions when he'd been violent – my mother covered for me and he never bothered to check. I'd come down here. I couldn't tell my mother what was going on – the more people that knew, the more people were in danger. By this time Ian had begun to get paranoid about Carl. We also knew Sidney would do anything to protect his beloved Ian. So it was decided that Lorraine would employ a private detective and report seeing a woman shot. We knew in the end the police would be told and it would be too late to look for forensic evidence. The beret and gloves were a sort of joke – we also tried to plant incriminating evidence. We were just not clever enough.'

'So what happened the night Lorraine was killed?'

It was Carl who answered this time. 'Ian had found out I

was back in the UK, but I was with my girlfriend. He may have thought I was at home. I think he came round to check for himself that Paula wasn't staying with Lorraine. Instead he found Lorraine semi-conscious on the sofa. Maybe she roused a little and he thought she was going to scream so he put his hand over her mouth – and finished her.'

'And the vodka?'

'Still a mystery,' answered David. 'But we do have a suspect smuggler. A taxi driver Lorraine had used when she was over the limit. Seems he's Polish and partial to strong vodka. We've yet to interview him.'

From the kitchen came the sound of childish laughter.

'It was *you* who ran me off the road, wasn't it, Paula?' I asked.

'I'm really sorry,' she said. 'I just meant to stop you. I was trying to see my children. I did ring 999 – a dead woman couldn't wait around – and I did see the car had righted itself and that you were still alive.'

'Gee, thanks – I was merely trapped,' I said.

Paula sighed miserably. 'I wasn't myself. I was terrified Ian would find out I was still alive. I'd hoped he'd be arrested straight away and then with Carl and Jem's help I'd be on my way to the Middle East. But it hasn't turned out like that – has it?'

My room at Sea Shells wasn't needed for a second night. The landlady seemed happy enough and so did Hubert, who hated to be away from home for more than one night. I'd explained the outcome once to him, as he'd missed the revelations because he was looking after Paula's children.

In the car on the way back he said, 'It was all a set-up then.'

'Yep. Lorraine didn't see anyone shot. The only coincidence was that Ian did break in on two occasions. Once when Jem was there and of course on the night she died.'

'So there were no silent phone calls or previous break-ins.'

'No. It was all a charade to get Ian off their backs once and for all.'

'And the items found in Ian Jenkins's shed had been a plant?'

'Yes. And the red beret and scarf were just a complication. I think they tried to be a little too clever.'

Hubert looked unconvinced. 'Maybe they did, but they very nearly got away with it.'

'I expect the charges will be fairly minor—'

Hubert, laughing, interrupted me. 'I don't think David will wear that, not after all that fruitless digging.'

'I'm wondering,' I said, 'if Ian will now come clean about Thomas and where he's buried.'

'I'm doubtful about that,' said Hubert. 'Maybe he doesn't know – and why should he make it easy?'

'Why indeed?'

We were nearing Longborough when he asked, 'Which one was Paula carrying on with, then?'

'I could be naive,' I said, 'but I don't think either of them. I think Jem was playing the knight and Carl was aiding and abetting the plan to ease his own conscience and release him from the grip of the past. With Ian in prison for murdering Paula he would have been home free.'

'Where does the gun-making come in all this?' asked Hubert, as he parked the car.

'I don't know,' I said. 'What do you need to make a gun, anyway?'

'A lathe, I suppose,' said Hubert, 'and the metal and—'

'A lathe would be heavy, wouldn't it?'

Hubert nodded. 'Well, yes – quite – what are you getting at?'

'Sidney Picton had a lathe in one of his outbuildings where, as boys, they made guns. Maybe if –'

'You're thinking –' He paused to stare at me. I smiled back, trying to feign innocence.

'Don't even start to think about it, Kate,' said Hubert with a face full of frown. 'I'm not doing any digging. Just ring your friend, the DCI.'

I waited for a few seconds and then made my suggestion. 'Couldn't we get a couple of gravediggers to move the lathe and start digging? There can't be a law against it.'

'I bet there is. Who's going to pay them anyway?'

'I will.'

Hubert, obviously in a mood, stomped into Humberstones and I didn't see him again for two hours.

He reappeared with Jasper, who jumped into my lap and began licking my face so excitedly that I wished a few members of the human male gender would react that passionately to me.

'I've been thinking,' said Hubert. 'If the police have finished in the Picton house, and in all probability, it's been left in Picton's will to Jenkins – it would seem the outbuildings don't really belong to anyone at the moment.'

'You mean you'll do it?'

'Not personally, and you're not going to know *when* they'll do it. I shall deny all knowledge and so will you, and you can pay my gravediggers.'

He wasn't a happy man, but this time I was sure the body would be there.

It was two days later when David phoned to tell me that an anonymous caller had led the police to Sidney Picton's outbuilding and the body of Thomas Jenkins.

'The stone being rolled away from a tomb I've heard of – a lathe, mysteriously removed, and some neat digging done is another matter and a very serious one.'

'I had nothing to do with it.'

'You're very quick to say that, Kate – a little too quick.'

There was a pause, during which I held my breath.

'I'll have to see you personally about this,' he said.

'At the station?'

'No. I'll come to you.'

He didn't give me a time to expect him and after a couple of hours I really began to worry. He hadn't sounded very friendly. Had I involved Hubert in a chargeable offence?

When he eventually turned up at eight p.m., he was in DCI mode and not smiling.

'You may not have dug that hole yourself,' he said, as I opened the door, 'but I bet you know the man that did.'

'I know nothing about it,' I said, with an extremely straight face.

'Perhaps I should have a word with Hubert,' he said. 'He usually knows what you get up to.'

'No . . . he isn't here.'

'That's convenient. I shall have to continue interrogating you – at our local wine bar.'

At that point there was a flicker of a smile.

In the bar I drank a glass of white wine slowly. I didn't want to slip up and give either Hubert or myself away. 'Strange,' said David, 'that thieves who come to steal a lathe should also dig such a neat hole and obligingly uncover a body undisturbed for twenty-seven years.'

'What can I say? I'm as puzzled as you are.'

'I'm not that puzzled. I'm just not delving too deeply into one of life's mysteries.' I began to relax. 'There was a big hole, too,' he said 'in the back of Thomas's skull. Ballistics think the calibre of the bullet will prove that the gun that shot Dorothy and Sidney was the same one used to kill Thomas.'

'For two men supposedly fascinated by guns,' I said, 'I'm surprised they didn't have their own collections.'

'Three men,' he corrected. 'Sidney's collection we found in the loft. Ian had a locked room at the factory with every sort of handgun you could imagine. Carl kept some guns at home, others with his girlfriend. We think Lorraine was seen visiting the factory to try to find where Ian kept his favourite gun. Carl has told us that Paula was convinced he'd kill them with the handgun he'd finally perfected. In her opinion it was his deadly talisman.'

'What about the gun found in the Jenkins shed?'

'That was one of Carl's. It was a hand-made job, but nothing special.'

'All this gun love sounds like arrested development to me.'

David's expression told me he didn't agree. 'If you forget they're killing machines and just look at them as objects, they *are* fascinating.'

'I can't forget what they do,' I said, 'what damage they cause. Like poor Thomas. That damage lasts. One violent death affects so many people.'

I was on my third glass of wine – and three should be my limit – when, as I was talking about Thomas, it reminded me. 'Do you think Sidney Picton was the only one who knew where Thomas was buried?'

'I reckon the only one who *didn't* know at the time was Carl.'

'You mean Dorothy and Patrick Jenkins *knew* where their son was buried?'

David nodded. 'Carl wasn't strictly family and he could have cracked under the strain. They couldn't take that risk. Better all round if he didn't know.'

'So Carl carried on his friendship with Ian?'

'He didn't have much choice. He saw for himself what Jenkins was capable of. He told me that even as a mercenary seeing cold blooded killers he thought Ian was the coldest killer he'd ever seen.'

'The psychologist was right,' I murmured.

'What was that?' he queried.

'Nothing – just thinking about the psychology of it all.'

He stared at me for a few moments. 'I'll drive you home now,' he said. 'I'm feeling a bit shattered.'

And that, I thought, was the story of my sex life – too tired, too drunk, not drunk enough or totally disinterested.

'What will happen to Paula and her children?' I asked, as he drove the short distance back to Humberstones.

'The kids are with Paula's mum and I reckon, in view of Ian's violence and threats, Paula will get probation or a suspended sentence. Probably she'll be charged with wasting police time.'

'Did she plan to leave the country right from the start?'

'No – she thought they had Ian stitched up, but it didn't work like that, so when it looked as if he might not be charged, Carl and Jem made arrangements for her to go to the Middle East on a false passport.'

'They'll be charged with fraud, then?'

'Depends on the Director of Public Prosecutions.'

At my door he hesitated. 'This case has come right in the end,' he said, cheerfully.

I was about to say goodnight when he said, 'A coffee would be nice.'

'I thought you were shattered.'

'A coffee might perk me up.'

I made him a coffee in my office and as I handed him the mug he put it down, saying it was too hot. 'We'll have to find a way of passing time till it's cool enough to drink,' he said, drawing me close.

We were happily passing time in a reasonably passionate clinch when I heard footsteps on my stairs. Moments later Hubert appeared at my door. I stepped back from David and wobbled on my still weak ankle.

'Simon phoned,' said Hubert. 'Wants you to ring him back.' He exchanged pleasantries with David and then left.

'Who's Simon?' asked David.

'Just a toyboy of mine,' I said, nonchalantly.

We resumed where we left off and I began to have a feeling that it was going to be my lucky night. Until, that is, a voice called out, 'Kate, pet.'

I swore under my breath just as Marilyn appeared at the door. 'Sorry to disturb you, dear, but Hubert wants to know if you two would like to join us for a drink.'

At that moment I didn't know who I was more annoyed with – Hubert or my mother. Either way the moment was lost. I gazed sadly at David for a moment. 'David doesn't drink,' I said, 'and he's just going.'

'I'll catch up with you, Kate,' he said, as he left.

I went straight to bed. There was no way I was going to share a nightcap with yet another gruesome twosome. But tomorrow is another day, as Hubert would say. And my first case back in the UK was over – not a glittering success, perhaps, in the annals of private investigations, but at least a criminal had been brought to justice.

The sound of my mother's laughter drifted through my open door followed by the soft pad of canine footsteps. As I lifted Jasper into bed beside me I reflected on how life never quite turns out as you expect, but a cold nose and a small warm body is sometimes compensation enough.